DEEP DIVE

Also by Chris Knopf

SAM ACQUILLO HAMPTONS MYSTERIES
The Last Refuge
Two Time
Head Wounds
Hard Stop
Black Swan
Cop Job
Back Lash
Tango Down

JACKIE SWAITKOWSKI HAMPTONS MYSTERIES
Short Squeeze
Bad Bird
Ice Cap

ARTHUR CATHCART
Dead Anyway
Cries of the Lost
A Billion Ways To Die

STAND-ALONE THRILLER
Elysiana
You're Dead

CHRIS KNOPF

DEEP DIVE

THE PERMANENT PRESS
Sag Harbor, NY 11963

For information, address:
The Permanent Press
4170 Noyac Road
Sag Harbor, NY 11963
www.thepermanentpress.com

Library of Congress Cataloging-in-Publication Data

Knopf, Chris, author.
Deep dive / Chris Knopf.
Sag Harbor, NY: Permanent Press, [2019]
ISBN: 978-1-57962-571-9
1. Mystery fiction.

PS3611.N66 D44 2019
813'.6—dc23   2019013732

Printed in the United States of America

To the brave people of Puerto Rico, who sing and dance with optimism in defiance of the heartless in Washington.

CHAPTER ONE

"I know I should call the police immediately, but I wonder if you wouldn't mind popping over for a moment to discuss before I do."

It was my friend Burton Lewis. He rarely called, especially on my cell phone, so it got my attention.

"What's up, Burt?"

He spoke clearly, though with a slight, breathless tremor in his voice.

"You know Joshua and Rosie Edelstein," he said. "I'm at their house. It's a situation."

"How bad?"

I knew the Edelsteins well, since I'd spent the better part of two years building all the cabinets and architectural detail for their custom oceanfront home. It was one of my most successful jobs, since I was working for my preferred general contractor, Frank Entwhistle, and Edelstein himself was an eager, grateful, and free-spending customer, my favorite kind.

"A houseguest. Appears to be dead. No, scratch that, is definitely dead. Along with the rhododendron he landed on. Right below his bedroom, two stories up."

"Did you just find him?" I asked.

"We did."

"Wait fifteen minutes, then call the police," I said. "Meanwhile, stay away from the scene. Don't touch anything, don't move anything, don't make any other phone calls, just stay in one place. Are there other guests?"

"Just his boyfriend. Of the moment," said Burton.

"Keep him with you, and away from the bedroom."

"Should be easy. We're on the patio and he's frozen in his chair."

"Does Edelstein have a lawyer?" I asked.

"I'm sure. Probably taxes and real estate."

"Call Jackie."

"I already have. She's Up Island, heading here fast."

"What the hell, Burt?"

"What the hell is right. Just please get here as quickly as you can. Three hysterical people are three more than I can usually cope with."

BURTON LEWIS was one of my oldest friends. A bona fide rich guy, he'd kept his name off "Richest Rich Guys in the Universe" lists since they started putting them together, a testament to how fervently, and powerfully, he guarded his privacy.

I jumped in my old Jeep Cherokee and tore off like a mad man toward the Southampton shoreline.

The Edelsteins had a security gate at the end of their driveway, but that night it stood open. I swung the Jeep onto the white pebble drive and fishtailed up to the giant post-modern house. It was lit up for a party, though only a few overpriced luxury cars filled the half circle in front of the house. Joined awkwardly by Burton's ancient, faux-wood-paneled Ford Country Squire.

The cops hadn't gotten there yet. When Burton appeared, I asked him what was up, and he just said, "Follow me," as he marched across the yard and around to the back of the house.

He held a modern LED flashlight that was bright enough to put a spot on the moon. I followed his silhouette.

He was right about the rhododendron. The houseguest was face up in the middle of the bush, which would have been bad enough if his body hadn't been twisted more or less the opposite direction. It was a tough old bush, brought in when the Edelsteins installed their instant mature landscaping. It had thick upward limbs, now crushed, with one of them protruding from the houseguest's thigh.

There was some blood as a result, which told me the guy was alive for a few moments after he hit the ground.

"I have to show you something."

He knelt on the ground and waved me to squat down next to him. He screwed the front of the flashlight to refocus it from a wide, diffused beam to a narrow spotlight. He cast the light on the right hand of the houseguest, which lay just clear of the rhododendron's shattered branches.

"Do you see that?" he asked.

I squinted at the brightly lit hand and said I wasn't sure. He took me by the shoulder and pulled me in closer to the body.

"Look," he said.

I saw something that looked like a shiny metal thing twisted around the dead guy's fingers.

"Okay, so what is it?" I asked.

He took a moment to answer, as if hoping I'd guess on my own. I looked at his face, partially lit-up by the reflection from the searing flashlight. His expression looked unfamiliar, one I hadn't seen in all the years I'd known him.

"Hate to say it, Sam, but it's my watch."

I'D QUIT smoking a few years before and tried not to think about how much a cigarette would help, sitting on the ground and waiting for the cops to arrive.

"What's the guy's name?" I asked him.

"Elton Darby. A colleague of the Edelsteins. I think Rosie was trying to fix us up, the existing boyfriend notwithstanding. You know how much I hate that sort of thing."

I did. Burton was the most circumspect man I knew when it came to his love life.

"How did the watch get there?" I asked.

"He pulled it off my wrist. Do we have to talk about the exact circumstances right at this moment?"

That surprised me. Because of course we did. The cops were on the way, and whatever he told them when they got there would have far more significance than anything he'd later say.

"Yeah, Burt, we do. Sorry."

He sighed.

"I can't. I need Jackie. It's too complicated to go into now."

Jackie Swaitkowski was a lawyer in a nonprofit firm Burton established to provide free legal service to indigent people on the East End of Long Island. Burton was the farthest thing from indigent, but he knew Jackie was the only one who would know how to navigate the situation. And she was devoted to him, for all they'd done together and all he'd done for her.

"Things got screwed up, eh?" I said to Burton.

"Yeah, Sam. They really did."

The trees over our heads lit up in a brilliant, fluorescent blue color, oscillating under the windswept leaves. Mechanical voices tore through the peaceful air, the product of bullhorns from the Southampton Village patrol cars swarming the Edelstein estate.

As we sat there waiting, I had to ask him something in the short time we'd have before the world lapsed into chaos.

"Did you do anything you shouldn't have, Burt? I don't care, I'll help you all I can, no matter what. Just tell me."

The light was dim where we sat on the grass, but I could see him slump down, the elegant man with whom I'd laughed through dozens of Yankees games, who'd retrieved me from suicide's reach, who'd secured my loved ones from imminent threat, and funded the rescue of countless victims of cruel circumstance.

"I don't know, Sam. I honestly don't know."

CHAPTER TWO

Southampton Town Detective Mike Cermanski looked like the kid in your high school class who was too scrawny to win a fight, but too wiry and vicious to lose. I stayed clear of those guys, or more often, made friends, since I was more or less the same way.

He always wore a dress shirt and tie. Never a sport jacket, or the athletic wear other detectives thought would impress the victims of their crime scene interviews. The spare, classic attire was less intimidating, since it made you feel he was a serious professional, and thus less likely to railroad you into ill-advised comments. Though the overall effect was somewhat compromised by the chunky service pistol holstered on his hip.

Long Island locution decorated his speech, but so did a respectful politeness, a presumption of innocence you couldn't help believing, even when your better mind knew you were being played.

He was officially in the town police department and we were in the village, a separate jurisdiction, only the village didn't have detectives qualified to investigate suspicious deaths, which I guessed they thought this was. That night he had the riveted attention of two billionaires, one of their wives, the victim's date, and me. Also one domestic servant, a Latina, who stood there still as a statue. It didn't seem to faze him a bit.

"So, everyone here heard the sound of glass breaking before you went around the house and found Mr. Darby apparently dead on the ground," he said, for at least the third time. "As far as you know, he was alone in the bedroom when the accident happened."

The little unhappy group agreed with that, for the third time.

Cermanski asked about Elton's circumstances. He was an employee of a nonprofit social welfare organization the Edelsteins had supported for years and had become a type of friend—subordinate, but welcome to their home for certain social occasions. This one featuring Burton Lewis, a potential donor whom Darby might convince the cause was worthy of support.

"Sorry, Burton," said Joshua, "but you know how these things work."

"Of course," said Burton. "I'd do the same."

"Worldwide Loventeers," said Rosie, clarifying things for Cermanski. "We're in twenty countries. Harnessing the power of goodwill for the good of humanity."

She used the tip of her middle finger to feel something on the side of her nose. It looked okay to me. So did the rest of Rosie. Though intimations of middle age had begun to haunt her eyes and thin, bloodless lips, she'd thus far resisted the siren call of plastic surgery.

Joshua shot her a weak, indulgent smile.

"Philanthropy," he said to Cermanski, further clarifying. "The Loventeers try to get the rich to give to the poor. Mostly successful. I'm on the board and chair of fund-raising. Elton was a Loventeers' staffer. Rosie and I make the pitch, Elton fills in the details."

Since fund-raising was central to the social ecology of the Hamptons—the rationalization for nonstop galas and conspicuous displays of financial prowess and prominent cheekbones—none of this was news to Mike Cermanski.

He wrote a few notes in his case book and flipped to the next page.

"So far as you all know, Mr. Darby was of sound mind," he said. "Not disturbed in any way, nothing that might have caused him to take his own life."

His date that night was Johnnie Mercado, maybe twenty years younger than Elton's forty-two. Johnnie told Cermanski he'd known Elton for a while and had never seen him show anything but robust health and good cheer. Often intense, but never self-destructive, in his opinion.

"I liked to cook for him," said Mercado, in a near whisper. "I'm a chef," he added to the group, which seemed to come as a surprise.

The Edelsteins exchanged glances.

"Elton was always high energy," said Joshua. "One of those type-As. But good at his job. Donors loved him. Always on stage. But we knew little of his private life. Rosie thought he was sad, right?" he asked his wife.

She was perturbed by the question. She looked at Burton, who seemed ready to say something, but I caught his eye and shook my head.

"He could be sad sometimes," said Rosie, without a lot of conviction. "It's not easy being gay. Hell, it's not easy being human," she added, glancing over at Burton. "He confided in me a little bit, but the relationship was asymmetrical. I'm a donor, he's a beggar. You know, professionally." She turned to Joshua. "That sounded terrible."

Joshua had likely been born with curly hair, but the thinning process had taken hold, and something akin to a perm had been installed to make the most of the declining resource. Over the years I'd known him, his hair had also lightened, leaving the overall effect of an orange Brillo Pad left too long in the kitchen sink.

He put his hand on Rosie's shoulder.

"We're all a little shook up," he told Cermanski.

"Sure. I get that," he said, flipping to another page in his case book.

It was a warm night in late August, but as always, the prevailing south southwesterly off the Atlantic kept the temperature in check. Since we were only a few hundred yards from the ocean, we could hear the steady churn of the surf. I could feel the dampness of the ocean breeze on my face, and imagined all the nice wooden stuff I'd built to decorate the Edelsteins' bountiful garden slowly succumbing to the corrosive salt air.

The crime scene investigation on the other side of the house was in full frenzy, with strobing lights in various colors, bursts of radio transmissions, and busy people in yellow jumpsuits going up and down the driveway carrying expensive-looking equipment. It was through this hubbub that Jackie Swaitkowski strode in her black, form-fitting dress and nose-bleed-high pumps.

She walked past me and the others and put her hand on Burt's shoulder.

"Let's go, Mr. Lewis, we're out of here."

Cermanski barely got the first syllable out of his mouth before she cut him off.

"Nice to see you, detective," she said. "Interview's over. Sam, care to join us?"

She half lifted Burton out of his lawn chair, and with arms locked, walked him back toward the driveway. The Edelsteins looked bereft, rightly so. Cermanski grinned at me but called to her.

"Nice to see you, too, counselor," he yelled.

I followed.

ISABELLA, BURT's housekeeper, and incidentally, chief-of-staff for his sprawling financial empire, was waiting for us at the front door of his house. Along with two cats, who curled around Isabella's legs and looked warily at the clamor heading their way.

Jackie walked Burton over the hundred-mile journey to the patio on the far side of the house and planted him in a white wicker chair. I took the one next door. Isabella repeated "What is it?" a few dozen times, until Jackie shut her up with drink orders.

"Now, Isabella," she said. "I'll explain later."

When she left, Jackie dragged a chair up to Burton and asked him to go through everything his memory would allow.

"Honestly, Jackie, not that much to go through. It was just a reasonably pleasant, albeit somewhat awkward, social occasion. I've only known the Edelsteins for a few years, since they built their house on Gin Lane. I'd run into Joshua in the city from time to time. He sits on various boards, financial companies, some of which are clients of ours. Easy going. I like him. Not sure about Rosie. Edgy woman."

"What about Elton Darby?" she asked.

The question made him uncomfortable.

"Deferential, but a little too inquisitive about one's private life."

"I know the type," she said.

"Nothing major," he said. "Just not my cup of tea."

Knowing Burton as well as we did, that brand of tea would have been closer to battery acid.

I pantomimed looking at a nonexistent watch on my wrist. His pained expression deepened.

"Somehow he got ahold of my watch," he told Jackie. "He was holding it when we found him."

Jackie cocked her head like a startled golden retriever.

"He was holding it?"

Burton nodded.

"Patek Philippe," he said. "One of the better ones."

Jackie Swaitkowski, born Jackie O'Dwyer, had been a real estate lawyer trying to figure out what to do with herself after her Polish-American husband stuck his Porsche into a tree at over a hundred miles an hour, when a series of events, mostly involving me, thrust her into the very different world of criminal defense. Burton had been looking for someone to represent his pro-bono law practice on the East End and Jackie turned out to be the ideal choice.

To say she was utterly devoted to both Burton and his good works was a vast understatement.

"Do you know how he got hold of it?" she asked.

Burton rolled up his shirt sleeve. There were deep, ugly red scratches down his forearm.

"He took it, believe it or not. Darby wasn't just inclined to stand a little too close. He made a pass. I pushed him away. He grabbed my arm, and when I shook off his hand, the watch came with it. I wasn't ready to share that detail with the detective."

"Oh, Burton," she said, getting up from her chair and walking out to the edge of the patio where she could look out into the night.

"Where did this happen?" I asked him.

"Outside the bathroom of a second-floor suite. He followed me and we exchanged words and he took my watch. Uncomfortable, to say the least. So I left him there. I tried to say goodbye to the Edelsteins but couldn't find them."

Jackie walked back toward us.

"Burton, where were you when Darby fell?"

"Walking down the front path toward my car. I heard a crashing sound and a muted thud. But not where it came from. I went back inside and heard lots of shouting and running about. It was a very confusing situation."

"Who found him?" I asked.

"The housekeeper. Violeta. I was right behind her, and then Rosie, but Violeta got there first. She was crossing herself and praying. I felt like doing the same."

Isabella showed up with refreshments which no one hesitated to accept. She stood as if ready to join the meeting, but Burton gently asked her to give us some privacy. She didn't like it, but left with quiet grace.

"We'll have to give a more detailed statement," said Jackie.

"I know," said Burton. "It's just the beginning."

The reason he'd founded a pro-bono defense practice in the first place was to be part of the other side of life while running up his late father's corporate law firm and real estate holdings into a multibillion-dollar enterprise. The pro-bono operation was a classic storefront in Manhattan, with Burton the only employee for the first few years. So he knew well the sequence of events that would relentlessly proceed from there.

Jackie's smartphone rang. On cue, it was the Southampton Town chief of police, Ross Semple.

We watched her listen, then heard her say, "Certainly, Ross. Tomorrow afternoon is fine. No, we'll come to you. But thanks for the offer."

If you spend enough time with a person, and I'd spent countless hours with Jackie Swaitkowski, you learn how to interpret their physical habits, the tics and gestures that run alongside verbal communication, often more telling. Jackie's hair was thick, strawberry blonde, and curly. When stress got the best of her, she used both hands to pull it back from her face. I watched her do this when she said, "We're going through everything again, everyone. And then again, before we get a little sleep and go over to see Chief Semple. I'll take notes. Sam, it's your job to bring coffee and keep Isabella from eavesdropping."

The first part of the job I knew how to do. The other, not so much.

Chapter Three

Mike Cermanski was one of the two plainclothes detectives on the Southampton Town police squad. The other was a blond bear named Joe Sullivan whom I'd known since first coming back to Southampton to move into my dead parents' cottage where I could embark on a new career of determined self-destruction.

In those days, he wore a uniform and drove a patrol car. Dedication to the job earned him his new position, a quality that figured largely in his wife's decision to lock him out of their house, leaving a suitcase on the front stoop along with a philodendron he'd brought into the marriage.

"Why the plant?" I asked him.

"She hated the competition."

In addition to our common marital fortunes, we shared an interest in working out at a boxing gym, where you could build your aerobic health and occasionally deck someone with few legal repercussions.

Having spent most of the night listening to Jackie working on Burton's version of events at the Edelsteins' house, I went there to clear my head before we reconvened that afternoon at the Southampton Town Police HQ. I was surprised to see Sullivan in sweats, pulling on a pair of sparring gloves.

"It's ten A.M.," I said. "You're supposed to be at work."

"No work for me. Ross put me on leave."

"What the hell for?"

"He said I've been putting in too many hours. But I don't believe him."

"You do put in too many hours," I said.

"Not the real reason. He wants me as far from this case as possible."

"What case?"

He stuck out his hands so I could lace up his gloves.

"Burton Lewis. What other case is there?"

"Because of me?" I asked.

"You, Jackie, Lewis himself. I'm too close."

"That's unfair."

"He's doing it for my sake," said Sullivan. "Partly. If anything leaks out of the squad room, it can't be because of me." He started doing a little warm-up dance, thumping his gloves together. "Want to go a few rounds?"

"I'm here for the steam bath. I guess you haven't heard anything."

"See? This is what I'm talking about. I don't have to hear anything to know this is as high profile as it gets, which means lots of publicity, which Ross hates even more than extra scrutiny by the DA, which comes with all the publicity caused by the DA talking to the press. You got your vicious cycle."

"What are you going to do with yourself?"

"Catch up on my origami. Maybe run for the Senate."

I'd stripped down and was fixing a towel around my waist when I said, "You could work for us."

"Nothing illegal, unethical, or inappropriate about that."

"Might be a nice change of pace."

I was at the door to the steam bath when I realized he was walking behind me. He held the door open and motioned me to go in. We had it to ourselves.

"Isn't this where Russian gangsters make all their deals?" I asked, sitting on the bench.

He stayed standing, his static bulk always ready to launch, nearly filling the room.

"I don't know anything," he said. "I only talked to Ross for a few minutes before he asked me to take a hike. On the department's budget. But I do have a feeling about this."

"I thought you might."

"You're not going to like it."

"Try me."

"Ross knows something you don't," he said.

"Not the first time."

"Something big."

"How do you know that?"

I knew it wasn't because he'd learned to read Ross Semple's mind. Nobody knew how to do that, and if they did, they'd regret it.

"Guess who I saw coming in when I was going out the door?" he asked.

"I love guessing games."

"Judith Paolini, assistant director in charge of the Manhattan field office of the FBI. And two of her top special agents. All that for a little old dive out a second-story window?"

WE DIDN'T expect and hadn't asked for any extra courtesies. Jackie's only concession to the seriousness of the moment was a pair of slacks and sensible shoes. Burton wore a few thousand dollars-worth of clothes designed to look straight off the budget rack, per Jackie's specifications. She frowned at my jeans as if wishing she'd done the same for me.

Ross, on the other hand, only owned ugly striped polyester shirts and ties from the set of a sixties sitcom, but it was his police station and he could wear what he wanted.

He waved us through the security door off the reception area as if impatient with a burdensome formality.

"Come in, come in. Who needs coffee?"

Everyone but I demurred, deepening Jackie's frown.

Ross settled us in interview room one—a spare, windowless box decorated with video cameras in every corner. I watched a camera follow me to my seat and gave it a little wave.

Cermanski was already there, relaxed in his chair, hands folded in his lap. His case book was open on the table. I nodded to him and he nodded back.

Burton sat at one end of the table, with Ross at the other. Jackie dropped the scuffed-up leather sack that mimicked a purse on the table. She extracted a yellow legal pad, and after a minute of tedious rummaging, came up with a pen.

"Even though I've given it before, I'll spare you the need to ask for my account of the other evening and just start at the beginning," said Burton. "If that's acceptable."

Ross leaned back in his chair, gripping the arm rests.

"Fire away, Mr. Lewis."

So he did, in quiet tones with precise inflections. There was nothing new for me to hear, so I admit my attention drifted. I saw in my mind's eye Burton working at his storefront criminal practice, earnestly listening to his indigent, mostly guilty clients, helping them build a convincing testimony out of raw incoherence. And Ross Semple during his days in deep undercover, in a dim room in the South Bronx, wearing sunglasses and long slimy hair, a cigarette hanging from his mouth, weighing bags of cocaine. I wondered if they ever crossed paths in those days, in or out of court.

Ross waited till the end of Burton's statement to ask, "Mr. Lewis, could you roll up your sleeves?"

Jackie sat up straight in her seat.

"What the hell for?"

Burton ignored her and unbuttoned his cuffs. Then pulled his sleeves up to the elbow. The red lines on his left forearm were obvious.

"The epithelials that we scraped from under Mr. Darby's nails will match your DNA, am I right?" asked Ross.

"Wait a minute," Jackie started to say.

"Undoubtedly," said Burton. "He grasped my arm and scratched me when I pulled away."

He described the scuffle in the hallway outside the second-floor bathroom, something he'd left out of his original statement. Cermanski asked why, and Burton admitted he should have mentioned it.

"He was trying to get the watch?" Cermanski asked.

Burton shook his head.

"No. I don't think so."

"Then what was he doing?" asked the detective.

Burton seemed unsure.

"I don't know. Just grabbing at me."

"Quite the altercation," said Ross.

"No," said Burton. "Not really. I don't know what he was thinking. Said he wanted to talk, invading my personal space. I must have reared back, and he tried to stop me."

Neither Cermanski nor the chief were easy reads, but they looked unsatisfied. The questioning continued along those lines, but it did nothing to change their mood.

"So you were already outside when Mr. Darby fell," said Cermanski.

"Asked and answered," said Jackie. "Multiple times. Make note of that and move on to something else."

Ross gave her a vague smile.

"Thanks for the insight, counselor," he said. "And help with the interview."

"You bet, Ross. That's what I'm here for."

Soon after, Semple checked his watch and said he'd promised to get us out of there in prompt fashion. None of us objected to being escorted from the building. Though before I made it out the door, he took me aside. Jackie stared as he led me to a private spot.

"Don't be under any illusion that I'll be helping you with this situation," he said to me.

I'd already told him we expected nothing of the kind and reminded him of that.

"Good, then you won't misinterpret the advice I'm about to give you."

I knew what his words meant, but there was no other interpretation than he was about to help us with our case. It didn't surprise me, since there was little about Ross that wasn't unexpected.

He shook a cigarette out of the pack in his shirt pocket and put it in his mouth, but didn't light it. It moved up and down when he delivered his counsel.

"Your client, Burton Lewis," he said, "and everyone else in that house last night, is lying."

Chapter Four

My ex-wife had urgent social aspirations. Having been born to a wealthy Boston family, and given the name Abigail Adams Albright, this was likely preordained. Family connections led her to Burton Lewis, who invited us out to his mansion in Southampton, sparing Abby the indignity of staying at my parents' tumbledown cottage in the North Sea area of the Town of Southampton.

She miscalculated Burton's interest in high society, which was close to zero, as well as her own ability to ingratiate herself into the East End's glitterati. To be fair, Burton did his best to make introductions, and was abidingly kind to Abby despite her transparent ambition, but I was the one who became his good friend, trading on our mutual interest in pool, the New York Yankees, woodcraft, and meandering, slightly sodden conversations about satisfying, though entirely forgettable, subject matter.

She never forgave me for this, though I'd committed so many unforgivable sins, it hardly rated notice.

When we divorced, I'd already blown up my corporate career, and was working hard on drinking myself into oblivion, so it was easy for the courts to give her the lion's share of our liquid assets and our big house in Stamford, Connecticut, which I later destroyed in a fit of misplaced initiative. I dodged a well-deserved prison sentence through no fault of my own, emerging with an old car, a young dog, and my parents' cottage on the edge of the Little Peconic Bay.

Things have improved somewhat since then.

Most notably in the form of Amanda Anselma, who lived next door and was a frequent presence bearing platters of unwholesome, delicious finger food and oversized biscuits for the dog, Eddie Van Halen, who would likely prefer the contents of the platter.

Since our properties shared the point of a peninsula that stuck into the Little Peconic Bay, we each had our own uncluttered view of the impatient water, so we alternated between two possible sets of Adirondack chairs to sit and discuss things, or just sit and quietly waste away the evening.

That night we were at her house with plenty to discuss.

"I'm just sick about this," said Amanda, after I'd shared everything I could about the meeting with Ross Semple and Mike Cermanski. Leaving out Ross's parting shot, for reasons I hadn't worked out in my head. It's not that I usually withheld stuff from Amanda, I just hadn't processed it well enough to answer her inevitable questions.

"After you, Burton's my favorite person," she added.

"Mine too."

"After me, you meant to say."

"I didn't say that?"

"There's no reason to call it anything other than an accident," she said. "In my opinion."

"Which is why there's no point in getting sick over it. You want the cops to do a thorough job so the conclusion is never in doubt."

"Doesn't mean I can't worry anyway."

"No. That's your prerogative."

The night was flirting with too warm, a light southwesterly doing little to sweep away the day's humidity. Amanda said it justified wearing a silky, floor-length thing she called a peignoir, which I liked looking at as much as saying the word with an exaggerated French accent. T-shirt and shorts were good enough for me. Eddie wore his standard fur coat, cut for the summer.

She held up the mangled remains of a tennis ball.

"If I throw this disgusting thing one more time, can we call it a night?" she asked him. He took a few steps toward the breakwater above the pebble beach, his eyes fixed on the ball, promising only to give an honest chase.

"Eddie's not bound by prosaic concepts such as 'one more time,'" I said. "He's transcended all that, recognizing that each toss is part of a timeless continuum, an eternal regimen of chase, secure, and return."

"I admit it feels that way."

She faked a throw to the right and threw it to the left. Eddie started to run off in the wrong direction, then stopped and listened. When the ball hit the beach, he turned and headed that way.

"You can't deceive the pure of heart," I told her.

"But you can fool them if you're fast enough."

The moon chose the next moment to clear a bank of clouds, surprising us with a bath of bright, colorless light. The peignoir was so white and her sun-scorched Italian skin so dark, the garment almost looked uninhabited. I reached over and caressed her above the knee, just to make sure she was still there.

When Eddie returned, I told him to cool it. He lay down with the ball under his chin.

"Why doesn't he ever do that for me?" she asked.

"I give him dog food."

"I feed him pâté. You'd think that would give me a leg up."

She raised her leg to demonstrate. The peignoir fell away as designed. This time the moonlight was enough to show her perfect contours. Perfect for me anyway.

"I'm not that easily fooled, you know," I said. "Impure as I may be."

"No, but you have your blind spots."

"Yeah? Like what?"

"Not what, who."

"Like who?" I asked.

"People you love."

"Like you?"

"So you love me. Now you tell me."

She stood and slipped off the peignoir. She balled it up and dropped it in my lap, then turned and walked toward her house.

"Bring that with you, would you?"

MY FIRST rule of driving into the city was to bring comforting reminders of home, like a large mug of coffee and the dog. To me, my aging Jeep Cherokee was solid, no-nonsense transport, but to Eddie, it was a thrilling, breezy playscape with seating and pacing options galore. I kept the windows down enough for him to stick his head out, but not enough to fit his whole body, never sure if some provocation from another dog in the back of a pickup would lead to a daredevil assault.

My object was the home office of Worldwide Loventeers, the nonprofit that had employed the late Elton Darby as fund-raiser in charge of major donors. A full staff of earnest youngsters worked the phones, put out e-mails, and made direct public solicitations, but only people like Darby were entrusted to squeeze out contributions from people like Burton Lewis. Those with oceans of tappable, tax-deductible largesse, the true lifeblood of any self-respecting charitable institution.

More specifically, I wanted to speak with his boss, a guy named Milton Flowers, who must have changed his name for professional purposes. I got the assignment from Jackie, who rightly chose to focus on the legal necessities of the moment, letting me put my PI license, recently acquired, to better use.

"Be nice to these people," she told me. "They do good deeds for a living."

"So no hitting or threatening."

"None of that. Just pleasant talk."

"Can I split infinitives?"

"Think passive voice. Like literally."

"That's a mission not accepted lightly."

Worldwide Loventeers looked out on its global territory from about fifty stories above Sixth Avenue in Midtown Manhattan. Expecting something more like a battered townhouse in the Village, it took a moment to adjust, and presented a challenge getting Eddie past the two guards at the security desk and into the elevator.

"Service dog," I told them.

"What're you blind or something?" one of them asked.

"Not that kind of service. More spiritual. He's here to interview Worldwide Loventeers."

They exchanged glances, as if they'd heard it all.

"I gotta call up there."

"Sure."

I gave them Eddie's full name, Eddie Van Halen.

"Like the musician?" he asked.

"Sort of. No relation."

He announced that Sam Acquillo and Edward Van Halen were in the lobby requesting entry. No distinct species identified.

"Go on up."

The office, like the building, was made of glass. Everything visible, inside and out, floor to ceiling. I noted that to the receptionist.

"We believe in transparency," she said, happy to repeat the joke for the thousandth time. "Who's your friend?" she asked Eddie. "Does he want a treat?"

"I'm all set, thanks," I told her.

Eddie knew that going to the city meant the indignity of a leash, the constraints of which he tested every few seconds. Though when I wrestled him over to the waiting room couch, he took it well, and even sat in front of me as if trained to do so.

The only thing floral about Milton Flowers was his complexion. A squat little guy, with a balding head sprinkled with oily dew, he reminded me of a materials fabricator I used to work with back at the company. His tie was loosened at his throat as if to relieve the pressure welling up from a pot belly well-defined under a straining dress shirt. Made me think he could lose twenty pounds with the prick of a pin.

"Mr. Acquillo?" he asked, walking up to me.

"Acquillo. With a C. Sounds like quill."

Eddie stood up and sniffed his trouser leg.

"Must smell my wife's cat. Thing's always trying to trip me. I'm a dog person myself," he added, adeptly scratching Eddie's ear as if to prove his bona fides.

"Sorry about Mr. Darby," I said. "Must be a shock."

"Freaking terrible. Let's go sit down. Bring the dog, unless he can help out on the phone banks. We take all volunteers."

He led me through the crystalline halls to a conference room staring into the building next door, also glass-walled, though opaque. Seemed like an unfair advantage.

"Joshua Edelstein told me you'd be stopping by," he said, as we settled at the conference room table. "I've already been through everything with the police."

"Sorry about that, but I'd like to hear for myself."

"I used to be a firefighter, so I get it. The insurance guys always wanted to get their own take on things."

He sat with his hands clasped on the table top, ready to serve. His glasses were too small for his face, which was too small for his head. He might have shopped at Ross Semple's favorite clothing store, a polyester-based holdout against the surging tide of natural fibers.

"Tell me about Elton Darby," I said.

"You're not recording this? I don't care if you do. For recollection's sake."

"I'll remember." I pointed at my head. "Steel trap."

"Mine's a sieve."

I didn't tell him that I liked to look at people's faces when they talked. Often said a lot more than their words, and more worth remembering.

"Darby worked for me, but we were basically on par with each other," he said. "I'm the inside guy, focused on the service providers; he was the outside guy, raising the money. I do phones okay, but he was Mr. Face-to-Face. Liked going to events and traveling around visiting people. Frankly, I'd rather pluck out my eyes with a fork than do that stuff, so there's your perfect team."

"So you got along."

His expression said they did, with reservations. He took off his glasses and dug a handkerchief out of his back pocket. As he wiped them off, I noticed how part of his thumb was covering a lens. I wanted to lean across the table and gently move the thumb out of the way. When he put the glasses back on, they still looked slightly glazed, as if the whole effort was meant to dim, or diffuse, the vivid, glassed-off surroundings.

"I got my CPA after quitting the department. Darby studied drama at Juilliard, so there you go. Not a lot in common, but there was mutual respect. Based on the fact that we hated doing what the other one had to do."

"So Darby was short on administrative skills."

Flowers chuckled.

"What administrative skills? Did he know what the word administrative meant? His assistant did everything but wipe his nose for him. Otherwise we'd never know what he was up to."

"But a good fund-raiser."

"Oh, yeah. Sometimes I had to close the sale for him, like when a victim sobered up and found the receipt for a one hundred K pledge stuffed in his shirt pocket."

He chuckled again, though with little humor.

"So a party boy."

He shook his head.

"Yeah, but not in the way you mean. I hate words like schmoozer and glad-hander. Undermines the seriousness guys like Darby put into their jobs. He was always on, always working the crowd. It's exhausting, never letting down. Even extroverts need a break."

"Did he ever take any?"

"Breaks? I don't think so. I made him go on vacation, but he just kept working. You could tell by looking at his expense reports, which I did with a magnifying glass."

"Padded?" I asked.

He unclasped his hands so he could point a finger, the former fireman emerging from his body language.

"No, Darby was sloppy, but honest. The fine-tooth comb was for his sake, not mine. He didn't know from auditors."

"Sorry," I said. "Mistaken inference."

He relaxed a little, but not much.

"This was an accident, right? Darby falling out a window," he said. "Edelstein didn't tell me much. Just that you were stopping by and I should talk to you. He's our biggest donor," he added, explaining the only reason I was sitting there.

"The cops haven't confirmed cause of death, but that's what it looks like. To me."

"What else could it be?"

I didn't see the point in keeping anything from him. Eventually he'd find out anyway.

"He went through a closed double-hung window. A six-over-six, it's called. Six lights top and bottom."

"With the wood things."

"They're called muntins. Make up the grid that holds the individual pieces of glass. People usually call them mullions, but that's a different thing. Point is, not that easy to just fall through. Takes some doing."

I could see him picturing it in his mind.

"For sure. So probably not an accident," he said. His expression changed again as he thought it all the way through. "Unless somebody pushed him."

"Nobody's saying that. Darby was the only one in the room when it happened."

"Ah," said Flowers. "I get it. You think Darby took the big leap. You're asking me about his mental state."

"I guess I am."

He started nodding, as if agreeing with his own thoughts.

"What's your interest in this? Protecting Loventeers? I think we can handle that pretty well on our own."

"I'm sure you can."

"My wife's sister killed herself last year. Looked to everybody like she had a nice life. Family, good job, no financial pressures, faithful husband, house in Montclair. Went to church, drove the kids to music lessons, big smile all the time. Went to a hotel and ate a bottle of sleeping pills. Left a note apologizing to housekeeping for the imposition. Nobody saw it coming, including my wife and all her friends. So don't ask me about Darby. I didn't know a lot about his personal life, and even if I did, it wouldn't mean a damn thing."

I tried to look through the smeared glasses for a better view of his mind. I felt like he meant everything he said, I just didn't think he was saying all he thought. Not surprising for a guy, who like he said, had an organization to look after.

"You work for Edelstein?" he asked.

"Indirectly." I didn't mention the finished carpentry I'd done on his house. "A mutual friend was at the house the night it happened. You could say I'm working for him."

For the second time, I seemed to confirm one of his suspicions.

"Reputation management," he said.

"I don't know what that is," I said, with all honesty.

"Sure you do. Your friend was around when Darby made a mess. You want to make sure none of it splashes up his leg."

Now that I knew what he meant, I guessed he wasn't wrong, exactly. Though Burton's reputation wasn't the only thing I was worried about.

"Darby had a date that night. A guy named Mercado. Ever meet him?"

Flowers gave an indifferent nod.

"Sure. I guess you'd call him a date. They were living together on the West Side. At least Johnnie was there the last time I dropped by with some paperwork for Darby. Looked pretty moved in. I met Johnnie last year at the Christmas party. Darby had his picture on the credenza."

Flowers pulled out his smartphone.

"Just checking the time," he said. "I should probably get going. You can always call me if you want more."

Sensing the change in dynamics, Eddie stood up from his spot in the corner and went to the door.

"You'll probably hear from me," I said. "Or maybe Eddie."

He took me all the way to the elevator banks before asking another question.

"This friend of yours at the Edelsteins' place. Wouldn't be Burton Lewis, would it?"

I hesitated, wondering if Joshua had spilled the beans. But then confirmed it.

"You asked me about Johnnie Mercado," he said. "I did see Darby at a restaurant with Lewis not that long ago. I figured he was just schmoozing an important donor, but now that I think about it, the whole thing looked kind of intimate, and you know, given Darby's and Lewis's batting preferences," his voice trailing off, but not his implication.

I just thanked him and took advantage of a waiting elevator to slip out of there.

Chapter Five

Elton Darby's funeral took place on a grass-covered hill somewhere deep in Nassau County. There were no trees within a thousand yards and the temperature was in the mid-nineties, simulating the prospects some of us had for the afterlife. Apparently not Darby, who according to the priest had led an honest and giving life, exemplary in every way imaginable, if you had a better imagination than I did.

I had no reason to doubt it. I'd never met him, in the strictest sense, and so far, the murmured commentary that reached my ears seemed uniformly grieving and sympathetic.

I was glad Amanda hadn't talked me out of wearing my off-white linen suit, a relic of Abby's enthusiasm for fitting me out for tedious garden parties. Though I stood out among all the black outfits, I could sense envious glances cast my way. Amanda wore something flowing and black, comfortable, flattering, and appropriate. That could have been the cause of the furtive glances, at least from the men.

The priest had an Irish accent and didn't hesitate to claim a deep kinship with the departed at hand, even though he'd never had the pleasure of knowing him personally. Apparently people of Irish ancestry also had special accommodations awaiting them in the hereafter, which made me wonder what was in store for Frenchmen like me. I guessed the cheap seats for all eternity, if I got that far.

Amanda gripped my arm tightly throughout the ceremony, either to keep her steady on those spiky black pumps,
or to encourage me not to huff or snicker, reactions any
religious service tended to bring out in me. Though I was
pretty content, knowing that the whole procedure would
be handled there on top of the hill, without the crushing
tedium of communion or any of the other baffling rituals
inflicted on the Roman Catholic bereaved.

My attention drifted away from the solemn priest toward
the faces in the crowd. I spotted Joshua and Rosie Edelstein,
who had a front row view. Milton Flowers was there standing with a woman who looked like a medicine ball with
feet, presumably his wife. Next to them was a long-limbed
guy in a silk suit that hung on him like a runway model's.
He occasionally gripped Flowers's shoulder as if to give
comfort, which Flowers didn't look like he needed. I caught
Mrs. Flowers frowning at the two of them.

It took a while to locate Johnnie Mercado, who seemed
to be hanging back, stone-faced, but clearly pained. I made
a guess at Darby's mother, who stood staring into the grave,
supported by another old woman who wore a matching
veil. Most of the others were people around Darby's age,
adults in the prime of their lives, looking fit and unsure how
to comport themselves with death all around.

We all held individual flowers handed out at the beginning of the service, and I was relieved to see the congrega-
tion tossing them onto the casket, which I took to mean the
ceremonies were all wrapped up. Even more encouraging,
the priest invited us to gather back at the cemetery's front
entrance where a tent had been set up with big fans and an
open bar.

"You did very well, Sam," Amanda told me as we traveled across the sweltering lawn toward the tent.

"Thanks, though I'm feeling dehydrated. Anything with
ice will do."

I lost Amanda along the way, but found what I wanted at the bar, really just a regular table covered in a white tablecloth. The bartender looked too young to be legally dispensing drinks, but maybe they broke the rules for funeral receptions.

"What do you got in a vodka?" I asked.

"Whatever you want, pal. Good stuff, not so good stuff."

"Family pays either way?"

"Yeah. I think you want the good stuff. Rocks with that or are you a straight-up guy?"

"Straight enough. Throw in lots a rocks."

The kid poured a small lake of Grey Goose from the neck of the bottle.

"You grow up in a bar?" I asked him.

"Yeah. How'd you know?"

"Sam's very intuitive," said Amanda, showing up behind me.

"What can I get the lady?" he asked her.

"If you mean me, ice water and a gin and tonic," she said. "In separate glasses."

"The good stuff," I told him.

He looked pleased with that, or maybe it was the five I stuffed in the tip jar.

"Where you been?" I asked her as we moved away from the bar.

"I was thanking Joshua Edelstein for letting me tag along. It's not every day I crash a funeral."

"I'm mostly a crasher myself. Jackie wanted me here to look over the crowd."

"And did you?"

"To the best of my ability."

The tall guy who'd been standing next to Flowers came up to us.

"Milt told me you'd be coming," he said to me, though he stuck his hand out for Amanda to shake. "Art Reynolds. Chairman of the board. Friends of the Edelsteins?"

"He is," said Amanda. "I'm just a hanger-on."

His grip had plenty of meat on it. I let him squeeze, not wanting to get into a contest when I was wearing my nice linen suit.

Closer up, he still looked comfortable in the million-dollar threads. Lots of reddish-brown hair, too reddish-brown, and fewer lines around the eyes than his face warranted. Unlike Rosie Edelstein, it looked like he'd had a little work, as they say out in the Hamptons, if you talk to people who care about those things.

I don't know what women consider attractive in men, it's always eluded me. But he did have one of those dimples in the middle of a heavy chin, like Cary Grant, who everybody thought was a handsome guy.

"Whose board do you chair?" asked Amanda.

"Worldwide Loventeers. By day I'm an attorney. And you?"

"Carpenter," I said for her. "We're both carpenters."

He didn't seem to believe me, which was okay, since Amanda was more of an all-around builder, though she could frame up a wall with the best of them.

"Quite a thing about Darby," he said. "He was a good man."

"That's what I keep hearing," I said.

"Joshua said you were a private investigator. You must do carpentry on the side."

"More the other way around. I did a lot of work on the Edelstein place."

"I've seen it. Impressive."

"Not too much flattery, please," said Amanda. "He's impossible enough."

"And what do you do when you aren't swinging a hammer?" he asked her, moving slightly between us, as if that might encourage me to go find another conversation.

"I do a lot of cleaning up," she said. "Especially at the end of the day. I suppose a lawyer would know something about that."

"Other people's messes?" he asked.

"Preferably."

"Are you replacing Darby?" I asked, trying to get Reynolds's attention. "I guess you have to."

"Unless I quit my job and do fund-raising full time," said Reynolds.

"You might consider that," said Amanda. She turned to him. "The messes and all that."

His smile was broad and pitched to engage, though not with me.

"I have another question for you," I said, still trying to retake the floor. "Will Darby have that whole hill to himself?"

It took a lot of Reynolds's self-possession to force out an answer.

"The hill is full of graves," he said. "Just no grave markers. It's cemetery policy."

"How do they know where everybody is?" I asked.

"Geo-location. Every grave has its own homing beacon."

"Get the heck out of here."

"How peaceful," said Amanda.

"You can also choose a meadow or a grove of trees. You'll love them. May I show you?" he asked Amanda, gently taking her elbow.

I watched the two of them move away.

"Don't love them too much," I said, just before they were out of earshot.

I thought I should go talk to somebody involved in our case, since Jackie would be asking me. I looked around and saw Johnnie Mercado over at the bar, a place I'd rather go anyway. I watched the bar kid pour him a stiff bourbon.

I reintroduced myself to Johnnie, though he seemed to remember me.

"In all the confusion over at the Edelsteins', I didn't properly tell you I was sorry for your loss," I told him.

"I think you did, but I appreciate it," he said. "Can't have too many sorries."

He had the type of Latino beauty that women would note as heart stopping, or further proof that all the best-looking young men in New York are gay. A mellifluous Spanish accent completed the picture.

"Anyway, you were busy being the only grown-up in the place," he added.

When he took a healthy pull of the bourbon his hands had a slight tremor.

"Nobody's prepared for that kind of thing," I said. "You did okay."

He managed a weak smile as his eyes scanned the crowd.

"Is there anything more awkward than a boyfriend at a dead man's funeral?" he asked.

"A girlfriend at a married man's surprise party?"

He thought that was great, the smile taking a stronger hold.

"Or a boyfriend," he said. "It happens, you know."

"I'm sure it does. So you don't know these people."

"I met his mother. She's the one in the veil. Her and Aunt Marcia, also in a veil. Don't bother trying to figure out which is which. They're interchangeable."

We stood quietly for a while working on our drinks. Partners in isolation, until I messed it all up by asking how Elton had been getting along at work. Mercado looked put off for a moment, but answered me.

"Not so great," he said. "He was always tense about his job, but tenser than usual lately. It was actually good in some ways. Seemed to want to have more fun. Get away from all the office bullshit."

"I guess even do-gooders have their own crap to deal with," I said.

"You think that's what they do? Good deeds? Pretty amusing."

Rosie picked that moment to roll up next to Johnnie and put her arm through his, the one holding his drink, causing some of it to splash on his silvery rayon pants. He ignored it.

"Johnnie, Johnnie, how are you feeling?" she asked.

"I'm okay, Rosie, Rosie. Still absorbing it all."

"Of course. Such a terrible, terrible thing," she said. "Thanks for coming," she added to me. "Is the darling Amanda here?"

"She was a moment ago," I said. I'd introduced Rosie to Amanda during a party of hers we'd stumbled into several years before. Rosie still had a suspicion Amanda was someone important, she just couldn't put her finger on why. I remained safely in the category of a working guy her husband had some confusing affinity for. She'd talk to me to uphold his support of the common man.

"Well, don't lose track of her. Attractive women are getting harder to replace," she said, meaning by me, who clearly didn't deserve Amanda's notice. Then she drifted away, leaving me and Johnnie alone with an unanswered question about the Loventeers's good deeds. Though I didn't get a chance to ask it, because Art Reynolds was standing near the food table trying to get everyone's attention. Amanda stood nearby.

He ran through the usual rehash of the sentiments expressed during the ceremony, nicely condensed, before leaving us with his gentle hope that we'd find a way to add to our latest donations to the Loventeers in honor of Elton Darby. No one seemed to be reaching in their pockets for a checkbook, but they took it well enough.

When he was finished, I looked around for Johnnie, but he'd melted into the throng. Amanda turned up instead, and that was the better thing.

"Pick out a nice place?" I asked her.

"I think maybe," she said. "I'll have to show you."

"Just give me the GPS coordinates."

"Mr. Reynolds wanted to know if I was married. I asked if he wanted to add me to the family plot."

"Might be a good real estate move. I was told these graves cost a king's ransom."

"I'd rather be back on Oak Point. For the time being."

Leaving it at that, we took off, making it out of there still in full possession of our earthly souls and disposable income.

CHAPTER SIX

I did a lot of work for Frank Entwhistle. That morning was no different, down in my basement shop with a roll of detailed architectural drawings from Entwhistle and a long list of expensive materials.

This was the part of fine woodworking that most woodworkers disliked, the nonphysical desk work of planning and calculation. But I liked it a lot, a holdover from my days as a mechanical engineer preparing to travel to a remote industrial plant that faced some inscrutable production breakdown I was paid generously to solve.

The answer was often hiding within the reams of technical specifications, if you had the patience and determination to plow through it all. Which I actually found more soothing than onerous. I called my approach guilty until proven innocent. The crime against an effective process had usually been committed before the mammoth facility was ever assembled, the fault of design engineers. It was worse when everything seemed to work fine, until it didn't.

I was thus engaged when my cell phone rang, reminding me again how much I hated those things. Unless I wanted to call someone from my car, a convenience I still marveled at. Like air travel. Didn't seem possible.

"Mr. Acquillo?" asked a woman with a low, hoarse voice, as if she'd expended her mortal vitality talking on the phone.

"Yeah. Who's this and how'd you get this number?"

"I'm calling from the office of Arthur Reynolds."

"Really. Is he in it?"

"In where?"

"His office. You said you're calling from his office."

"On behalf of Mr. Reynolds's office."

"Oh. You should tell Mr. Reynolds."

"Tell him what?"

"That his office is calling people. I wouldn't stand for that."

"Mr. Reynolds asked me to call you. To set up an appointment."

"Sorry. I'm not taking new clients."

"This is for you to see him."

"I've already seen him. Once is enough. If he wants to talk to me, he can call me himself. And tell his office to stay out of it."

"Is this Samuel Acquillo?"

"Just Sam. My parents couldn't afford two syllables. I'm hanging up now."

Which I did, though it took a few minutes to regain my concentration. Just enough time for Reynolds to get the message and figure out how to use a phone all by himself.

"Hello, Sam?" he asked. "This is Art Reynolds. Chairman of the Loventeers."

"I remember you. An expert on cemeteries."

"I was hoping we could have a conversation," he said.

"Sure. I'll talk to anybody. As long as I know what it's about."

"I was hoping to meet in person. When will you be back in the city?"

"I'm never back in the city. I live in Southampton. I can give you the address."

"Oh," he said, disappointed.

"You ever hear of the Pequot? It's a joint in Sag Harbor. I can meet you there."

"I thought you said Southampton."

"The Pequot's my business address. When's good for you? How about tonight?"

"I'm not sure."

"Check with your office. It seems to know everything."

"Would any other time work for you?" he asked.

"I don't think so. How about seven o'clock? Seven works for me."

"Will Miss Anselma be joining us?"

"That's up to her."

"Charming woman."

"If you like the type," I told him, and hung up, then turned off the phone and struggled to return to the alpha state of unhindered clarity, with eventual success.

AMANDA WANTED to know if Reynolds had asked for her specifically. I said yes, and that he thought she was charming. She had to concur.

"You don't get to be a chairman of the board without keen powers of observation," she said.

"Any idea why he'd want to talk to me?"

"When we were on our walk he tried to find out every which way what you were about. I guess I disappointed him."

We were out on Amanda's patio waiting for the sunset to make an appearance over the Little Peconic Bay. I'd already invited her to go to the Pequot with me, but just then broke the news that Art Reynolds might be joining us. We were dressed for the occasion, which meant the way we dressed for work. Jeans, boots, and T-shirts flecked with paint and dried glue. Amanda had her hair tied back and makeup minimalist. Though freshly showered, contrasting with the

Pequot's regular clientele who usually showed up straight off the fishing boats.

The owner, Paul Hodges, was an old friend of mine, going back to when I was a kid growing up in North Sea, when I wasn't in the Bronx. In his seventies, he'd turned over management to his daughter, but was often there for dinner and to encourage the preservation of the Pequot's ambience, which was to say, obstreperous and unrepentant.

You got there by sneaking past the few houses held on to by Sag Harbor natives, defiantly holding their ground against the tidal forces of heedless prosperity overrunning the rest of the Hamptons. Then you went under a narrow bridge and onto a spit of land where the fishing charters plied their trade. Once a lively little commercial enclave, they'd traded harvesting cod and fluke for the striped bass, blue fish, and tautogs favored by sportsmen. It wasn't what any of them preferred, but it kept the boats running and the families fed and educated.

The decor and basic menu had been established some-time in the 1950s, and Hodges never thought it worth tam-pering with a successful formula. I'd driven us there in my father's '67 Pontiac Grand Prix, which I kept in decent mechanical shape, deferring unnecessary body work until a future date I'd already determined to be never. It made find-ing a parking spot wide enough to contain the stately vessel a challenge, but I never worried about the consequences of doors swung by drunken sailors trying to plot a course into their pickups.

Hodges's daughter, Dorothy, in the command position at the bar, nodded to us when we came in, our regular drinks dispatched to one of the waitresses a few seconds later. The lighting had always been just within the range of normal vision, if your pupils were racked open to full stop, but that night it seemed dimmer than usual.

Dorothy came over to watch the waitress set down our drinks.

"You could go blind in this place," I told her.

"What you don't see can't hurt you. You wanna know the specials?"

"I thought everything was special."

"My brother just brought over a pail of flounder caught a couple hours ago," said the waitress. "Can't get any specialer than that."

"We'll take it. Whatever way suits the chef," said Amanda.

"That'd be cooked," said Dorothy.

I asked if her father was around. She said he was in the kitchen shelling clams.

"Tell him we're here, if you would," I said. "Just wait till he puts down the knife."

Amanda reached out to touch Dorothy's forearm and said, "That's new."

There wasn't much of Dorothy's skin left to decorate, so it took a keen eye. She was pleased.

"It's a dodecahedron," said Dorothy. "A Platonic solid with twelve faces. Two D, unfortunately, but you get the idea."

"What does it symbolize?" asked Amanda.

"A woman nearing middle age who thinks she can still hold her liquor on a date with a geometry professor."

"Is that why it's Platonic?" I asked.

"No, but it's what I tell my father."

Not long after, Hodges emerged from the kitchen, drying off his thick arms with a paper towel. His hair started thinning out years ago, but then held on, leaving a fine mist of white tangles. Face like a ceramic gnome, you wondered how he could have produced a lean and angular daughter like Dorothy, a woman whose comeliness seemed impervious to the color-shifting hair, facial jewelry, and swirling, chaotic tattoos.

He drew himself a beer and came over to our table.

"Dottie told me you were here," he said. "I hope you're having flounder. Got a ton of it back there. Cheap too. Unless you want to call it sole, in which case we'll have to double the price."

"So business is good," said Amanda, looking around at the tables and booths filling up with the sunburnt, aromatic trade.

"Yeah, they keep coming in here," he said. "Despite our best efforts."

We caught up on our latest news, leaving out the matter of Elton Darby. It made me lose track of time, so I didn't have a chance to warn Hodges about Art Reynolds, who suddenly appeared at the door of the restaurant wearing a pair of salmon-colored slacks, light green polo shirt, a white cashmere sweater tied around his neck, and a vague look of dread.

"You gotta be kidding me," Hodges whispered.

"He's with me," I said. "Nobody fuck him up."

He was about to spin around and take a powder when I got to him.

"So you found the place," I said, slipping between him and the door.

"There's no sign," he said. "I took a chance."

I tried to remember if there ever was a sign.

"Come on in. We got a table."

He pointed toward the parking lot.

"I have a colleague with me. He's waiting in the car."

"Room for him too. How do you feel about flounder?"

I half expected him to bolt when he had the chance, but he came back in with an even taller guy, this one with a linebacker's build, wary eyes, and skin that hadn't spent much time outside. He wore white on top and black on the bottom, as if he'd just come from waiting tables somewhere

in Southampton Village. Reynolds introduced him as Mikolaj Galecki. His handshake was soft and loose, which was
good, since his hand was almost too big to grip.

"Mikolaj drove, I navigated. Pretty successfully, if I do
say so."

Hodges had beaten a retreat before we got back to the
table, so there was room for four. Amanda let Reynolds take
her hand as if he were going to kiss her ring. Galecki just
gave her a quick nod.

"Are you sure this is the best place to talk?" Reynolds
asked, reluctantly taking a seat.

I looked around the noisy restaurant.

"Not holding any of them back," I said.

Our waitress cemented things by taking drink orders.
Reynolds wanted to know what they had in a red, and
she told him wine. He thought that sounded fine. Galecki
ordered a beer. They passed on food.

"Are you also with Loventeers?" Amanda asked Galecki.

He looked over at Reynolds, who said, "He works for
me. Personal assistant."

"And translator," said Galecki.

"He speaks ten languages," said Reynolds. "Very handy
in Europe."

"And Brooklyn," said Galecki.

"*Serait-il utile a Montréal?*" Amanda asked, wondering
about Montreal.

"*Seulement si vous pouvez tolérer l'accent Canadien,*" he
said, a jab at Canadian French.

"Sam's mother was French Canadian," she said.

I told him I never understood a word she said.

"*Je n'ai pas compris un mot qu'elle a dit.*"

"Oh, no, I'm surrounded by polyglots," said Reynolds.

"I dislike that word," said Amanda. "Sounds like an
affliction of the throat."

Our flounder showed up, providing a timely break in the conversation. Reynolds urged us to go ahead and eat, something I was already starting to do.

"Why don't you tell me what you wanted to talk about," I said to Reynolds, between bites.

Reynolds settled himself back in his chair, as if preparing for an arduous task.

"It's delicate," he said.

"I'm not," I said. "Just say it."

He made a little sigh, resigned to the inevitable.

"How well do you know your friend Burton Lewis's private life?"

An unanswerable question, since I didn't know much, though I couldn't imagine who knew more.

"It's none of my business," I said. "And none of yours."

Reynolds agreed that was true.

"But it is of material importance to the police," he said.

"So talk to them about it."

Galecki, never quite comfortable in his chair, rolled his shoulders, like fighters do before a workout. I took a closer look at his face. His nose was even bigger than mine, and just as crooked. One ear might have been a little puffy, and some of the flesh around his eyes. He rested a bear paw on each knee. Poised.

"I'm trying to help you," said Reynolds.

"And yourself, I suppose," said Amanda.

"Everyone loves a win-win," he said.

"What does your win look like?" I asked him.

"It doesn't involve negative publicity for the Loventeers," he said. "We've been lucky so far. I hope to keep it that way."

It felt a little like a poker game, where my opponent knew my hand, but for me, all the cards were blank. And I sure as hell couldn't read his. I bought some time by savoring a mouthful from the mountain of flounder piled on my plate. And then some more by waving to our waitress to ask for another round. Reynolds covered the tab.

"So what do you want me to do?" I asked him, after the waitress left.

"Absolutely nothing," he said. "I think that's the point. If everyone just stays calm and quiet, this will all blow over. Burton Lewis is in no danger here, I can assure you. Darby's death will be ruled an accident and that will be that."

Amanda asked him why he was so sure. He looked at her indulgently.

"Some of us just know things," he said. "I know about you, for example," he said to me. "Very persistent, I think is the term."

"We prefer pigheaded," said Amanda.

"It might have served you in the past, but not this time. Keep looking and you won't like what you find. In fact, you will achieve precisely the opposite result of what you hoped for."

When I was at the company, I liked nearly everyone but the people in charge of what I did. Not so much because they told me what to do, but for those times when they told me what I couldn't.

"You need to talk to Jackie Swaitkowski," I said. "I work for her."

"Of course you do," said Reynolds. "This wine really isn't half bad," he said, taking a sip, looking at it, then downing the glass. "So I think we understand each other."

Rarely had a statement brandished less truth.

"I hear you," I said, a noncommittal trick I'd learned from my ex-wife, who had a lot of expensive psychotherapy to back her up.

Hodges must have sensed it was time to come back over to our table.

"How're you folks doing tonight?" he asked Galecki.

"We're achieving peace and understanding," he said.

"We could use a little more of that around here," said Hodges, running his eyes around the bar and grill.

"I can handle that for you," said Galecki, with another, more subtle roll of the shoulders.

Others have tried, I thought, knowing the measure of a roomful of commercial fishermen.

"Well," said Reynolds, "we should let you get back to your evening out."

"But you just got here," said Amanda.

"I can be back whenever you want," he said to her.

Hodges was leaning on the back of my chair. I could feel him stiffen.

"Consider yourself invited," he told Reynolds. "Maybe next time you can have something to eat."

"I'm sure that would be quite an experience."

He wiped his face carefully with a napkin, refolded it, and put it on the table. Then he stood up, simultaneously with Galecki, as if they had it choreographed.

He said good evening, nodding at each of us, then they left. Hodges waited until they were out the door to say, "You're going to tell me what the fuck *that* was about."

"As soon as I figure it out myself," I said, taking a sip, then downing the rest of my vodka.

CHAPTER SEVEN

Jackie's office was the whole floor over a Japanese restaurant in Water Mill, a hamlet just to the east of Southampton Village. Her apartment was connected to the office, making it a seamless warren protected by an elaborate security system. I'd installed the system, so I knew how to get around the touch pad, though I always pushed the doorbell at the bottom of the outside stairway, mindful that a crucial part of Jackie's defenses was a military-grade Glock 10 mm semiautomatic pistol, always within easy reach.

I doubted she'd ever shoot me, though it was Saturday morning, which meant a Friday night out with her boyfriend, and bleary eyes had made greater mistakes.

"Do you know what time it is?" she strained to ask through the intercom.

"The crack of nine A.M. I have coffee. Enough for three."

She buzzed me in.

A giant was waiting for me at the top of the stairs. Her boyfriend, Harry Goodlander, was tall enough to crouch through doorways, with a wingspan rivaling Wilt Chamberlain's. Luckily, we'd always been good friends, despite Jackie telling him at the outset of their relationship that I came as part of the package. We shook hands and he led me into the office.

Harry was in boxers and T-shirt and Jackie had on her flannel pajamas, the ones with cartoon dogs scratching themselves in dilapidated rooms under bare light bulbs.

I told them I was feeling overdressed.

"You're welcome to go," said Jackie. "Just leave the coffee."

She made places for us to sit by clearing stacks of papers off a pair of opposing love seats that provided the fiction of a client meeting area. Harry sprawled out and Jackie sat cross-legged like a Buddha.

I told them about my chat with Art Reynolds at the Pequot. Partway through, Jackie came up with a pad and pen and took down notes.

"I'm not happy about this," she said.

"Tell me why," I said. "Then it's my turn."

She chewed the butt end of the pen.

"Everybody knows things we don't know and they don't want to tell us."

"Art says it's for our own good."

"Do you believe him?" she asked.

"No. But maybe it's for Burton's good."

"I don't believe that either. I'm his lawyer. If anyone should be privy to all the information, good or bad, relating to this case it should be me. I don't like swinging-dick Manhattan lawyers claiming they have everyone's best interests in mind. Usually that means it's his own self-interest that's at stake. What do you think?"

"That's what I think," I said. "Reynolds pulled out the old carrot and stick approach. Protecting Burton is the carrot, Galecki the stick."

She told me that Burton's legal status was reasonably sound, on the face of it. No one at the Edelsteins' house saw him walking away at the time of Darby's death, but no one could claim otherwise. Neither had anyone seen him scuffle with Darby, or even heard them exchange heated words. Though Burton and the Edelsteins had an agreeable relationship, they weren't that close, Burton's support of their favorite charity peripheral at best. It was their hope that the evening would draw him in closer. None of which would compel them to lie in his favor. If anything, Darby was their boy, crucially important to the organization, and thus of greater value to them. And greater still to Mercado, naturally.

"Which would make it easy if it weren't for one thing," said Jackie.

"The Southampton police," I said. "Ross isn't buying any of it, and if he's been hosting Judy Paolini from the FBI's Manhattan field office, he's not the only one."

Jackie squinted her eyes at me, as she does when she wants me to complete a thought.

"The last thing we're going to do is back off," I said.

She nodded, and Harry Goodlander said, "There's a surprise."

Before we had a chance to feel too noble, the Suffolk County district attorney charged Burton Lewis with voluntary manslaughter in the death of Elton Darby.

There are rituals attendant to an arrest that Ross was willing to forgo as a courtesy to Burton and the rest of us, but Burton wouldn't hear of it. So Jackie and I were at Burton's house when Mike Cermanski showed up with a patrolman. Burton put his hands behind his back and Cermanski cuffed him, helped him get in the patrol car, and they drove off with Jackie and me following behind.

Jackie was crying, from a combination of frustration and grief.

"This is so fucking ridiculous," she said.

"Burt won't stand for preferential treatment," I said, a half-truth. I'd never seen him wait for a table or hesitate to fly out to the Hamptons in a helicopter, rattling the plates of the beleaguered neighbors of East Hampton Airport. On the other hand, he founded his pro-bono practice to compensate as much as possible for his clients' structural disadvantages, and his standing with them was pure.

At the Southampton Village station, he was gracious and calm, bantering with the young sergeant given the task of shooting mug shots and taking fingerprints. When they were finished, we walked upstairs to the courtroom where the judge was processing a long line of drunk drivers and other traffic offenders. We waited our turn, and Jackie stood with him while the ADA read the charges, and the judge set a million-dollar bail, which Burton posted electronically with a push of a button on his smartphone.

Egalitarianism only goes so far.

"I'm going to want that back," he told the lady at the pay window, giving her a broad smile.

"Just stick around, sir, and I'm sure they'll be good for it."

He sat in the back of Jackie's Volvo station wagon when we drove him home.

"Well, that was exhilarating," he said, opening the window to get a blast of fresh air.

He'd forced Isabella to stay in New York to avoid histrionics, so it was just the three of us banging around his kitchen, into which you could fit my entire cottage, where we put together a light meal to eat at the counter.

Jackie tried to get him to review the facts of the case one more time, but he made her stop.

"I've already said everything I can say. Let's just get on with it."

"I just have a few questions, Burt," I said. "Then I promise to shut up."

He stirred a bowl of fruit and yogurt longer than necessary, then said, "Of course."

"How much do you know about Worldwide Loventeers?"
He shook his head.

"Precious little. Which is what I've been donating to them, to answer your next question. I like to keep my philanthropy focused on a few organizations I know really well. Joshua and Rosie are reputable people, somewhat silly as they are, and it doesn't hurt to be courteous with the neighbors."

"What about Art Reynolds?" Jackie asked.

"Never met him. His firm is heavy into corporate tax, so theoretically a competitor, though we operate at a slightly higher level."

"He said he cleaned up messes," I said.

"It's what we all do," he said. "There's nothing messier than the law."

I let him eat for a few moments, then asked, "Had you met with Elton Darby before that night?"

He took even longer to answer this time.

"I did, Sam. We had dinner on a few occasions. I'm not by nature an overly social person, so it gets boring, especially in the city."

I would have guessed lonely as well, but didn't say it.

"So not just a matter of getting hit up for a big donation," said Jackie, softly.

He nodded.

"Not just, though that was always a subtext. Too bad you never met Darby. A very engaging fellow. Tightly wired, but a real smart ass. I'm a bit of a sucker for people like that."

Jackie looked over at me and I acted like I didn't know what she meant.

"But that was it," said Jackie. "Just dinner."

He dropped his spoon in the yogurt bowl and took it over to the sink.

"That was it," he said. "Just dinner."

We intended to leave him alone at that point, but when we went out to her Volvo, we were met by a half-dozen cars pulling into the circle in front of Burton's house, followed by a white van showing the call letters of a New York City TV station. Seconds later they had us surrounded, sticking mics and cameras in our faces.

Jackie stood there refusing to say anything other than no comment while I moved to the side and called Joe Sullivan. I explained to him the situation.

"Any reason why you couldn't hang out here and look after Burton?" I asked him.

"None I can think of. We're allowed to do off-duty security work. Ross will be okay with it, especially since I'm persona non grata around the HQ. That's Latin, right?"

"*Illud est verum.* Now would be a good time to get over here. We gotta go and we're not leaving Burton alone with these predatory birds."

"Give me a few minutes."

I went over to where Jackie was holding off the legions and told her we needed a bit of time for Sullivan to get there. She nodded and turned to the reporters.

"Get out of my face and back in your cars," she told them. "Then out to the street. This is private property and if you aren't gone in two minutes the Southampton police will be climbing up your ass and a civil action will be headed toward your owners faster than you can say 'Fuck that Pulitzer.'"

They complied.

"I guess Art Reynolds got his bad publicity after all," I said, watching the caravan exit down the long driveway.

"All it takes is a criminal charge. Public record. Some intern, or junior schlep, at the local paper was probably monitoring court proceedings. She should get a job, or a raise, or a gold star."

"Things are different now."
"They are indeed."

I WAITED until Sullivan got there lugging big canvas bags full of portable security gear and ordnance. It wasn't the first time I'd recruited him for security detail, most recently at Amanda's house, so I knew the drill. I had to clear everything with Burton, of course, but he seemed relieved, and grateful for Sullivan's company if not his unflinchingly protective embrace.

I worked my way through the pack of media at the end of the drive with no fatalities and drove the five minutes from Burton's house over to the Edelsteins' on Gin Lane. When I got there, the gate was closed, and no one answered when I hit the call button. I could see their cars in the driveway, so I hit the button again, with no result. Then I pressed it again for about ten minutes until Joshua's angry voice came through the intercom.

"Who the hell is there?" he yelled.

"Sam Acquillo."

It was quiet for a moment, then Rosie came on.

"Go away, Sam. Joshua doesn't want to talk to you."

"I want to talk to him."

More silence, then Joshua said, "My attorney has instructed me to remain silent on all matters relating to the Darby incident."

"You mean when he incidentally ended up expiring in the middle of your shrubbery?"

Rosie came back on.

"Go away, Sam, or I'm calling the police."

Joshua was next. I wondered if they were crouched down next to each other or speaking from different rooms in their colossal coastal mansion.

"I'm sorry, Sam," he said. "I really am on lawyer's orders. I had a rough morning. You don't know. They grilled me for hours. I thought it was just a friendly conversation, and the next thing I know, it's like *Marathon Man*. I'm not used to this shit."

I rested my head on the pillar that held the iron gate, the intercom a few feet away. I'd built the gate in my shop and installed it myself. I felt around the cedar shakes that covered the pillar, checking my work. I put my shoulder against it and pushed, testing the lumber I'd pounded into the ground as structural support. No give.

"You sold him out, didn't you," I said.

Another long pause, long enough that I thought they'd finally figured out how to mute the intercom. But then he came back.

"I told the truth, Sam. Unless this country's gone totally authoritarian, the truth still matters. I know we said we hadn't heard Darby and Burton arguing, but we did. You couldn't miss it. Shouting and banging around. And then this big crash. It took a bit for Rosie and me to figure out where all this was coming from. Rosie decided to run outside, so I went upstairs and found the broken window. I looked out and saw Burton and Violeta standing over the body. The poor girl was beside herself. Rosie got there moments later and was horrified. Burton was cool as a cucumber. I don't care what I said before, that's what happened. I'll swear to it in front of God and any court in the land."

While he spoke, I could hear Rosie yelling something in the background, solving the puzzle of their individual locations. I was trying hard to hear Joshua, so I didn't make out what she was saying, until she took her turn at the intercom.

"Listen, mister," she said. "We've all had enough drama for the day. I for one am planning a quiet evening on the deck over the ocean and you should too. Tomorrow cooler heads will prevail and we'll move on from this."

I set my shoulder against the gate pillar again and put some effort into it. I was about to give up when I heard a crack and was gratified to feel it a little unsteady to the touch.

"Sam? Are you there?" Rosie asked over the intercom. "Sam? Sam?"

I let her keep calling as I walked away.

Chapter Eight

My efforts to contact Johnnie Mercado were getting me nowhere. A Google search turned up a pair of Johnnie Mercados in New York, one on the Upper West Side at about the right age, but no phone number or e-mail address. I could probably find him through the Edelsteins or Loventeers, but those weren't good options at the moment.

The only thing left was to drive back into the city. Not my usual thing, as I'd told Reynolds.

I checked in with Joe Sullivan, who was entrenched at Burton's house, along with Isabella, who seemed to be accepting the intrusion as a necessary thing. How they'd get along over time was anybody's guess.

Jackie agreed that tracking down Mercado was a good idea, especially given our truncated conversation at the funeral. So I took off in the Jeep, leaving Eddie in command of Oak Point and Amanda thankfully back attending to her construction projects.

I'd lived long enough to see the Upper West Side go from scruffy to gentrified to out-of-reach for ordinary people, if there were any of those left in New York City. The GPS on my phone told me where to go, where to park, and if I wanted, have lunch with specified cuisine and pricing options. I guess if I'd wanted a pair of local bearers to carry me to Mercado's apartment, that could have been arranged.

It was hot in the city, which meant it was a special sort of oppressive, odiferous heat. I wore a baseball cap and a pair of shorts with a hammer holster built in, though I left the hammer at home.

Mercado's name wasn't on the buzzer outside the apartment building, but Darby's was. I pushed the button, but got no response, so I sat down on the stoop and waited, grateful to be in the shade.

Eventually one of the building's tenants showed up—a young woman wearing a pair of denim overalls and a wide-brimmed straw hat. She made it easy by asking if I was waiting for somebody.

"Johnnie Mercado," I said. "Was living with Elton Darby in 3C."

"Poor Elton," she said. "Terrible thing."

"You knew him?"

"Just from the laundry room. Talkie guy. Fun, but a little jacked-up all the time. I wondered if it was coke. And actually pretty flirty, in a boy way, but only when Johnnie wasn't around. I guess he might have been a switch-hitter. I know a few."

"Do you know where Johnnie's working?"

"He's a sous chef somewhere downtown, but don't ask me where."

"I was going to ask you. Do you think I could give you a note to drop in his mailbox? I'll let you see what it says."

She said sure and watched me write it out on a sheet of paper torn from the little notebook I kept in my back pocket.

"Johnnie: Please contact Sam Acquillo asap. Important." And included my phone number and e-mail address.

"You're from Out East," she said.

"Southampton. I'm a carpenter."

It was always important to set one's socioeconomic status with a new person, since the word Southampton could have you living on the ocean or in a run-down rental with ten other people.

"Can you believe some rich guy threw Darby out a window?" she asked, taking the note from me.

"I don't think that's a sure thing quite yet," I told her, not wanting to get more into it than that.

"They seemed happy," she said.

"Who?"

"Elton and Johnnie. I'm not sure Elton was the faithful type, but when I saw them together they looked pretty lovey-dovey. No way he'd kill himself." I was reminded of Milton Flowers's sister-in-law, but didn't think it worth bringing up. "Why do you want to talk to Johnnie?"

"I met him at Elton's funeral. Just wanted to follow up on our conversation," I said. "He asked about restaurant gigs out in the Hamptons, and I might be able to help him," I lied.

"He'd like that," she said. "They had one of those relationships where Johnnie was the serious one, responsible, but could never find decent work, and Elton made all the money and was a total nut-boy. In a ha-ha way, not like a depressed nut."

I watched her through the door window stuff the note into a mailbox before using a key to open her own. I waved and she waved back. Then I sat back down on the stoop, deciding to give it another hour or so, before retreating back to Southampton. I didn't have long to wait, though, because the woman came back out again, looking concerned.

"Hey, Sam. Can you come up here? Something's goofy."

I followed her up the three flights of stairs and she guided me to apartment 3C. We stopped at the door.

"Notice anything?" she asked.

I didn't at first, but then I did. And I knew what it was. I pulled out my phone and called 911.

"Is it what I think it is?" she asked. I nodded. "Shit."

I gave the dispatcher the address and told him we probably had a dead body behind a locked door. The woman
listened with her hand over her mouth, out of fear or revul-
sion, or both.

"I grew up on a farm," she said, explaining how she
knew. In death, all God's creatures end up smelling more
or less the same.

I called a friend of mine in the NYPD, told him what
I thought was going on, and asked if he could get to the
responding cops so I could look over their shoulders. The
woman listened to my side of the call with some curiosity,
and suspicion.

"You a cop?" she asked.

"Private investigator."

"I thought you were a carpenter."

"I'm that too. Mostly that. The cops will want to talk to
you when they get here. If my buddy reaches them in time,
I can help make it easy."

"Nothing's easy," she said, and I couldn't disagree.

True to her farming heritage, she stood her ground
when the cops arrived with a crowbar and busted open the
door. People describe a wave of strong odor as a wall, and
that's what it felt like. The cops had been given a heads-up
about me, and they just asked to see my PI license and let
me stand in the hallway with the woman, who continued to
show remarkable fortitude. I couldn't see much from that
vantage point, but I could hear the cops call it in, and knew
enough of the code numbers and acronym-filled nomenclature to tell her it was a white male, mid-thirties, in the
bedroom, apparently battered, though early decomposition
made it hard to confirm.

When the cops set about securing the scene, they had us
move away from the door to the end of the hall, where one
of them took our statements. The woman learned a lot more
about me, though not enough to have her feel like I'd totally

bamboozled her with my story. I made sure to include the bit about meeting Johnnie at the funeral and my efforts to get all the facts straight in Darby's death. I didn't have to say that Burton was my friend, or that I was working for his lawyer. I could fill that stuff in later with my buddy on the force.

I wanted to take a direct look at the crime scene, but didn't push it with the serious-minded cops, and I trusted their CSIs and medical examiners to observe and interpret far better than me. So I just left them and the late Johnnie Mercado's neighbor to her disrupted day. Surprisingly, she stuck out her hand to shake.

"I wish I could say nice to meet you," she said. "But that's not your fault."

"Sorry."

"Elton and Johnnie. Boom-boom. Just like that."

I wanted to give her reassurances that these things don't just happen, that there was something purposeful behind it all, but if she'd asked what, I wouldn't have had an answer. So I just shook her hand, thanked her for her help, and drifted on out of there.

I TOOK the subway over to Worldwide Loventeers where I hung out with a Nigerian guy selling umbrellas and native art, manufactured in China, so I could stake out the entrance of their office building. He tolerated my company, especially after I bought an umbrella, suggesting that all the hot weather was a sure harbinger of big rainstorms to come. I would have opened it to create a little shade and maybe draw in a few more customers, but I didn't want to catch the attention of Milton Flowers, whom I finally saw at a little before four in the afternoon, making a break for it.

I pulled my baseball cap down low on my forehead and followed as far back as I dared. He moved quickly enough for a wide little guy, so we kept a steady pace all the way to the subway entrance. I tightened up the distance as we trotted down the stairs, and took a few anxious seconds buying a ticket while Flowers used a pass to move through the turnstile. I guessed he was heading downtown and was rewarded by seeing him on the platform checking his phone like 90 percent of the other subway passengers. This let me close in without notice so I could board the same car.

After the doors shut, I sat down next to him.

"Hi, Milt," I said.

He jumped a little.

"Shit, you startled me."

"Sorry. Where're we headed?"

"I'm going home. I don't know where you're headed."

"With you. I thought maybe we could get a drink on the way. I'll buy."

"I don't think so. What're you doing here?"

"I was planning on talking to Johnnie Mercado, but when I got to his apartment, he was dead. Probably beaten to death. So I thought I'd use the time to talk to you instead."

"Jesus Christ. You're kidding."

"I'm not. I'm the one who called the cops."

He seemed equal parts frightened and annoyed. I considered trying to calm his fears but decided against it.

"I just want to talk," I said. "Burton Lewis has been charged with killing Elton Darby. And now an important witness is also dead. You can understand why I have questions."

"That's your problem. Nothing to do with me."

He was wearing a short-sleeved shirt and tie, another thing that reminded me of the rank-and-file engineers back at the company. Contrary to popular myth, you didn't see many pocket protectors, though a lot of their pockets had ink stains from pens stuck in with the caps off.

"Ten minutes," I said. "What can it hurt?"

"My wife is waiting for me," he said.

"Invite her along. I'll pay for her too."

We endured a few stops with commuters getting on and off, some of them eyeing our seats with weary envy. I tried to guess his destination, answered when he stood up on the approach to Spring Street and Lafayette. I stood up next to him.

"This isn't going away," I said. "We'll have to talk eventually. Why not now?"

He didn't answer, but let me follow him up to Spring, where he walked with authority into a little bar that was filling up, though still with a few empty booths. He sat with his back to the door, and I was happy to sit across from him, always wanting to see who was coming and going.

He waved at the bartender and signaled for two of something he must have usually ordered. I hoped it was drinkable.

"I liked Mercado," he said. "More than Darby, to be honest. Good kid. Not that I didn't like Darby as well. I told you that."

"You did."

For some reason I hadn't remembered that he had a moustache, more grey than black, that was slightly bigger than something Hitler would wear. I noticed it when the beers arrived, cold and foamy straight from the tap.

"Art Reynolds came to see me out in the Hamptons," I said. "Do you wonder why he'd do that?"

Flowers looked settled in with his beer in his favorite spot, as if achieving refuge from the overtaxed burdens of his day-to-day life. I thought it might discourage him from talking, but it had the opposite effect.

"I can guess," he said, "but you already know. For the record, I gave him my resignation today. Sent it by e-mail. Haven't heard back, but that's not unusual. Art always expects a speedy response and never gives one back in return. Just another power thing."

I told him I liked his choice in beers. He said it was a special brew the owner of the place mixed up in his basement, probably illegal. Then he told me his old fire station was only a few blocks from where we were sitting. That on 9/11 he was in Asbury Park with his wife on vacation. Most of his mates perished. He tried to get there, but it was too late. All that was left was the giant mound of rubble and a whole lot of smoke, and even the cops he knew wouldn't let him through the roadblocks. They told him to go back to New Jersey and wait for news.

"I slept in a church that night," he said. "Episcopalian, even though I'm Catholic. I spent most of the time comforting the priest, or minister, or whatever you call those people. We got soused on communion wine. Worst shit I ever drank."

I couldn't add anything to that, so I just sat there and listened, slowly turning the tall glass of beer in the slick on the table.

"I'd already decided that I was quitting the department and going to work for God," he said, "though the priest really helped put it over. The whole thing sounds really stupid, so I don't normally talk about it. Seeking out God after being spared from a horrible death that swept up your best friends. The guilt, the need to do something different with your life. I hate hearing all that crap when other people talk about it, but that's what happened. I had the accounting degree from night school, I just needed to do the CPA exam. I like numbers. Math is math. The same numbers will always add up to the same thing. It's about the only thing a person can believe in. My only job criterion was working for people doing some good in the world. I started with the Salvation Army, then went to the Red Cross, and some other nonprofits you never heard of, till landing with the Loventeers. You're wondering why I'm telling you all this."

"Cause I'm a good listener?"

"You are, but that's not why. You're going to want me to say why I quit the Loventeers, what the organization is like, how Darby got along with other employees, all that stuff. Which I'm not going to do. Whatever I told you already is all you're going to get from me."

Without taking his eyes off me he twirled his finger in the air and the bartender said coming right up. Flowers said it would have to be his last one, since his wife really was waiting for him.

"She won't have a bite to eat until I show up," he said. "Thinks it's rude. I tell her I don't care, especially if she's hungry, but she has her principles. Like I have mine."

"Like not talking about your employers," I said.

"Nothing bad about my employers. I'll tell you good things all day and night."

He said I could find it all on their website, but their main mission was fighting poverty in remote rural regions around the world. Improving health care and nutrition, advancing economic well-being, making the world a better place.

"I guess that's noble," I said. "Unless it helps people get away with bad things."

"Here's another of my principles," he said. "My family comes first. Then God. If he doesn't like that, I'm sorry, but there's no sense lying about it since he knows everything."

"I don't get the connection. You won't talk about the Loventeers because of your family?"

He looked at me with the indulgence you'd reserve for a child or golden retriever.

"How long you been in the private detecting business?" he asked.

"Officially? Not too long. My friend Jackie Swaitkowski talked me into getting my PI license. She thought it would keep me from getting in trouble with the cops. Not sure it would have made much difference."

He drained off his beer, looking at the bottom of the glass as if another swallow might magically appear.

"Then I got some advice for you," he said. "Just let all this alone. No way they're going to convict a big wheel like Burton Lewis. Surprised it got this far. There's nothing you can do but make things worse for everybody."

I thanked him for his excellent advice, assuring him I would back off as soon as the earth reversed its axis and the Mets won the World Series. He told me he wasn't surprised.

"You got a family, too, though, right?" he asked. "Everybody's got people they'd rather not see hurt. That's the real higher power. Bigger than yourself."

I ran through a mental checklist. My daughter and her boyfriend were in France. Amanda was two hours away. Probably still at her project, a tear-down in Sag Harbor. Burton was with Sullivan, both secure. Jackie? Who knew?

I left him at the booth and went out to the curb. I called Nathan, Allison's boyfriend. He was reasonably glad to hear from me. I asked how they were doing, if everything was okay, nothing out of the ordinary.

"Should there be?" he asked.

"Probably not," I said. "But I'm hiring some people over there to look after you for a little while. Expect to be contacted soon. Do you know the name of Allison's pet hamster?"

"I do. Don't ask me why."

"They will too," I said. "They'll stay in the background, but if they want you to do something, please do it. Meanwhile, just stay tucked in for a few hours."

"I know what to do," he said.

"I know you do, and so does Allison."

I got off the phone so I could make another call. In a few minutes, things in France were underway. You could say I was an overly protective father, though once I wasn't, and it almost cost me my daughter.

I called Amanda.

When she answered the phone I said, "You once told me how much you love staying at Burton's house."

"Oh, please. Not again."

She knew what I was going to say. That I couldn't concentrate on helping Burton if I was worried about keeping her safe. She didn't ask me to explain over the phone the sudden concern, only that she looked forward to an interesting conversation.

"You bet. Sullivan's already at Burton's. I'm sure you can have your regular bedroom. Isabella still has a big stock of dog biscuits."

"When were you thinking we should go?"

"Nowish?"

Milton Flowers came out of the bar as I was finishing up with Amanda. He stood with his hands in his pockets and just looked at me. I stared back at him.

"I rest my case," he said, then strolled off like he was taking a Sunday walk in the park.

CHAPTER NINE

I called Burton Lewis and told him to expect Amanda and Eddie showing up within the hour.

"Seems like an uptick in precaution," he said. "Not that I don't enjoy having those two around."

I asked him if he ever met a guy named Mikolaj Galecki, friend of Art Reynolds. I described him as best I could. He said he hadn't.

"I haven't spent much time with Reynolds," he said. "Only at charity events. I noticed he always had a different young lovely hanging off his arm, not always his wife. Quite the rake."

There was a lot more I wanted to ask him, but not over the phone. I hated talking on the phone, with only words doing all the work. Though one question popped out of me.

"Say, Burt, you sure you don't know more about the Loventeers, what they actually do?"

"Just what I already told you. They had the Edelsteins' imprimatur, which is good enough at that point. I haven't given enough to bother vetting them beyond that."

When we got off the phone, I called Jackie and gave her the rundown. I was able to get most of it out despite frequent outbursts of "Jesus Christ!" and "Son-of-a-bitch!" whenever I was forced to take a breath.

"I could get through this faster if you stopped interrupting me," I said.

"I'm not interrupting. I'm actively listening."

Before hanging up, I gave her an assignment, tracking down Mikolaj Galecki.

"I thought the tracking down part was your part of the deal," she said.

"Not when you need investigative software. That's a job for you kids."

"You can't hide behind ignorance forever," she said.

"I didn't know that."

My NYPD friend was a detective named Bill Fenton. I got involved with him when my daughter, Allison, was beaten up in her apartment on the Upper West Side, not far from Darby and Mercado's place. I called him and he agreed to meet me at a joint where we'd spent some time in the past, close to where he worked and full of other cops, so pretty safe, unless it was the cops you were afraid of.

It was within easy walking distance of Flowers' favorite hangout and he was already sitting there when I arrived.

He'd lost some weight since the last time we got together. Other than that, still had the same lively aspect of an aging French bulldog.

"Yo, Sam. What's with the PI ticket?"

I explained Jackie's rationale for making me official, which I still didn't quite buy. Neither did Fenton.

"Won't help you much around here," he said. "Might even hurt. Unless you're retired police, or military, or something like that."

"So not mechanical engineer."

"Maybe. Your boy John Mercado got quite a workover."

He said they found him on his bed, where he was likely murdered. Strangled, beaten, fingers broken—probably defensive wounds, along with the bruising on his forearms.

"Dressed?" I asked.

"Yeah. I think he was dumped on the bed to keep things quiet."

He said there was no evidence of a robbery. Mercado's wallet and smartphone were still in his pockets. Laptops and electronics everywhere, sterling silver in the cupboard. No forced entry. I tried out the scenario.

"People come to the door. Maybe just one guy. Mercado recognizes him, lets him in. Guy pulls gun, directs Mercado to the bedroom, where he grabs Mercado by the throat, forces him on the bed, and finishes him off, choking him with one hand, socking him with the other."

"That's pretty much how I see it," he said.

"Would take some strength."

"And experience."

"So a professional hit."

"That would be my opinion," he said. "The victim either knew the assailant, or had reason to let him in."

He said they were running prints and collecting forensics, but not to expect too much.

"If the pro theory is right, there'll be nothing," he said, then got a little more serious. "What's your interest in this anyway?"

I'd been introduced to Fenton by Joe Sullivan, and he came with an okay from Ross Semple, so that meant a lot. Though Fenton was a twenty-year veteran of the New York City streets, so wariness was built in.

I told him the story of Elton Darby going out the window and my friend Burton Lewis getting indicted for it, which had led me to Johnnie Mercado's door.

"I read about that in the *Post*. I think the headline was 'Billionaire Gets Top Billing for Charity Heave-Ho,' or something like that."

"Mercado was there, but he wasn't a direct witness. There weren't any, if you believe the others in the house.

Even if Mercado had been a direct witness, we know definitely that Burton didn't drive into the city to knock him
off."

"How come?"

"Joe Sullivan's hanging out with him in Southampton.
On paid leave."

I explained Semple's decision to give Sullivan a vacation, which made sense to Fenton.

"He's just protecting his cop along with the investigation. Sullivan should give him a big hug."

"I'd like to see that."

I asked if he knew anything about the Loventeers, which
he didn't. Or Mikolaj Galecki. Nothing there either.

"I could run a search through our databases, and Interpol, if that'd help," he said. "Likely find out more than your
lady lawyer."

"That'd help a lot. And don't call her a lady. Not to her
face anyway."

I thanked Fenton by picking up the tab for his burger
and two double bourbons. That pleased him, I think. He
said he'd call me with whatever he learned. I said I owed
him one.

"Don't worry. It's like the Mafia. Someday you'll get a
knock on the door and it'll be payback time."

By then it was getting late enough to dodge the commuter
traffic heading out to Long Island. So I beat it out of there
and made it to Burton's in good time.

"Who's there?" Isabella barked at me over the intercom
at the gate.

"Sam."

"Sam who?"

"Acquillo," and spelled it for her.

"Then you're pronouncing it wrong."

I wondered how many times we'd have to have this debate.

"Just open the damn gate, Isabella. Or I'll have Sullivan shoot you."

"I don't think so," she said. "He's the polite one."

"Then I won't forget to thank him."

I'd noticed the absence of media at the end of the driveway. It was good to live in the age of the twenty-second news cycle.

Sullivan met me at the door, and as we walked the long road to the patio at the other end of the house, I filled him in on Johnnie Mercado.

"That puts a wrinkle on it," he said.

"Could be a coincidence. The director of the Loventeers quit today, before he found out about Mercado."

"Another coincidence?" he asked.

"Maybe. *Cum hoc, ergo propter hoc.* Correlation doesn't always equal causation."

"Soon as you say something I understand, I'll probably agree with you."

I asked him how things were going around the old mansion.

"Burton's kind and considerate, Isabella suspicious, and Amanda's cranky. Not at me, mind you. Eddie's clearing rabbits out of the flower gardens. The cats have disappeared, not hard in a house like this. Basically, all quiet on the western front."

I told him I'd spent some time with his friend Bill Fenton, who said he'd nose around for us. Sullivan told me Fenton's wife had died a few months before.

"Didn't show," I said.

"They grow 'em stoic on the NYPD."

"You lost your wife and you're pretty stoic," I said.

"She threw me out of the house. Important difference. Though if she hadn't, I might've killed her, and then we'd have more of an apples-to-apples comparison."

Burton, Amanda, and Eddie were on the patio when we got there. Burton seemed glad to see me. Amanda was too brimming with unspoken words to give more than a quick peck on the cheek. Eddie brought me a new ball to admire.

"He's been digging them out of the underbrush next to the tennis court all evening," said Burton. "I won't have to replenish for years."

"I thought he was chasing rabbits," I said.

"They're in full retreat."

Isabella showed up on cue with her traveling food cart, which I was glad to see, even if she wanted to swat my hand when I reached for a hot spring roll. I really didn't want to drag myself through another debriefing, but I owed it to them, so I did. Burton seemed to absorb it all, then saved the situation by declaring the subject dead for the rest of the night and launching us down the path of desultory and meaningless conversation on the current state of arts, culture, and major league baseball.

We all jumped aboard the evasion and distraction railroad and thus fully depleted our energies, and Burton's wet bar, before staggering off to bed and our respective apprehensions.

"ART REYNOLDS wants to date me," said Amanda, when I awoke to her sitting up in bed reading the *New York Times*.

"Really."

"He called me on my cell phone, a number I only give to my closest friends and clients, by the way, and said he had two tickets to that Broadway musical no one can afford to go to. He said one of them had my name on it. I don't know how it got there."

"You gonna go?"

"I've been debating it."

"With whom?"

"Me and my alter ego, the one who goes on dates with handsome, rich, and powerful men from the city."

"You know he's married."

"I do. He said she has her social life and he has his."

"You might call her to confirm," I said.

"And spoil all the fun?"

I swung my legs out of bed and went into the bathroom to throw cold water on my face. I looked up at myself in the mirror. After several decades of doing this, I still didn't like what I saw. Especially the broken nose, which hadn't seemed to repair itself, despite subtle urging.

"He didn't seem to notice I'm also already in a relationship, to use the modern nomenclature," she called to me.

"You are?"

"That was my understanding."

I stuck my head out the bathroom door.

"So what did you tell him?" I asked.

"I'd think about it."

I went back in the bathroom and took a shower. Like all Burton's bathrooms, there was plenty of room in the shower stall for a junior varsity volleyball team. I would have invited Amanda, but she was still reading and grappling with her dilemma. The bathroom came equipped with all the necessities, though the hairbrush had a hard time with my disreputable mess of curly hair, surprisingly undiminished in volume and tenacity, if losing color, now nearly all the way grey.

"You seem to completely lack the capacity for jealousy," she said, when I came out of the bathroom, wrapped in a terry-cloth robe with enough heft to endure an arctic winter.

"I'd never stand in your way," I said.

"The last time someone tried to pursue me, he ended up dead. You were indicted."

"And acquitted," I reminded her, in case that important detail had slipped her mind.

"I think I should go," she said. "You'll want to know everything you can about him. I can report back. Like Mata Hari."

I actually didn't like the sound of that, for reasons beyond jealousy. In fact, the whole thing caused my heart to climb into my throat, or drop to the earth and burrow underneath. It was hard to tell.

"It might not be safe," I said. "In fact, I think it's anything but."

She arched her eyebrows, in a way I always adored, even when they were arched unhappily at me.

"I can't take care of myself?" she asked.

"You can."

"You don't think so. Otherwise I wouldn't be here. The concern is fine. The presumption intolerable."

I sat on the bed and took her in. This was one of my favorite things, looking at Amanda. No one had more thick and luxurious hair, tending toward brunette, with scintillations of red, tumbling in big waves down over her shoulders. Olive skin like mine, but with eyes made of an almost unnatural crystalline green.

None of it would have mattered if there wasn't such a powerful dose of pained brilliance and vitality behind those eyes, but just the sight of her never grew old.

Like Allison, I'd almost lost Amanda, not that long before. Another head wound, but this one from within, a cluster of tiny brain tumors that would have driven her insane, and then killed her, if we hadn't made it to the ER in New York City at just the right moment. She still had the lingering trauma to deal with, mine was more subterranean. Or not.

"Let me know how it goes," I said. "If you want. Just leave the dog with Burton."

I got dressed and went downstairs to where Sullivan had set up his command post, a pair of big flat-screen monitors hooked up to sensors and video cameras distributed around the property. He didn't have to watch every move— programmed alarms would let him know if something was amiss. Otherwise he'd never be able to sleep or take a few moments to catch up in the bathroom on *Hard Case Cops Weekly*, or whatever else kept him interested.

"Isabella made a few gallons of coffee," he said. "If you drink some of it, I won't have to listen to her bitch about all the wasted caffeine."

"I'll do my part. Amanda's probably going back to her house. Don't try to stop her or have her monitored at work."

"I could have told you that."

"You did, sort of. *Que sera, sera.*"

"I know what that means," he said. "Fuck it, she's on her own."

"Not exactly. More like, 'how people want to live their lives is not up to you.'"

I went straight to the job I was working on and spent a joyfully distracting day taking measurements and jawing with Frank Entwhistle on the best strategic approach to the customer's fine woodworking aspirations. I left at the end of the day with a manifest of needed materials and a series of drawings already cooking in my head. To scale.

Back on Oak Point, Amanda's lights were on, but she didn't come visit me above the breakwater. I had Eddie at my feet, retrieved from Burton's. I'd picked him up before heading to North Sea. I'd only brought him to Burton's with the expectation we'd all hunker down in safety, but now that I just had the two of us to look after, it wasn't worth it.

Eddie could stay with me and be no worse for it. At least in my mind.

So all I had to do was finish off some bourbon left over from who-knew-when, which seemed like a worthy pursuit, if only to clear space for happier times.

Chapter Ten

The next morning, I made it to the hardware store in South-ampton right as it opened. The store was a family business that had been there a long time, so it was a real hardware store crammed with every imaginable item, useful for the building trades as well as the summer people who considered the experience of buying utilitarian goods a type of adventure. Most of these folks, who often came as couples, showed up after a sixty-dollar breakfast at one of the sidewalk cafés, so guys like me knew to scoot in early.

The sales clerks were clustered around the middle of the store drinking coffee and gearing up for the day. I usually knew where to grab what I was looking for, so they just said good morning and commented on the cooler day. Eminently helpful and patient—whether a builder needed to configure an elaborate set of cabinet hardware or a benighted flower from the Upper East Side was looking for a "thingy"—these were men and women who had seen it all and been asked every question there was to ask, and yet approached their duties with unflagging enthusiasm.

I loaded up on miscellany, then went to the cash register that fronted a wall of nuts, bolts, and screws in boxed order, maintained that way by keeping customers from touching any of the merchandise. I told him what I needed. He got the right box down on the counter and I pointed out the proper nut and bolt combination.

"Stainless steel," he said. "That'll cost you almost two dollars."

"Means you guys can make payroll this month."

"Is this for a job or your boat?" he asked.

"The boat."

"Oh, then that'll be twenty bucks."

I was on my way out the back of the shop when I saw Violeta, the Edelsteins' housekeeper, approaching the door. She recognized me, and hesitated, as if not knowing whether politeness called for her to say hello or avert her eyes.

I said hello in Spanish.

"Qué bonita mañana," I told her. What a beautiful morning.

This brightened her up and she answered in the same language, happy not to struggle along in English.

"Especially since it's been so hot."

"I apologize, but I don't think I know your last name," I said.

"Zaragoza. Violeta Zaragoza."

I loved the way that sounded, but didn't say it, not wanting her to misinterpret my intent. Intentionally demure with no makeup and hair pulled back, and wearing a loose lightweight polyester jogging suit, young and as pretty as her name, and thus likely subject to endless flirtations, in a variety of languages.

"I'm sorry you had to go through all that the other night," I said. "I'm sure it was awfully shocking."

She looked down at the ground and nodded.

"Such a terrible thing. I couldn't believe it."

"Burton Lewis said you were the first to find him," I said. "I think that makes it worse."

She agreed, though said the worst for her was speaking to the police. She said it was hard to find the right English words, and even though Cermanski was being civil, his eyes were stern and unwavering.

"I'm sure that was rough, but that's just him doing his job," I said.

"I'm Puerto Rican, but sometimes people make you feel like you shouldn't be here. So many undocumented."

I told her I hated that as much as anything could be hated. She smiled at me.

"I know. You are always respectful. And I hear you talking to all the men working on the house, like you are one of them."

I asked her how the Edelsteins were doing, not knowing if she'd overheard our last conversation over the intercom. It didn't seem like it, though her face clouded over.

"It's not the same. They are very unhappy all the time. The señor mostly stays in the city and the señora eats by herself when he's here. I shouldn't tell you that."

She looked like she was actually relieved to talk about it, however tentatively.

"That's okay. I know you're just concerned about them."

She gave me a hard look, the type that suggested she was weighing just how much to trust the respectful Anglo.

"Not really, Mr. Acquillo. I'm afraid."

With that, she darted into the hardware store. I followed her to the housecleaning department, which was conveniently in the back of the store, away from the gathered sales clerks.

"I'd like to talk some more, if that's okay," I said. "Could you meet me somewhere? Jackie Swaitkowski, the lady lawyer you saw that night, will be there."

She looked over my shoulder toward the front of the store and shook her head.

"I've already talked too much. My mother always said that about me. My mouth and my brain need to be better connected."

"You said you're afraid. That's a big thing to say. It's a miserable thing to be alone and afraid. We can help you.

Give us a chance." I took the store receipt out of my pocket and wrote Jackie's address and phone number on the back.

"Give Jackie a call. She's a good egg," the rough translation of a Spanish idiom.

"It has to be soon," she said. "The señora is away until tomorrow. It's how I got to go out and do some things on my own."

"The sooner the better," I said. "You can come to Jackie's office in Water Mill. The entrance is in the back. No one will see."

The calculations going on behind her eyes were vastly deeper and more complex than anything I could likely imagine. What showed was an electrified admixture of hope, wariness, and dread. She took the pen out of my hand and wrote a number on the receipt. She tore it off and handed it to me.

"It's my mobile," she said. "If you don't hear from me in an hour, you call. If I don't answer it's because I can't. Or won't."

She looked around me again and shooed me away. I did as she asked and called Jackie as soon as I reached my Jeep. It was only eight in the morning, so I knew I'd reach her.

"Wa," she said, answering the phone.

"I'm coming over. We have to meet someone in an hour. At your office."

"It's the middle of the night."

"Maybe in Japan. Here it's time to get off your ass and seize the day."

She muttered some other incomprehensible complaint and I hit the end button. I decided to give her about a half hour, time I could use to procure coffee before driving over there, a trip the summer traffic doubled the usual time to travel. I had my own circuitous short cuts, but there was no way around the painful crawl down Montauk Highway to Jackie's home and office over the Japanese restaurant.

She buzzed me through the outside door and accepted the coffee as a peace offering. Dragging herself out of bed was hard enough, but she'd also forced herself into a semi-professional skirt and blouse. I filled her in.

"Do you think she'll call?" she asked.

"I do, though she's got a bad case of approach-avoidance. Having Joshua and Rosie out of the house gives her a deadline. Might force the issue."

We only had a little while to find out, both of us jumping when a lively rendition of "The Flight of the Bumblebee" came out of Jackie's smartphone.

I only heard Jackie's side of the conversation, but it was promising. Jackie used her most reassuring voice, steady and mature. She looked at me and nodded when she said, "We'll both be here. See you then."

It took another hour, but when Violeta got there the arrival was worth waiting for. She wore a short white dress printed with giant flowers of red, yellow, orange, and green. Her jet-black hair was coaxed into soft waves, accented by curved eyelashes and full ruby lips. Silver high-heeled mules supported shapely young legs.

Though I always had a sense she was an attractive woman, I was used to her in a black-and-white house-keeper's uniform, deliberately designed to dissolve into the background of lawn parties and intimate gatherings in one of the Edelsteins' many casual seating areas.

This time I thought it was okay to point out the obvious.

"*Hola*, Violeta. You look like a million bucks."

"I hope you don't mind," she said, as I led her up the stairs to Jackie's office. "I never get to dress like a human being when the señor and señora are at the house. I feel sad for these clothes that just sit there in the closet."

"Lucky for us," I said.

When I introduced her to Jackie, we learned Violeta's English was far better than she thought it was, which was typical of Puerto Ricans, even the less educated. English was always in the air on the island, on signs and piped in from Miami, and now streamed to computers and smartphones, entirely unavoidable.

We settled in Jackie's client lounge, a pair of love seats facing each other within a fortress of stacked boxes and miscellaneous clutter. The women engaged in some banal small talk, each complimenting the other on their hairstyles, nail color (Jackie didn't have any polish on, so that was easy), and choice of shoes, Violeta clearly getting the upper hand on that as well. Jackie asked how long she'd worked for the Edelsteins, how she got the job, the usual. Turned out her sister, who had a housecleaning business, had told her about the full-time maid gig. She'd been there nearly four years. Jackie went with the flow, as artful as she always was when a client was involved. When it seemed Violeta was completely at ease, Jackie gently asked her to tell us about that night at the Edelsteins', just as she described it to the police.

Violeta tucked the hem of her sundress under her thighs before answering, still leaving an ample amount of tanned leg. Jackie didn't swat me, like she usually did in these situations. Though she didn't have to. I really was trying not to look.

"I was talking to the young man," she said.

"Johnnie Mercado," I said.

"Him," she said. "We heard this big crash, but we couldn't tell where it came from."

"Where were the señor and señora, and Mr. Lewis?" Jackie asked.

She shook her head, concentrating on her memory.

"I don't know. They were moving all around the house."

"Running?" Jackie asked.

"Not exactly. Moving quickly. The señora always moves like a frightened rabbit. She has the energy of a thousand people. I can't believe it sometimes. If I had that much money, I would sit in a big comfy chair and eat all day. But this is her way."

"So you don't know where Mr. Lewis was when you heard the crash?" Jackie asked, as if it was an incidental question.

"He ran right up after I saw the gentleman lying in the bushes. He held me and let me cry into his shirt. It was so terrible. He told me not to look."

"So Rosie came after that," I said.

"She did. Very soon after."

"What did she say?" Jackie asked.

"She said, 'Burton, what have you done?'"

"What did Burton say?" I asked.

"Nothing. He was still comforting me. He ignored the señora, like he usually did."

"How much of this did you tell the police?" Jackie asked.

"All of it. Though I'm not sure they understand me. I was nervous and the young policeman was very . . ."

"Intimidating?" Jackie asked.

"I don't know what that means. He was quiet, but strong," she said to me in Spanish.

I defined intimidating in Spanish. It took a few words.

"Yes, that's right. What Sam said."

"What about before Mr. Darby fell," I said. "The Edelsteins said there was a lot of yelling from upstairs. Between Darby and Lewis. Did you hear that?"

"Oh, my God, yes," she said, folding her hands primly in her lap. "They sounded very angry with each other."

Jackie frowned, which I didn't want Violeta to see, so I grabbed her attention.

"Could you tell what they were actually saying to each other?"

She nodded.

"Mr. Lewis said that Mr. Darby was a sick pervert, *that* I remember. Mr. Darby called him a hypocrite. He used another word along with hypocrite, but I think you know what I mean. He said Mr. Lewis couldn't hide behind his money forever. That the world would know soon enough just what sort of man he really was. Mr. Darby was very excited, I think you would say."

The cloud over Jackie's face got even darker.

"What did Mr. Lewis say to that, if you remember?" she asked, through nearly clenched teeth.

"He said, 'Not if I have anything to do with it.' A little while longer, we all heard the big crash."

Violeta looked over at me, as if seeking my approval. I gave her a big indulgent smile, which she seemed to like. She smiled back for a moment, then cast her eyes down to her lap, as if catching herself in an indiscretion.

"And this is what you told the Southampton police?" Jackie asked.

"Of course. You cannot lie, isn't that true?"

She looked at me again, as if I was her reliable validation. I nodded, because she was right. You cannot lie.

She asked Jackie if she could have a cup of coffee. Light, with no sugar. Jackie jumped up as if shot from a spring, realizing she'd never offered any. She apologized all the way to the office kitchenette with its oversized drip-brewed coffeepot. While Jackie was on this mission, Violeta asked me in Spanish if she was still doing the right thing. I said she was.

This seemed to make her more relaxed. She sat back in the love seat and let her dress pull up and legs spread just enough for me to see a pair of cotton panties. I probably shouldn't have been looking in that direction, but it's what I saw. I pretended I hadn't, but Violeta looked at me like it was a sealed deal.

Just in time, Jackie came back with a tray full of coffee and a selection of decorated sugar cookies.

"Did you notice anything uncomfortable between Mr. Lewis and Mr. Darby before the event?" Jackie asked. "How did they get along?"

Violeta thought about that.

"They were just talking," she said. "But now that I think about it, Mr. Lewis only spoke to the señor and señora, while Mr. Darby tried to speak to him. I didn't think anything of it at the time, because Mr. Lewis was the important man, and Mr. Darby was just a worker. The señora tried hard to keep Mr. Darby in the conversation because she could tell he was unhappy. They were very good friends."

"Darby and Rosie Edelstein?" Jackie asked.

Violeta lost some of her composure.

"Here I go again, like I told Sam, I talk about things I shouldn't."

Jackie nearly fell off her chair assuring her she could share anything she wanted with us.

"Many times when the señor was in the city, Mr. Darby would come to visit the señora."

It took Jackie and me a few moments to process that.

"Visit, as in come over to say hi, or, you know, visit, visit?" Jackie asked.

She looked at the floor.

"He didn't always leave until the next day."

"An omnivore," I said.

Violeta looked confused, so I gave her a rough translation.

"Mr. Darby was a very energetic and reckless man," said Violeta. "He let his interest in me be known, as well, but I wish it had been his boyfriend."

"Johnnie Mercado," Jackie said.

She smiled.

"A very handsome man. Mr. Lewis might have ignored Mr. Darby, but he definitely talked to Mr. Mercado. He asked me to make sure Mr. Mercado's drink was always full. I was happy to do this."

She sat back in the love seat, pleased with this recollection. Not so Jackie.

"So you're telling us that Mr. Lewis was paying special attention to Mr. Mercado throughout the evening," she said.

"Oh, yes. Who wouldn't?"

We asked her to think about what else might have happened that night that struck her as odd, or worth mentioning, but that was all she had. As far as I was concerned, it was plenty enough. Jackie thanked her, and then asked if she would repeat all of this in court. Violeta took a deep breath and said she would do whatever she should, because even if people acted like she was a foreigner, she was a citizen.

We both thanked her again, and I walked her down the stairs.

"I like Miss Swaitkowski," she said, before leaving. "She seems like a very calm, reasonable person."

I said she certainly was, and went back up the stairs to confront anything but.

Chapter Eleven

A few days later I was sitting in the cockpit of my boat, the *Carpe Mañana*, which was berthed next to Paul Hodges's big motor sailor, close enough to toss incisive commentary and uncleaned fish between the vessels.

Hodges was chopping vegetables and drinking from a German beer stein big enough to hold a small keg, and I was just drinking. It was well past dinner time, but I wasn't hungry, or just impatient to get underway with the nightly obliteration of memory and good sense. Hodges had a grill mounted off the stern of his boat smoldering with red coals, the destination of the hacked-up beans, peppers, onions, and carrots on the cutting board.

"I figure two cups of veggies counter the negative effects of about a half pound of steak, if taken in close chronological proximity," he said.

"I think there's a lot of solid science to support that."

"I actually like eating plant life," he said. "Of course, I also got fat on rations over in Vietnam. So I suppose I can eat almost anything."

"Anything?"

"I draw the line at raw octopus, which is a delicacy among certain Far Eastern connoisseurs. It's a consistency thing."

"Too rubbery?"

"Consistently tastes like shit."

I looked around our little marina, still lit by the fading day, but cooling as the sun fell behind a stand of big maple trees. A gentle breeze was a nice touch—warm, but vigorous enough to stir the water in the channel and the hearts of us sailors confronting dusk and another indecisive slice of existence. The American flags up on masts and mounted on sterns and pulpits flapped their irregular rhythms.

"Nice night," I said.

"That's what the weather people are claiming. Good till the weekend, when with any luck, the rain will come and drown the summer people."

"You don't really mean that," I said.

"I don't. They pay the bills out here. I only wish they'd just send over their money every spring and leave us alone to spend it as we wish."

"On beer, steak, and chopped vegetables?"

"That'd be my plan."

Eddie and I came over to the boat after seeing Amanda pull out of our shared driveway in her little Audi, wearing a dress I'd last seen on one of the rare occasions we'd gussied up to eat dinner at an overpriced seafood restaurant less than a mile up Noyac Road. I only saw the top of her, but it was enough to spark the memory. I remembered how the dress delineated all her curves and contours. And the look on her face when she came downstairs, enjoying my unabashed appreciation.

All I got this time was a glance of her passing down the drive, dust from the unpaved surface flowing behind the Audi like a dingy contrail.

Whatever brooding concerns I might have had at that moment, Eddie's only agenda was challenging the seabirds flying around the marina to life-or-death combat, without many takers. He'd been throwing down the same gauntlet for several years, and they were used to it by now.

I looked up and saw him staring down at me from the cabin top. I realized that even if I wasn't hungry, he probably was, not enduring the same existential angst, his hopeless competition with the water fowl aside. I kept a few cans of dog food onboard, so the situation was easily remedied.

"What's this thing with Burton Lewis and some fancy gentleman getting tossed out a window?" Hodges asked. "You involved in that?"

"First off, fancy gentleman sounds like a pejorative, and Dorothy would kick your ass if she heard you say it. If I don't get there first. Secondly, Jackie's defending Burton in this thing and I'm helping, and no, he didn't do it."

Hodges sat silently for a few minutes, then said, "Got nothing against them."

"Good. Then don't say fancy gentleman."

"Can I call you a fucked-up drunk?"

"Yes, but only under certain circumstances."

"Like what?" he asked.

"When I'm sober."

He left me alone for a while after that, until he said, "That sophisticated man with the sweater tied around his neck, who I would never describe as being all that fancy, had a pretty big dog looking after him."

"Bigger than me."

"Bigger than you and me put together. Glad there wasn't any trouble."

"Me too," I said. "He could have done some damage."

"Not likely. Dottie had her hand on the shotgun the whole time he was there."

"Explains the lousy service."

"Nah, that's standard of the house."

I took Eddie's dog bowl full of food up to the bow so he had plenty of room to eat. He growled at a family of Canada geese nosing around the sea grass on the other side of the channel.

"Relax, handsome. They got better things to eat than this."

Then he turned toward the dock, his tail wagging. A guy in a priest's collar was standing there waving.

"Sam Acquillo?" he called out.

"That's him," said Hodges.

I walked through the standing rigging to the stern of the boat where it was pulled up to the dock.

"Do you have a couple minutes?" the priest asked.

"More than a couple, depending on what you have in mind."

"Just a message to deliver," said the priest.

"Not from God, I hope," said Hodges.

The priest smiled.

"Not directly, though you never know."

"Come aboard," I said, and watched him navigate the dock ladder and step across the transom, tentatively, as if expecting the boat to suddenly toss him overboard. I gripped his sleeve and helped him into the cockpit.

A little younger than me, with brown unkempt hair, extravagant eyebrows, and an oversized moustache, laugh lines radiated from the corners of his eyes, amused at his own unease.

"Not used to the world shifting under my feet," he said.

"That's the norm out here on Hawk Pond," said Hodges.

He introduced himself as Jeremiah Swanson, though I could call him Jerry. I asked him if he'd like a drink, and he pointed to my plastic glass.

"One of those would be great if it's what I hope it is."

I took him down below where it was warmer, but out of interference range of Paul Hodges. Jerry said it was remarkably cozy. I turned on a couple fans and built us some vodkas on the rocks.

"I suppose you could take a boat this size around the world," he said.

"People do, all the time. I'm happy taking it around the Little Peconic Bay. So what's up?"

He sat on one of the settees in the salon and I sat across from him.

"I was sent here by an acquaintance of yours. My message for you is pretty brief, but I'm on strict instructions to keep it that way."

"Heard it in confession?" I asked.

"We handle confessions in the Episcopal faith without the special furniture, but the same basic rules apply."

"I know who was doing the confessing," I said.

Jerry took an appreciative swig of the vodka.

"I imagine you do, though I can't confirm it."

"So what's the message?" I asked.

"'Puerto Rico.'"

"That's it?"

He nodded.

"A lot of effort to tell me two words," I said.

"He didn't trust any other approach. He believes there are no secure communications these days, so he wanted to go old-fashioned."

"Sending a priest is a nice touch," I said.

"He didn't send me. I volunteered. Not a bad place to come to in the summer, though you need to do something about the traffic."

"I'm working on it. Should we stipulate that's all the information you plan to share?"

"That was the deal, though we can play twenty questions."

"Love that game," I said.

"First ask me if I think his intentions are benevolent."

"Are they?"

"Yes. It won't solve his moral dilemma, but I convinced him doing something was better than doing nothing. He knows something is wrong, but not exactly what. What's frightening is he doesn't know what others think he knows."

I told him he had to give me a bit more than that, to honor the rules of twenty questions.

Jerry sighed, and said, "The day before he resigned, he was contacted by the domestic partner of the man who fell from the window. The partner said he had disturbing things to share about the Loventeers, and wanted management to be aware. He said he'd also reached out to members of the board. My friend decided to quit the organization rather than become complicit in any way, but then the partner is murdered. It's complicated, but the net is a conscience in pain competing with a lot of fear."

"A big night of soul-searching?" I asked.

"A pair of nights, though searching souls is sort of my regular day job."

Finished with his dinner, Eddie bounded down the companionway. He greeted Jerry as if hoping to be rescued from his desperate captivity. I didn't have the heart to tell the priest this is how he greeted everybody.

"I used to have a dog who looked just like you," he told Eddie. "Only not as gallant."

"I'm glad you added that."

When Eddie grew tired of his own obsequiousness, I asked Jerry, "Just how bad is it? For the sender of the message?"

"Bad. Living in fear is no life at all. Especially fear for one's soul."

"Anything else you can tell me, without making me guess?"

"Sadly, no. I've already stretched my mandate to the breaking point. It must have been the vodka."

He downed the rest of his drink and got up to leave.

"Though I do have an opinion about vacation travel," he said. "Even in the summer, the heat is bearable in the Caribbean, and the deals, especially after Maria, are fantastic."

I stood in the cockpit and watched him climb in his car and drive away. I looked over at Hodges, who was busy grilling his vegetables.

"I'm not even gonna ask," he said.

"Bless you."

I WENT and got my laptop computer from the cottage and dragged it over to the boat, noting in the process that Amanda's Audi was still gone from the driveway, not that it shouldn't have been. Wi-Fi at the marina wasn't great, but good enough to move as fast as I was on the computer, which wasn't very fast. This was the sort of chore I depended on Amanda to help me with, having come late to the digital party and still getting used to making everything work, however poorly.

On the other hand, I once used a bank of mainframes at the company to engineer advanced hydrocarbon processing, so how hard could it be?

According to their official website, Worldwide Loventeers was founded by an English botanist and his wife, whose frequent research trips to remote, undeveloped regions of the world had ignited their compassion for people in daily need of nutrition, medical care, and basic education. A familiar story. Their twist on allaying these ills was to establish an all-volunteer organization made up of like-minded altruists, willing to give freely of their time and fund their own expenses, as a sort of tithing, presumably cementing their commitment to good works.

Volunteering With Love was the organization's original name, streamlined sometime in the 1980s, probably by a guy in the marketing department hoping to give a modern kick to their fund-raising, another element of the group's model. You didn't have to actually suffer the inconvenience and discomfort of a Third World posting if you just wanted to write a tax-deductible check. Consequently, about 80 percent of their volunteers were now manning phone banks in offices like the one in Manhattan, soliciting the guilt-ridden and taking in contributions.

Since field workers supported themselves, this money was dedicated to other general expenses, like food, water, and medical supplies. The idea was that the built-in subsidy of the organization's operations meant a far greater percentage of your contribution would be dedicated to essential supplies, a bigger bang for the giver's buck.

I moved off the official website and friendly commentary and down through layers of Google hits, going several pages in before uncovering complaints, though most of these involved logistical hiccups, illnesses contracted on the job, or easily countered gripes from the field, like, "I really didn't think I should have to pay for *everything*. Why not a small stipend?"

I did come across a news article noting one of a half-dozen missionaries murdered by a gang of insurgents in the Congo had originally come to Africa by way of the Loventeers. Another article from a few months before reported that the director of the Loventeers' campus in Puerto Rico had died of an apparent suicide.

Other than that, the cyber sphere was remarkably free of bad news about the Worldwide Loventeers.

I left the search and booked a plane ticket for San Juan, Puerto Rico.

Chapter Twelve

"Permission to come aboard," Amanda called from the dock the next morning.

Eddie jumped off the quarter berth and leaped up the stairs to the cockpit, effectively granting her request. She was in her regular work clothes—boots, jeans, and white T-shirt covered by a light baseball jacket against the moderately cool morning, the sun still getting ready to break through the horizon.

"You're up early," I said, helping her down the dock ladder.

"Implying I was up late."

"Assuming."

"That's fair, but look at my eyes. Are these the eyes of a sleep-deprived woman?"

Nothing about her looked sleep-deprived, though I wasn't sure I'd know how to determine that.

"I didn't go," she said, following me down into the galley to get the coffee-making underway.

"To the play?"

"To anywhere. I called him on the way in and said I was heading back to Oak Point."

"Okay."

She banged around the cabinets above the range, pulling out the plastic coffee *preseur*, ground beans, and a tea kettle to boil up the water. She looked up at me where I was sitting inside the companionway.

"It was a foolish thing to do," she said.

"Agreeing to go or canceling?"

"Don't get all rhetorical with me, Mr. Acquillo. You know what I mean."

"You don't have to explain anything to me," I said.

"I know, but I will anyway. You don't have any cream around here, do you? I don't understand how an otherwise cultured person can drink coffee without cream."

"Not that cultured. For example, I hate musicals."

"You have greater deficiencies than that, but we won't go into it at the moment. Not when I'm trying to apologize."

"You are?"

I went below and took out a sweatshirt to put on above my boxer shorts. I stared at the tea kettle, hoping to force it into a fast boil.

"The neurologist said I might have to deal with excess impulsivity," she said.

"Is that what it was?"

"I choose to think so. If you can't blame bad behavior on your brain tumors, what good are they?"

We left it at that until we each had our coffee, with Amanda grousing over the necessity of emergency powdered cream.

"Didn't you used to make that stuff in one of those petrochemical plants?" she asked.

"Sure. A byproduct of the distillation process. We got asphalt the same way."

Her jacket was made of silk, though long given over to rough service on her job sites. Scuffed up and nearly shapeless, on her it looked like it belonged in a designer's fall collection.

"I try too hard to protect you," I said. "It's smothering."

She wasn't the kind of woman who pretended to be independent, but actually hoped someone would swoop in to look after her. What she actually hated was being looked after.

She put her hand up to my cheek.

"Enough of that," she said. "Tell me why your computer's on the boat."

I told her about the visit by the Reverend Jerry Swanson, the message, and who and what I figured was behind it.

"So, of course, you're going," she said.

"I'll leave Eddie with you. Isabella will just make him fat."

"Please be sure to come back," she said. "I'm not sure you're entirely replaceable."

"Don't try too hard to find out."

WHEN I called Jackie, she was swimming a quarter mile out in the ocean.

"How is that possible?" I asked.

"Waterproof phone and headset," she said.

"That's nuts."

"Would you feel that way if you couldn't reach me?"

I asked if she could tread water for a few minutes so I could brief her on my meeting on the boat with Jerry Swanson.

"Not a problem. I float like a cork."

I shared the story Milton Flowers told me about his 9/11 epiphany while drinking sacramental wine with the Episcopal priest, which had seemed irrelevant before. She agreed it was a worthy lead to pursue.

"I gave you a credit card for expenses that you never use," she said. "Use it this time, just keep the receipts."

I reminded her that she was going to track down Mikolaj Galecki.

"So far, nada," she said. "Either that's not his real name, or he's not in any of my domestic data bases. Nothing on Google that fits the description. Does your detective friend Fenton have access to Interpol?"

"He's already checking with them. Meanwhile I want to chat with Ross Semple. If that's okay."

"Since when do you ask permission?"

"This is your rodeo. I'm just one of the cowboys."

"Right. It's okay with me. Just get him to tell you everything he knows and don't tell him anything."

"Okay," I said. "I think I can remember that."

"If we're done here, I've got to swim back to shore. Just stay in touch."

"I promise."

"*Vaya con Dios.*"

I DROVE back to the cottage so I could leave Eddie and pack a bag. I had some time to kill, but I wasn't in the mood to go down to the shop and work on my drawings. Instead, I went out to the Adirondack chairs above the breakwater. Eddie lay at my feet, not bothering to provoke me into tossing golf balls, or gnawed-up chunks of driftwood. As usual, he knew my mood.

Before I'd blown up my corporate job, left Abby, and spent a few months of blacked-out rest and relaxation, I hadn't been a very good student of my own mind. Setting and achieving goals had been an adequate stand-in for contemplation. It was only after I'd given myself a life sentence served at my dead parents' cottage on the Little Peconic Bay, that I took the trouble to study why my emotional condition had become such a shredded mess, a toxic waste dump of blunders and regret.

I never really came up with an answer, but at least I developed a process for self-examination, which involved important props, in particular those Adirondack chairs above the breakwater and medicinal overdosing on Absolut vodka. That day I left the booze in the house and relied solely on a view of the bay, which expressed an irregular pattern of calm water, interrupted here and there by patches of tiny herring-bone waves. The signs of light and variable winds, common that time of year. With the breeze so unevenly dispersed, the sails on one sailboat stood upright, while another, blessed with a freshening puff, heeled slightly. A motorboat, uninfluenced by the whims of the wind, struck a straight white line across the blue water.

The sun was hot enough to force me to raise the big market umbrella that Amanda had added to the setting, a complement to the three chairs, two side tables, and wicker basket filled with tossable objects in various states of disintegration.

The tide was low, revealing a band of rotting shellfish and seaweed, the aroma from which failed to deter a scattering of families and solo sunbathers from setting up along the pebble beach in front of the breakwater. A tall, skinny old guy was passing by on a paddleboard, taking advantage of the relatively calm waters. He caught me looking at him and waved, a sailors' custom, so I waved back. It meant we were both fine and in no imminent danger, which was a comfort considering my state of mind.

You've heard it noted that time is a river, though what is overlooked is all the sediment the river leaves behind, diverting the path, obscuring recollection. Experience emboldens when it's not taxing resolve, eroding vitality.

I'd learned that illusions were handy for motivating action without the inconvenience of accepting reality. If I'd ever had any of those illusional helpers, they were lost in the muddy river. I'd been driven by some indeterminate fury, propelled by an eagerness for combat, with correspondents aplenty. No need to go looking for a fight, they were always there at the ready.

Maybe that was good enough. Let externalities control the process. Keep cause and effect in close harmony. Leave solipsism to people who need to create their own conflicts to make up for the absence of involuntary penalty.

I went back to the cottage to pack my bag, determination and ambivalence picking up the rear.

THERE'S SOMETHING about the weather out on the East End of Long Island and what it does to the light. You hear about it in art galleries back in the city, and in real estate brochures trying to sell houses worth more than a small country's GDP, but the hype insults the reality. It really is different, and if you live out here, you know that. But you don't talk about it, for fear it will jinx the experience, and God will take it all away from us.

It was one of those mornings as I drove off Oak Point, heading west toward JFK airport and parts south.

Still late summer, the sun was hot on the windshield of my old Jeep, but the air coming in through the partly lowered windows was dry and riding the torrents of a northeasterly breeze. They were playing jazz on some college station up in Connecticut that my radio struggled to pull in, but it was clear enough for me. I didn't want to hear anything else. I just wanted to drink my third round of coffee and dream of unfiltered Camels, something I'd forsworn, hoping abstention wouldn't wreck the perfection of mornings like this.

My muscles were vaguely sore from the work I'd been doing for Frank Entwhistle lately, something I was trying to get used to. It was just age, which I was grateful I'd lived long enough to experience. I didn't deserve it, having been spendthrift with my natural gifts, profligate in exhausting my reserve of inherent vitality. Though I could still heave four-by-eight sheets of plywood around like graham crackers and outpace any of the eager Latino guys on the job sites, causing them to yell, "*Viejo loco.* Hey, old man. You making us look bad!"

It didn't come easy, but I wasn't ready to let down for anybody, in any language, of any age or recognizable ethnicity.

I just had to collect the aftereffects the next day, shake them off, and go back to work.

Though I was grateful to just sit and drive and feel the wind from the open windows batter the inside of the Jeep, competing with the crying alto saxophone on the radio.

I already missed Eddie, left behind on Oak Point with secret access to the cottage, where he'd wait for Amanda to show up with an evening meal and inappropriate treats. But of course I worried about him, just like I worried about everything I'd grown to love. This was the ultimate penalty for living past my expected time stamp, this tendency to horde precious beings, as if my wanting would absolve them of injury or need.

No delusion there, no introspection necessary.

Chapter Thirteen

I used to relax on airplanes until a night in Omaha, Nebraska, when the pilot was forced to land in a whiteout, a weather phenomenon involving snowfall of such ferocity that visibility goes to zero. He didn't mean for this to happen, thinking the blustery snow had moved away from the airfield, but there it was, a surprise appearance minutes before we were supposed to land.

The pilot was about to abort, and was in the process of doing so, when the ground came up and met the landing gear, deciding the issue for him.

It was a while ago, so training and technology have likely made this a remote hazard, but in those days the result was essentially a crash landing, complete with oxygen masks and luggage disgorged from overhead and flight attendants screaming only a little less earnestly than the passengers.

I bit halfway through my tongue and it felt like my lumbar had popped up into my brain stem. After the initial thud, the plane, thrown into reverse under excess throttle, shuddered and oscillated down the runway, eventually skidding off into the snow drifts, where we were greeted by a fleet of emergency vehicles rushing up with spinning lights and square-jawed first responders eager to catch us at the bottom of the inflatable escape slides.

Flying never had the same allure again.

None of this would likely come into play on the flight from JFK to San Juan, but that was immaterial to the part of my brain that had been on high alert ever since that single formative event, ever-present after nearly a million miles of air travel.

Fortunately the trip to San Juan was a night flight, and Burton's expense account included a bottomless liquor tab.

I ordered the first round in Spanish, which caused the flight attendant to ask what part of Mexico I was from. I told her I was all American, though I'd started out in Quebec. After that, she said everything in beautiful Parisian French. Everyone's a showoff. She also sold me a ham sandwich in a cardboard box with a little tub of medicinally flavored mayonnaise.

"*Delicioso*," I told her.

"*Oui, très délicieux.*"

I walked off the plane at the Luis Muñoz Marín airport and wondered, now what? I wound my way through the throngs of Puerto Ricans and off islanders coming and going to the car rental area, where I asked at the first counter what they had in the way of a four-wheel-drive vehicle. They had several, with options boiled down to big, medium, or small, and I picked the middling one, not knowing the girth of the roads to come.

The guy at the counter asked if I needed insurance. I told him I wasn't sure.

"Where is the señor staying?"

I showed him on a map where the Loventeers' campus was located, up in the hills near the town of La Selva Bendita, the Blessed Jungle. He looked concerned.

"Let me show you our premium plan."

He also made a reservation for me at a resort hotel in the Condado area of San Juan, a good place to alight and gather myself before moving inland. I think he was pleased I didn't hesitate at the choice, hoping maybe I'd just settle down and spend time at the beach with a flow of mojitos and give up on this mountain exploration.

I was traveling light, with just a duffel bag packed with a few clothes wrapped as a buffer around my tablet and laptop. I used the phone itself to guide me on the quick trip to the hotel, during which I marveled at the insulated comfort of the modern SUV, almost asphyxiating on the new-car smell and getting hypnotized by the display of state-of-the-art LEDs.

I called Amanda to complain.

"What's the world coming to?" I asked her.

"The world is coming along fine. You just need to get out of North Sea once in a while."

"I remember when Dubai was a colorful little trading town selling pearl necklaces and smuggled gold."

"My mother remembered cows grazing on dune grass in Southampton Village," she said. "What's your point?"

"How's Eddie?"

"Voracious. Can't understand why he doesn't gain weight."

"He's on the Beach Foraging Workout. Great aerobics bolstered by meals of rotting sea life."

"I might try it," she said.

"Not necessary. You look great."

"You think so?"

Amanda knew, intellectually, she was an extraordinary specimen of middle-aged loveliness, but was still a bit insecure about it, which no amount of reassurance would ever completely dispel. Not vain, exactly, but unsure how to traverse the inevitable transitions to come.

"I do."

We ambled through meaningless conversation until I arrived at my hotel, when she let me go. The reception area was open to the outside, allowing a silken breeze to animate huge potted palms and shuffle the paperwork when I was signing in. A tiny young woman with eyelashes to her forehead tried to fill me in on all the hotel's seductive amenities, but I told her I was just stopping over on the way to other parts of the island. She showed no disappointment.

"Maybe a little swim before you go," she said. "The sea," pointing a long, thin finger to the north, "or the pool, open twenty-four hours a day. We have towels."

"And a bar?"

"By the pool."

It had what looked like a thatched roof, wicker stools, and a floriferous jungle of local plant life taking up most of the space. I sat down and impulsively felt the surface of the bar, made of joined planks of dark tropical wood sealed under about an inch of clear urethane.

"Like what you feel?" asked the tall, shaggy Anglo bartender.

"I do. Not easy to get this stuff so smooth."

"Local craftsmen, dude. Rebuilt this whole place after Maria in, like, six months. Where you from?"

"New York. It's hotter up there," I said.

"PR, man. Fucking great weather year-round, if you don't mind the occasional Category 24, end-of-the-world, zombie apocalypse fucking hurricane."

"You were here?"

"Oh, yeah. Had this shack over in Loíza, which is down the coast from here, but super funky, you know, like Venice Beach meets the Ninth Ward meets, I don't know what, Oahu? Not much there is exactly built to hurricane specifications. Spent the whole storm in the bathroom, which was cool, since I had a place to pee. Until water came up through the john, which wasn't so cool. Biggest problem was keeping my man Drunk Carlito's face above the water, since he was passed out the whole time. After the wind stopped, we went outside and like the bathroom was the only thing left standing."

I asked him what they did after that.

"Drunk Carlito asked if it was okay for him to take off all his clothes, and I said, Carlito, man, that is *totally not okay*. But he said, the world's been destroyed, like it sort of was, so we can do what we want. Which I almost believed until the US Army eventually dropped out of the sky and informed us otherwise. Do you want another one of those Swedish vodkas? I'd do 'em myself, only they overstimulate the gastric juices."

I got another round and ate some food to soak up the consequences. The bartender, whose name tag identified him as Slope, coasted by once in a while to check up on me. I asked him how he ended up in Puerto Rico. He said that had yet to be clearly determined.

"I was rehearsing with a band in a house on the Outer Banks, then I was here. The stuff in the middle is a little vague. Memory can play tricks on you."

"What happened to the band?"

"Not sure about that either."

I asked him about La Selva Bendita, where the volunteers had their local campus, without mentioning the organization by name.

"*No bueno*," he said. "Maria kicked the shit out of them. Why do you ask?"

"Read about it, that's all."

"No place for touristas, amigo. Stick around here. We got the Caribbean and a pool."

"So I've been told."

I let him get back to his other customers for a while, then when he wandered back, asked him where I could buy a used four-wheel-drive vehicle to replace my rental before traveling up into the mountains.

"Why do you want to do that?" he asked.

"Don't want to call undue attention to myself."

He studied me with a look that didn't need interpretation. Then said, "Well, it's pretty simple. You find a car in the want ads or online. You go meet with the owner to check it out, do a test drive, squabble over the price, all of that. Then both of you go to *Obras Públicas* to pay off any fines he's got piled up. When that's paid off, you'll have to buy *sellos*, these stamps that show you're in the clear. Then both of you just have to stand in line for about a week to get the title, though you'll have to prove you're a resident of PR. After that, you pay for the car, then go get an emissions inspection, which usually amounts to a guy in a gas station charging about twenty bucks to glance at the car and say it's all shipshape. Then you need to go to another *colecturia* office to buy a *marbete*, a sticker you put on the window, which proves it's registered and covered by liability insurance, which'll cost you another hundred and fifty bucks, or so. Then you drive off a happy new owner. Piece of cake."

"Or?"

"I get my man Drunk Carlito to rent you his spare Wrangler for about forty bucks a day, paid in advance. With another two thousand in collateral I'll hold onto till you get back."

"You can make that deal on your own?"

"I make all of Carlito's deals. Since he's, like, drunk all the time."

The transaction moved fluidly from there, since the white Wrangler was in the parking lot and the hotel was able to use my credit card to advance me the necessary cash. I asked Slope how he was going to get home, and he pointed to the street in front of us.

"Bus station four blocks thataway, on foot. Exercise will do me good," he said, handing over the keys. "If you get busted for anything, I'm saying it was just a loan to avoid any accessory-before-the fact shit. Appreciate you honoring that."

When he went back to the bar, I examined my new ride, which was in reasonably good shape, if you overlooked dinged fenders and the subtle whiff of mildew, apparently from losing part of the soft top in Maria. It was a stick shift, like my Cherokee, and the gauges looked to be in familiar places.

I cleaned out an assortment of local and imported beer bottles and cans from the back seat and trunk area and went back inside to sign for my bar bill. Before heading to my room, I asked Slope if he had a first name.

"Slippery," he said. "But no need to stand on formalities."

Chapter Fourteen

I turned in the luxury SUV at the rental company's San Juan office, checked out of the hotel, and tossed my duffel bag in Carlito's Wrangler.

I wore a white T-shirt, jeans, and the lightweight hiking boots I used on the job. My first stop was a hardware store, where I bought a one-inch-diameter wooden dowel, a coping saw, and a roll of duct tape. I cut the dowel down to about eighteen inches in length, wrapped one end with the tape, and stowed the result under the front seat.

The air was wet with wind-driven humidity, the sun behind a veil of haze. I had the radio on, trying to keep up with the rapid-fire, English-infested Puerto Rican Spanish. The GPS on my smartphone plotted the course, but I kept track with a paper map open on the passenger seat in case the signal failed.

As I moved from the traffic-clogged highways around San Juan, then onto the minor arteries, and finally entirely rural roads that wound their way up into the hills, the Puerto Rico of my prior visits emerged. I remembered a dense tree canopy and exuberant tangles of tropical foliage, much of which had made a spirited comeback, I was happy to see. Stalwart plastered concrete and cinder-block structures painted faded shades of yellow, gold, green, and pink, stood defiant in the midst of the destroyed flora spilled around the properties, much of which had been gathered into piles to await further resolution.

Blue FEMA tarps were in evidence on pitched roofs, but so was new metal and tile. Other buildings were dejected wreckage—crumbling, abandoned, and left for dead. I wondered how long they'd stand there and how deep their local stories would become.

The Jeep's capable traction in four-wheel-drive soon proved its utility over roads that were never a model of fine finish, potholes and crumbled shoulders now abundant and treacherous as I climbed farther up. Not an uncommon vehicle in those parts, it drew little notice. I probably wouldn't either, curly-haired and bent-nosed as I was, looking Latin enough to pass for a native.

A dog, about Eddie's size, though skinny and short-haired, walked out into the road and stopped, looking my way with hostility shaded by indifference. Slow moving as I was, it wasn't hard to pull up to a halt. I waited him out, finally tapping my horn, which resigned him to moving on along.

I could easily imagine some muttering under his breath.

As I came up to each crossroad, I consulted the GPS, which gave me the answer. The mechanical voice mispronounced the street names, but was close enough for me to decipher what to do. There was no setting that would tell it to speak like a regular Puerto Rican.

About two hours in, moving at about ten miles an hour max, I could see that I needed another half hour to get even close to my destination, assuming increasing up and down travel, shown as a curvy line on the GPS map. So I began to look for a place to stay the night.

I asked Google its opinion of my options, and it just sent me back to the north coast. I would have appreciated, "Sorry, man, you're on your own." Since I was.

I still had solid cell service, surprisingly, and was tempted to call Amanda, but thought better of it. Nothing I could say would make her feel better about me being here, and it would only make me feel worse about not being there.

Little businesses still appeared at intersections, so I pulled into a tumbled-down *colmado* of indistinct character to consult.

After buying some water and a bag of *alcapurrias*, I asked the kid at the cash register if he knew where I could put in for the night. He asked me if I was from Mexico.

"Nah," I told him in my inflected Spanish. "I'm from New York. Most of the guys I talk to are Mexican, or from Central America, and that messes with my accent."

"My Uncle Xavier lives in Brooklyn," he said in English. "No one here understand him anymore. Talks like a Yankee."

"So do you," I said. "Which is good, since the Yankees are going to win the World Series this year."

"You better believe it," he said. "My cousin has a tourist hotel in La Selva Bendita. I think they're open. I can call her and ask."

I gave him my smartphone and he punched in the number. After a few moments of back and forth, he handed me the phone. "She say maybe."

The woman on the other end of the line sounded tired.

"How many nights?" she asked in Spanish, without preamble.

"Just tonight, I think."

"Pay in cash. Power may be on, may be off. We have candles."

"That's fine. Just need a bed."

"We have a generator, but you'll have to pay for gas," she said.

"That's okay. Probably won't need it."

"Give me back to my cousin."

The two of them seemed to be catching up on family matters. The kid looked at me when she was talking and nodded his head, saying something like, "Seems okay. Just an old guy from New York."

After hanging up, he pulled out a road map and showed me where to go. It was farther up into the hills, with a little road winding through lots of green shading.

"People go there for the rain forest," he said, "though to me it's just the *campo*. Full of things that bite."

"Thanks for this," I said, handing him a twenty-dollar bill, to his pleasant surprise. He suddenly looked more cooperative.

"I can take you around here if you want," he said. "We can look for monkeys."

"There're no monkeys in Puerto Rico."

"Escaped from medical labs, man. They're out there."

"Maybe later. I know where to find you."

"*Planet of the Apes*, man, I'm just saying."

Night had fallen, and it took about a half hour to wend my way up the narrow road, once paved, but now little more than a gravelly path, to a house lit up within the tangled overgrowth as if signaling the way.

An angular, black-haired, middle-aged woman wearing shorts, flip-flops, and a faded "I Love New York" T-shirt came out to greet me.

"I only have a *casita* over there," she said, pointing down a pathway. "It has a bed and running water, everything clean."

"*Eso es todo lo que necesito,*" I told her. That's all I need.

"So walk this way," she said, with a big wave of her arm.

I followed her carrying my duffel bag. Ten minutes later, we arrived at a hut that reminded me of the motel cabins in the Hamptons that proliferated before the war and were still plentiful when I was growing up. One room with a bed and desk, plus a separate bathroom with sink, toilet, and shower. Smelled moldier than my Wrangler, but no leaping or soaring insects within view. The lizards had already headed for their escape routes.

I gave her the night's rent in cash and reemphasized my appreciation for her hospitality. She wasn't impressed, but spoke as if she was.

"We're working hard to get up and going again," she said. "Tell your New York friends. Remind them Puerto Ricans are American."

"I will."

She looked both dismissive and reluctant to leave.

"What are you doing here?" she asked.

I had a cover story ready, though it embarrassed me to use it.

"I'm writing an article for a newspaper."

Her disdain deepened.

"You know how many of you assholes came through here after Maria?" she said, in perfect, accent-free English.

I was tired, unnerved by the strangeness of driving up into the hills and finding a home for the night, which might have influenced my response.

"I don't know," I said. "A couple thousand? I'm here on a follow-up. Just tell me what you want and I promise it'll get into my story."

She examined me the way Slippery Slope had done back at the bar in the fancy hotel.

"What happened to your nose?" she asked.

"Busted in a professional boxing match. By a Filipino guy named Rene Ruiz. I still managed to knock him out, though he lives on every time I breathe."

"I think you're lying," she said.

"Not about the nose. Just let me go to sleep and I'll be out of your hair by the morning."

She went into the bathroom and came back holding a white towel, which she tossed in my lap.

"Be sure to do that. You stink of trouble."

"I'll wash it off. Promise," I said, holding up the towel.

Before she could leave the little room, I said, "Not all trouble is bad."

She had a broad face, unaccustomed to subtle expression, though it almost seemed to give up a little.

"We'll talk about that if I ever see you again," she said, softly closing the door.

I OVERSLEPT the next morning. I dreamed of missing trains and losing valuable possessions. I protested loudly, but no one seemed to care. At one point, Eddie was lost in San Juan and Amanda unable to call me back on my smartphone, claiming technical incompetence, which in the dream I thought was a subterfuge. Art Reynolds was hanging behind her, grinning.

I woke in a sweat. The bed, made up of coarse cotton, was soaked through. Wet and hot inside the sheets, my face was cool, and my arms, out in the air, were blanching from the cold. It was confusing.

The nasty dreams, conflating with reality, lingered. I yelled "Jesus Christ" into the air and heard "He is our Savior" in return.

The casita's owner was outside my door, knocking. I got into my jeans and T-shirt and answered.

"Wanted to be sure you're not dead in there," she said. "You said you'd be long gone by now."

"Sorry. I overslept, something I never do."

"Travel will do that. Happens to me when I go see my sister in Cincinnati."

"I'll be out of here soon as I can."

"My nephews are up at the house. They'll see that you are," she said, and stalked away.

True to her word, a pair of young guys were leaning against the front of the Wrangler, arms folded in a caricature of dimwitted pugnaciousness. One taller than the other, with more or less the same-looking face. Each wore a baseball hat from competing National League teams. I walked past them and opened the Jeep, putting my duffel in the back. The shorter of the two stepped around and stood in front of the driver's side door.

"Good morning, guys. How's it going?" I said in Spanish.

"You got to leave," said the guy in front of me, wearing a Phillies cap.

"Happy to do it, soon as you move out of the way."

"Maybe quicker if we carry you," said the other one, a supporter of the Mets.

"Feet first," said Phillies cap.

"Doesn't seem all that efficient," I said. "Why don't I just drive away?"

"We want to know what you're doing in La Selva Bendita."

They were different heights, and the shorter one much heavier, more fleshy than toned.

"I want to know why the swallows always return to Capistrano," I said, "but I'll probably never find out."

"That's not an answer."

"Yes, it is. But what about, I'm just passing through?"

"Why stay here?" one of them asked.

"It's a nice place. And your aunt is a nice lady."

"She don't like you," Phillies cap said in English.

"That's too bad, since I like her. Why the attitude? I'm just trying to leave."

The tall guy in the Mets cap moved next to his brother, too close to get his longer arms into play. They had their fists partially raised, but the way they stood and their foot placement were all wrong. Amateurs.

"You might not know about Capistrano, but are you familiar with Newton's Laws of Motion?" I asked them, stepping away from the car and flexing my hands. "Number three is 'for every action there's an opposite and equal reaction.' They teach you that in school?"

"Newton who?"

"Sir Isaac. Famous for his apple."

They separated a little, which was actually better for me, though it was clear we were about to get into it. It didn't make me happy, so soon after waking up with my head still full of jittery nightmares.

"You're talking nonsense," said Mets cap.

"You're a dumb fucker," said his brother, or the equivalent in Spanish. "Dumb fucking gringo."

"That's an ugly word. I don't like it," I said.

"See if you like this," said Phillies cap, taking a swing he'd telegraphed all the way from San Juan. I blocked it with my left and stuck a right jab in his nose, which I know from personal experience hurts like hell. He stumbled back and fell over his own feet.

"Newton's third law explained," I said. "I punch you, you fall down."

Which is what I also did with Mets cap, who went over like a tree.

I could tell that Phillies cap was neither stupid, nor lacking in courage, though practice in the ring might have improved his effectiveness. He scrambled up onto his feet, and thinking he had a weight advantage, bent over, and came in swinging blind. Blind being the operative word. I stepped aside and let him go by, then swiveled and hit him in the right kidney. This also really hurts, which is why boxing rules say you can't do it. Not that we didn't try anyway.

He grabbed his side and stood up straight, exposing his face, which allowed me time to gather up a cowboy round-house, which I used to launch him off his feet and back onto the ground, where I hoped he'd stay. Just in case, I got my homemade club from under the driver's seat and stood at the ready.

"You fucking idiots, what the hell are you doing?" their aunt yelled, running down the front path holding a broom.

"I was trying to leave," I said, though she ignored me and went after her nephews, whacking them with the broom. I have a pretty good command of colloquial Spanish, even the Puerto Rican variety, but she called them things I'd never heard before.

"I said to make sure he leaves, not get into a fight, *imbéciles!*" was the gist of her complaint.

Not caring how the conflict might resolve, I just got in the Jeep and rode away, flexing my right fist to make sure I hadn't broken anything. Except for a small cut on my knuckles, all was well.

"So much for undue attention," I said out loud, the kind of thing I'd say to Eddie, but he wasn't there.

I wound back down the bumpy, narrow, barely manage-able road, keeping the rest of my thoughts to myself.

Chapter Fifteen

It took about a half hour of rotten roads and up and down driving to get to the entrance of Worldwide Loventeers, Puerto Rico Campus, in La Selva Bendita. I drove by without looking closely and stopped where a guy was working on the side of the road. He had a big wrench on a piece of pipe sticking up out of the ground; I assumed a well head, but it could have been anything. I asked in Spanish where a man could get a drink in those parts.

I didn't need one, but there's no better way to approach unfamiliar terrain than via the local bar. He gave me directions to a place called El Rancho de Velilla down the road where I could get lunch and a beer. He said it looked like a house, but if you went around back, there were outside tables and a bar tucked up under a freestanding metal roof, since Maria had blown away the original building. He said to get the *arroz con habichuelas* with chopped-up sausage.

Everything was as advertised, though he'd failed to mention the gutted carcass of a small car up on jacks in front of the place. Two of the plastic tables were occupied by men hunched over their meals beneath fresh orange and red umbrellas. I sat at the bar under the improvised shelter, somewhat upwind from the wood-fried grill, and asked the barmaid for a Medalla Light to go with my *arroz con habichuelas*.

She left me alone to eat so it wasn't until she cleared the empty plates that I asked about Worldwide Loventeers, and if they employed people from around the area.

"They do, thank God," she said. She described how Maria had virtually wiped out the local plantain plantations and all the little businesses that served the agriculture business, making the Loventeers one of the few places to find work. She wasn't sure if they took Mexicans without visas, assuming my status from my accent.

"But if you have English and education, they might not care," she said, more advice than speculation. She left the bar for a moment and came back with a ragged printout that listed employment opportunities on the campus. As she suggested, there were plenty of openings to work in the office, requiring good English skills, but also in construction, all trades welcome. I asked about that and she said they were still rebuilding after the hurricane, and most of the local tradesmen had left for the coasts where the need was vast and the money far better.

"My brother is in Mayagüez fixing roofs for the university," she said. "Our mother still has a FEMA tarp on hers, but I don't blame him. We're happy to get money sent to us every month. It paid for gasoline for the generator until the power came back on after nine months. My mother refuses to leave her house. She's afraid if she leaves they'll never let her come back."

She drifted away to help other customers, and when she came back I asked her how most people fared in the storm.

"They say it sounds like a freight train, but no freight train is that loud. Our roof stayed on, but water came in from all sides and from up above. I keep thinking it's almost over, then it gets worse. And this is for hours. Ruined everything. My plants with flowers, all gone. I don't even know what they're called so I can get new ones. Our neighbor next door was very old and had a machine to give him oxygen.

So without electricity he died in about two days. We buried him in his backyard, because there was nothing else we could do since the bridges were all gone and there was no gasoline for the cars anyway. We might have starved if my husband hadn't grabbed up a few baskets of plantains and bananas before the storm. We collected rainwater to drink and cook, and washed in the river once it calmed down."

I guessed she was somewhere in her thirties, and as with so many of the hurricane survivors, too poor or too stubborn to abandon their old lives, Maria had beaten her up, but had failed to douse her spirit.

"When they finally came with water and gasoline, we had to stand in line for hours. So we brought along radios and Medallas so we could make noise and dance to the merengue and bachata, two wings of the same bird, to pass the time. Because this is what Puerto Ricans do."

I thanked her for the meal and information and left a sturdy tip. She thanked me, and wished me luck, since that was a commodity in even less supply than a waterproof place to sleep.

No PLAN is perfect, but at least I had the basic outlines of one when I pulled up to the locked gate. It would involve creating a false identity, something I had little practice in, with every word spoken in Spanish. Though I had grown up with a number of kids in the Bronx and Southampton who had pursued careers in illegality, most of whom were fluid and adept weavers of fanciful selves. The trick was to stay as close as possible to the truth.

"I'm a builder looking for work," I told the white-shirted security guard at the gate.

"What sort of work?" he asked.

"Carpentry, if it's available, but I can do anything."

He looked in the back of the Wrangler.

"Where are your tools?"

"Stolen," I said. "One reason I need the job."

He stepped out of earshot and called someone on a hand radio, eventually nodding at me and opening the gate. He had me stop just inside and wait for another guard to escort me onto the grounds. I thanked him, which only elicited a slight shrug and a stern expression on his face. The universal language of security guards the world over.

The next guy was older, but a little friendlier and more forthcoming. He had a Wrangler of his own, which I followed down a curved drive to a squat metal building identified as the security office. It looked new, though temporary, the kind often used as office space on a construction site. The reception area was a small room with two desks heaped with papers and printed manuals. A rack on the wall was filled with walkie-talkies with a sign-in/sign-out sheet posted next to it.

I stood and waited for about ten minutes before a third man arrived, this one in a short-sleeved shirt and tie. Young enough to still be in college, by appearance, and positively ebullient compared to the security force.

He introduced himself as Daniel Osterman, executive director of the Loventeers' Puerto Rico Campus, and shook my hand.

"Carlito Montaño," I said, the first big, but essential lie.

He led me to a canteen, with a sink, vending machines, coffee maker, and the sour smell of past meals. We had the room to ourselves.

"So please tell me, Carlito, how you came to be way up here in La Selva."

I gave him my story. I had been working on a condo complex in Condado and was stupid enough to go out drinking at some crummy place just south of there with a few other carpenters from the job. It was a tired, but reliable story of fumbling with my car keys, getting hit from behind, and waking up with a bad headache and all my tools taken from the Jeep. I was tired of that job anyway, tired of the city, and generally bored. So I packed a bag of clothes and took off, only stopping when I came to the bed-and-breakfast, where I spent the night, and then was directed there by the barmaid down the road.

"You're a carpenter?" he asked.

"I am, but I've done it all at one time or another. I'm not great with plaster, careful, but too slow, and not much of a painter. But I can lay up block, or brick, and level concrete. Metal work is okay and I can run electrical and plumbing. But finish carpentry and building cabinets are my main skills. I've also managed crews in Mexico and the US."

He looked pleased by all this, literally jumping around in his seat when I mentioned finish carpentry. Or maybe that was just youthful energy. I made sure my hands were always well in view, nicked, scarred, and covered in calluses, my forearms overdeveloped from constant manual labor. I was braced for questions about work visas and certifications, but they never came. Nor any prying about how I ended up in Puerto Rico. It told me how badly the Loventeers needed help with rebuilding, and their current relationship with official propriety, which was casual at best.

He left me alone with the coffee maker and a bag of Café Rico, which I turned into a dense and bracing black brew. I was on my second cup when he came back with a guy whose balding head was framed by thin, white hair, though by the overall look of him, not much older than me. He had even less concern about my documentation, but there was another hitch.

He was a Mexican.

I'd spent a number of years going in and out of an oil refinery just over the border with Texas, so it gave me a place to be from, and a vocabulary rich in industrial Spanish. He looked satisfied enough, especially after I gave him a loose résumé of my experience with hammers, power tools, arc welders, and electrical testing gear.

So I got the gig, along with a plastic name tag with my photo and a room in a bunkhouse with a freestanding closet and sink, showers, and toilet down the hall. My new boss waited for me outside while I stowed my stuff, taking a few extra minutes to tape the laptop to the back of the closet. Then we stopped off at a construction shed where he gave me a leather nail bag with a built-in hammer holster, and we put together a canvas satchel filled with carpentry tools. Plus a circular saw and a battery-powered drill for driving in screws. Basic, essential gear.

"We're putting an addition on the hacienda," he told me, adding that they had a temporary shop set up on the job site.

To get there, we got back in our vehicles and I followed him farther up the hill through splintered and truncated foliage, though still dense, and covered in bright-green new growth. At the top of the hill, the world was transformed.

The gravel road became a paved driveway that led up to a circle in front of the stucco hacienda, painted a brilliant white, with a grand staircase leading up to the second story, three-sided porch. Large, tapered columns supported the porch roof, which had been recently reshingled in a rust-red asphalt made to resemble tile. Tall double windows were open to the porch, and ceiling fans turned listlessly overhead. To either side of the stairway, giant palms and floral shrubs—lobster tails and birds of paradise—screened and blocked access to the first floor.

It was a big building, easily ten thousand square feet viewed from the exterior, though I knew there was probably a center courtyard behind the facade, carving out some of that space. Behind the hacienda, other buildings were attached, suggesting years of progressive add-ons. Some of these had freshly troweled-on stucco, others plain cinder block, all recently painted the same eye-searing white.

My new supervisor, Ramon, led me down a path and around to the back of the complex to another attached extension, this one a single story made of cinder block in the process of being sheathed in stucco.

Inside was one big room, about thirty feet by forty feet. Two-by-fours and finish lumber were stacked on the concrete floor. Overheard the roof structure was a truss-style that could handle the span without vertical support, this one held together with metal plates and straps, and an abundance of through bolts. All covered with metal roofing panels on top.

"Gusts up to two hundred miles an hour," said Ramon, anticipating my question. "Any more than that, the world is probably coming to an end anyway."

The temporary shop he described was in a far corner. It had a table saw, cut-off saw, a compressor with a collection of nail guns, and a workbench made of plywood and sawhorses. My natural habitat.

"So what are we doing here?" I asked.

"Making the inside. I have drawings."

He spread out rolls of plans pulled from a big cardboard tube. They were professional architectural renderings, detailed and precisely drawn using draftsman software. The kind of thing I worked with every day.

We held down the corners so I could give them a good look over.

"Okay," I said.

"Okay what?"

"I can do it. Any helpers available?"

"You're looking at him."

"Good. Let's start tomorrow after I've had a chance to plan the approach. Unless you've got one in mind."

He shook his head.

"I'm a stone mason. My plan was to figure out how to fashion wood without cutting off my fingers."

"So you've already learned lesson one."

Left alone, I laid out the first steps and did an inventory of tools and supplies. There was enough to get through the initial framing. I listed what was needed to take it from there.

Not that I ever thought I'd get that far.

Chapter Sixteen

A week later, Ramon and I had framed up all the interior walls. It was only then that the executive director found a moment to wander into our work space to appraise the progress.

"Lookin' good," he said in English, examining the interior framing that defined rooms and hallways, door openings, and support for future mechanicals. I acted like I didn't understand him. "Nice work," he said in Spanish, making a pantomime of swinging a hammer.

"*Gracias.*"

"Ramon tells me you're a very good carpenter."

"He's the skillful one. Easy to work with," I said, with all truthfulness.

"If you have a moment, I'd like to get your opinion on something."

I said sure, and followed him into the main building. We traveled through a windowed passageway to a heavy door that he opened with some effort. On the other side I was assaulted by a blast of air-conditioned air and a sudden drop in ambient noise. There was deep carpet on the floor, curtains made of floral fabric pulled back from the windows and heavy wooden desks occupying an open space filled with young men and women, dressed in shirts and ties, sensible skirts and pale blouses, flat shoes and clear complexions, some Latino, some not.

They spoke in barely audible Spanish and English. Computer screens were lit up and hands danced over keyboards. Some wore earbuds, the delicate wires draping down their chests like high-tech necklaces.

As I walked through the room, I felt like a mountain ogre spreading sweat and sawdust in my wake. The men tried to smile as I passed by, the women diverted their eyes. I adjusted my tool belt to keep it from knocking into anything.

The eyes following the executive director were a mix of amusement and disdain. One of the men flicked his hand under his chin. A woman next to him swatted him, looking both wary and filled with fun.

"It's in here," said the director. "A silly thing, but it's driving me nuts."

It was his private office, a monkish spare room with the cloying mildew smell that seemed to permeate much of the island. He pointed to a bookcase behind his desk, which was sagging noticeably to the right, the side facing the window.

"I'm afraid it's going to fall," he said, a legitimate fear. The swaybacked shelves and vertical supports were soft to the touch.

"Rot," I said. "The whole thing has to be replaced."

"I know," said the director, ashamed to face the inevitable. "Can you do it?"

"Of course. A lot of these books will have to be thrown away."

"That's okay. I don't read them anyway. I inherited all this."

"How long have you been here?" I asked, taking a chance with a personal question. He actually lightened up.

"Three months, two weeks, and a day. Not that I'm counting."

"You're a good man to be doing this important work," I said, trying like hell to sound sincere.

"That's what I keep telling myself."

Someone knocked on the door, an imperious little tap-tap-tap. The director looked wearily at the door.

"Yes, Ruth."

A large woman with an English accent came in clutching a loose pile of papers. She wore a print dress a size too small and a hairdo a few sizes too big. She was around fifty and all her weight was above her waist, the type of shape I always feared would topple over at a moment's notice.

"Daniel, we need to get these reports signed and sent off. Oh, sorry," she added, seeing me there in the room.

I smiled down at the floor, the dutiful servant.

"He's here to fix my bookshelf," said Daniel.

"*¿Inglés?*" she asked me.

I shook my head.

"People are coming, you know that," she said to Daniel. "Everything has to be in perfect order. We can't disappoint."

"We won't," said Daniel, with a kind of exhausted resolve.

The woman inhaled a deep breath, then barked out, "Are you a dedicated Loventeer?"

"I am," said Daniel, proclaiming with shoulders suddenly straight and proud.

The woman's view drifted over to me, pausing longer than I wanted. I kept my eyes averted, fiddling with my tool belt.

"I'll be in my office next door," she said to Daniel, though still peering at me. "I don't want people like this in the hacienda," she added.

I smiled at her like she'd just given me a wonderful compliment and watched her spin around and leave.

RAMON WAS pissed that I'd been pulled off the big job to make a new bookcase for the executive director. I couldn't blame him, having known that rage from similar situations back in corporate America. All I could do was promise to build the thing after hours from the available supply of finish pine.

"Won't take long," I said. "It's just a bookcase."

As promised, I waited till it was time to knock off, then asked which of the finish lumber I could use for the book-case. We'd had another good day and I was sorry to remind him of the director's request.

With a lot of muttering and unnecessary struggle, he came up with enough eight-foot, three-quarter-inch pine boards to complete the task, seemingly among the knottiest in the stacks. As we laid them on the worktable, I asked him a question.

"Say, Ramon, I see people working in the office, but where are the ones being helped?"

"At the Caring Center. That's all separate," he said, jerk-ing a thumb over his shoulder. "In another place down the hill. Why do you ask?"

"Just curious. I thought I'd see kids running all around."

He grinned at that, though not sympathetically.

"Maybe that's why they put them there. They don't like the noise."

"Whatever," I said. "Just seems odd."

Ramon's frustration with the director's bookcase seemed to deepen into hostility.

"Lots of odd things about the Loventeers, Carlito. Better not to be too curious."

"Can't help it. It's my nature."

He told me the old proverb about the scorpion and the frog, which I hated from the first time I'd heard it, but pre-tended to thank him for his advice. Then before he left me to get on with my night job, said, "Don't make this thing into a work of art. They don't deserve it. The motherfuckers," he added, in English, like a true kid from the neighborhood, which made me feel strangely homesick.

"Fuckin' A, brother," I said, and we executed an awkward, painful fist bump.

THE BOOKCASE was ready the next morning.

It wasn't much of a structural wonder, pieced together with a little glue and a finish nailer, but would stand up to your average rows of books once it was screwed into the wall.

Ramon reluctantly agreed to go into the hacienda to fetch the executive director. I told him the sooner I got it installed, the sooner we could get back to the job at hand. Soon after he came back to say the director was away from his office, but we should just lug the bookcase in there and to hell with permission.

We almost made it to the executive director's office when two oversized guys in tropical shirts stopped us in the middle of the open area full of millennial worker bees. They spoke to us in English, but it wasn't hard for either of us to understand.

"Get that goddamned thing out of here."

Ramon struggled with his limited English to describe what were doing. The two guys seemed less than sympathetic. One of the kids from the office stepped up to help, explaining the situation to the two tropical shirts.

"Tell them it will only take a few minutes," I said to the kid.

One of the tropical shirts moved us along with an impatient wave. The other followed us a few steps behind. The director's door was unlocked, so we let ourselves in. They stood outside while we pulled out the old bookcase, stacking the books in a corner in two piles, one good, the other irredeemably foul.

When we had the new case firmly attached to the wall, the guy was still waiting outside in the hall. With no words passing, he escorted us all the way to the big office area, then left us to go the rest of the way on our own. I told Ramon to go ahead of me.

"I need to take a piss," I said. He was troubled by that, saying I could just go behind the new building. I opened the door and gently guided him out. "I'll only be a few minutes."

I made it all the way back to Director Osterman's office unmolested, so I kept going. I followed the hall past other enclosed offices, pausing when I heard voices coming from around the next corner. I strained to hear. From the sound of it, it was a gathering of English speakers making small talk, though I couldn't make out specific words.

I went ahead and turned the corner.

It was a sumptuous room with a ceiling high enough to hang a chandelier, under which was an ornate Mediterranean dining room table laid out with serving platters filled with breakfast food. The two tropical shirts were there juggling small plates and cups of coffee, and two other guys, much older, in polo shirts and khakis, differing only in shades of tan. More interesting were the half-dozen Latinas they were speaking to, very young, wearing heels they could barely stand up in, wobbling like newborn fillies, and the kind of dresses you'd see lined up at the door of a Manhattan nightclub.

Some of the women held coffee cups, but only the guys were eating. It was about all I could take in before the big-haired woman who didn't like the way I looked strode into the room and saw me standing in the doorway.

"What the hell?" she asked me, in low tones, though delivered like a shiv in the chest.

"I'm sorry. I was just looking for a place to go to the bathroom."

"This isn't it," she hissed, moving close enough for me to smell the perfume that went with her overdressed outfit. "Get the hell out of here."

I didn't bother apologizing again, not knowing how it would come out, before returning the way I came. As I moved down the hall, I passed a men's room, and now in the mood, finally took that piss.

Ramon was pulling wood out of the fresh stock when I got back to the job site. If he was annoyed with me, it didn't show. It wasn't long before we were back in the rhythm of the work—measuring, cutting, popping in nails with the pneumatic hammer.

I ATE dinner at El Rancho de Velilla that night, then hung around nursing Medallas and watching an old Yankees game with the sound turned off on my smartphone. Not entirely satisfying, but killed the time, so I was back in the bunkhouse after eleven.

I'd picked up a pack of cigarettes at the bar, and went outside to light up the first one I'd had in a few years. I wondered if it would reignite the habit, wondering if the bartender Slippery Slope would have an opinion on the matter. In any event, there was no better excuse should anyone pass by and ask what I was doing outside well after hours.

As I stood and smoked, I looked around the tree cover and utility poles in search of little red lights that might give away security cameras or motion detectors. I assumed they were there, but took the chance of wandering away from the bunkhouse toward the closest building abutting the hacienda. I got as close as I could without leaving the path and stood there listening, though hearing nothing more than the coqui, the little frogs that provide the soundtrack for the island's countryside, and other nocturnal creatures in the surrounding rain forest.

I smoked one more cigarette and was about to go back to the bunkhouse when I heard a door opening. Two women, backlit from the door, stepped outside, speaking to each other in unintelligible whispers. They sounded like excited kids. Moments later, I could see the burning ends of cigarettes. Sisters in crime, I thought to myself.

I walked back up the path, not waiting for them to finish their smokes. Satisfied that sometimes hunches work out exactly as planned.

I spent another hour online after successfully using my smartphone to link up with the Internet. I went to Google Earth and in a few minutes, zoomed in on La Selva Bendita, and using the GPS map as a guide, found the Loventeers' campus. Even with Maria's savage pruning, there was still plenty of canopy cover, but I could make out the roof of the hacienda and bits of the adjacent buildings. Remembering Ramon's thumb gesture, I moved to the southeast and saw the roofs of other buildings, and the bright blue, rectangular telltale of a swimming pool. I could also see fragments of road surface, showing that the working portion of the camp had its own access road.

I pinned and labeled the entrance in the GPS, logged off, and went to bed.

Abandoned by sleep, at a loss for waking dreams, I lay there and thought of the Little Peconic Bay, wondering how it was getting along without proper supervision.

Chapter Seventeen

Daniel Osterman, the young executive director, wore awkwardness like an itchy shirt. I knew what he wanted to talk to me about, but I was up on a ladder and made him work for it.

"It would be better if you could just come down," he said.

I finished driving in a nail and did as he asked.

"Obviously you've encountered Ruth Bellingham," he told me when I got there. "She wanted me to fire you."

I tried to look sheepish, apologetic, and a little defiant all at once. Not sure which of those showed as intended.

"I don't want to make trouble," I said. "I need the work."

"We need you to do the work, which is what I said to her. But we can't have people just wandering around inside the main building. You understand that?"

"Of course you can't. Especially with the big boss around."

He didn't exactly know how to respond to that.

"Ruth's not the big boss, but she works for them in New York. She's escorting some very important people. That's what she does. It's a very demanding job, and she's a demanding person."

I reassured him as well as I could, offering to paint the new bookcase if Ramon could dig up some paint. That was apparently the worst suggestion I could have come up with.

"No, no, no. We'll manage that ourselves, thank you very much," he said, too loudly, as if it made his lousy Spanish more coherent, then he beat it out of there.

Ramon shook his head but kept the unspoken remonstrance to himself.

OVER LUNCH I asked Ramon if he ever did any work at the Caring Center. He nodded as he swallowed a mouthful of a three-meat sandwich called a *tripleta*.

"They did better in Maria," he said. "The hill blocked the wind. But there was still plenty to do. Nice people. They were grateful," implying a contrast with our current supervisors.

"What sort of folks are they looking after?"

"The poor. In this part of Puerto Rico, it's hard to tell the poor from the rest of us, but they find a way to do it."

"Families? Women and children? Daddies and mommies?"

"And grandmothers. No single men."

"But single women," I said.

"Indeed. They have their own dormitory up here in the hacienda."

"Why the separate housing?" I asked.

He shook his *tripleta* at me, grinning. He called me a nosy bastard, using a local colloquialism that sounded nothing like what it meant.

I let him eat in peace for a while, then asked, "Did you leave any tools on the job at the Caring Center?"

"Nothing we need here. Maybe the impact drill. I love that tool."

"We definitely need an impact drill, Ramon. Why didn't you tell me we had one of those?"

He looked a little embarrassed.

"I told you, I'm a mason."

"I'll go get it," I said. "Just tell me where it is."

"You'll have to ask the executive director," he said. "He'll give you a permission slip."

"I've worked on military bases with less security than this place."

He let that slide by, but changed the subject.

"Where were you born, actually?" he asked.

"Montreal."

"I thought maybe America. New York."

"We moved to New York when I was a little kid," I said. "Never left."

He nodded, happy with his guess. He let a little more quiet form around his thoughts.

"Don't ask the executive director," he said. "You can buy a pass at the security hut for forty bucks. Just keep it hid in your palm."

"I know how to do that."

"I imagine you do. I'll give you directions to the maintenance shed. And the key to open it up."

We finished up the rest of the day's work with no more mention of the impact drill or countries of origin. But before I left for the day, Ramon stopped me with a hand on the shoulder.

"Your Spanish is pretty good, but you won't fool another Mexican," he said. "Some of us not desperate for construction help might be offended."

"Okay, what do you suggest?"

"Try French Canadian. It's the truth and you sound like one anyway."

"*Merci beaucoup, mon ami.*"

THE NEXT morning, instead of going to the job site, I drove the Wrangler down and around the hill to the entrance to the Caring Center, as I'd accurately guessed from Google

Earth. There was no sign, but they had a similar gate with a security hut. The guard, big around the waist, looked a little imposed upon by my arrival, a bad sign.

"I forgot to get a pass from Director Daniel, but I'm really in a hurry," I said, after he took a few hours to waddle over to the car window. "Can you just let me in?"

"Need a pass," he said.

"Can't get one till tomorrow."

I explained our work up at the hacienda and the need for a special tool left here on the Caring Center grounds. He looked at me as if he was listening, then said, "Need a pass."

I opened my hand to show him the folded twenty-dollar bills.

"Would this work?" I asked.

He reached a meaty forearm through the window, but I moved my hand out of the way.

"Need a pass," I said.

He went into the hut and came out holding a small slip of paper. Before passing it to me, he rested his hand on the butt of the gun stuck in his holster. That this simple transaction could falter enough for him to actually shoot me was sobering. I reached out my hand to shake, and he took it, allowing me to transfer the forty bucks. He gave me the permission slip and let me through the gate. No friendly waves were exchanged.

The Loventeers' landscaping standards took a decided turn for the worse, though the grounds were clean and uncluttered. I pulled over to consult Ramon's map, especially helpful since there were no signs to direct anyone anywhere.

There were kids, however, which I discovered soon after in teeming numbers at a big playground featuring wooden structures designed for sliding, climbing, swinging, balancing, and breaking bones big and small. The decibel level was commensurate with the activity, supporting Ramon's theory of why they were down there on the side of the hill.

I stopped at the first sight of an adult, a blonde Anglo woman wearing blue-jeans shorts, white tank top, and a weary expression. I decided to forgo the Spanish and just thrust out Ramon's map and ask, "Can you tell me where this is?"

She took the map.

"That's the maintenance shed. You maintenance?"

"I am. I guess."

"You guess?"

"I'm here to work on an addition for the hacienda. What do you need maintaining?"

"My self-control, unless someone from on high fixes the damn thermostat in the nurses' quarters. Parboiled brains make for lousy caregivers."

"Take me to the shed and I'll look at the thermostat. No guarantees."

She came around to the passenger side and got in.

"You can fix it by looking at it?" she asked.

"That's stage one. We'll take it from there."

Closer up she was more of a grey-blonde—straight, unmanaged hair pulled back by a fabric-covered barrette. Weathered skin, pale blue eyes like Jackie Swaitkowski's. And like Jackie, hovering in that border territory between young and not-so-young anymore.

The roadway curved between low-slung, cinder-block buildings with flat concrete roofs, which helped explain their durability. Each was labeled with a big number and the name of a local bird: Pitirre, Guaraguao, Reinita, Zorzal, Chango, and so on.

More kids and presumably their grownups were milling around, kicking soccer balls and wielding plastic baseball bats, chasing each other with the random logic of universal childhood.

"Are you one of the sweltering nurses?" I asked.

"I'm their supervisor. Much worse."

"How long have you had the problem?"

"Pre-Maria," she said. "Which is to say, a million years ago."

"I started last week."

"So I don't blame you."

"Please don't."

She directed me to the shed with hand signals. On the way we passed the pool, filled to the brim with Loventeers beneficiaries. Next to that was a large eating area covered by a metal frame protected by taped-together blue tarps, under which people were served some type of stew from large cauldrons.

"You look after a lot of people," I said to the woman.

"It's what we're here to do. Most of us anyway."

"Who do the others look after?"

"Themselves."

The impact drill was where Ramon said it would be. I also picked up a few tools I might need to work on the nurses' thermostat.

"Do you have a name?" the woman asked me.

"Sam Acquillo. Though up at the hacienda they think I'm Carlito Montaño," I said, feeling the honesty gushing from me in a single cleansing release.

"I'm Charlotte Ensler. Everywhere."

I don't know why I felt full trust in her from the moment I saw her walking along the gravel road, or if it had more to do with my own state of mind, which had been strained to the breaking point by maintaining an artifice. It wasn't that I was committed to saintly rectitude, I just never saw much advantage in misrepresenting myself. I always felt if you didn't like something about the way I was, that was either my fault, or yours, and either way, I could give a damn.

"Why Carlito?" she asked.

"I rented his Jeep. If they checked the plates, I needed to have the same name."

"I'm sure that's not the only reason."

I didn't know how to explain further without feeling ridiculous. On the other hand, once you start babbling the truth, it's hard to stop.

"I'm nosing around the Loventeers as part of an investigation. I work for a defense attorney back on Long Island." I gave her the broad outlines of my signing up for the construction job the week before after a brief stop in Condado where I secured the Wrangler courtesy of Slippery Slope and his good friend Drunk Carlito. I left out everything that came before.

"It'd be swell if you kept all that to yourself," I said.

"Why are you telling me?"

"I'm trying to figure that out myself. Guess I'm tired of speaking Spanish."

She laughed.

"I'm tired of switching back and forth. After four years of this, the novelty wears off."

We arrived at the nurses' dorm. She led me to the thermostat, a commercial version behind a locked plastic box, which she slapped open with the palm of her hand, then waved me forward.

"I'm assuming private investigators know something about thermostats," she said.

"I knew the guys who ran the company that made this thing. Capable, but not much imagination."

I fiddled around for a moment and knew immediately what the problem was.

I unscrewed the face and dug around the delicate wires until I felt the culprit. I pulled it out and showed Charlotte.

"A battery?" she asked.

"We just did the easy part. The hard part is getting a replacement."

"Shit."

I told her I could have one by the end of the day, but she'd have to let me feed her dinner if she had any hope of getting it.

"Isn't that extortion?"

"Fair trade. Do you have a car?"

"I can borrow one."

I fiddled with my smartphone until I came up with a restaurant that seemed as safe as any.

"Can you meet me there?" I asked.

"Will you be interrogating me?" she asked.

"I will. After plying you with the drink of your choice."

"Or drinks."

I put the thermostat back together and let her affix the plastic cover. Then I went back to put in at least part of a good day's work.

THE PLACE I picked was about twenty miles by car and a light-year of socioeconomic status away from El Rancho de Velilla. Open on three sides with a massive bar made of carved tropical wood anchoring the fourth, there were views of the Caribbean from nearly every angle, and the trade winds stirred the air to perfection.

The tourist trade, so vital to Puerto Rico's survival, created plenty of ironies. One being the existence of places like this, featured in magazines catering to the ultra-rich, cheek by jowl with unrelenting poverty. The roads leading there were just as beat up as anywhere else in the mountains, but the parking lot still had its share of Mercedes SUVs and Land Rovers. Proving the wealthy will go anywhere for a four-star dinner, if only to brag about it later.

I felt a little out of place in the wardrobe department. All I had with me were blue jeans, but I'd shaved and put on my best black T-shirt. Charlotte was waiting at the bar, not much more decked out than I was in a buttoned-down collar shirt, tan skirt, and sandals. She said she was glad I'd shown up, since she'd already invested my money in a piña colada and was about to up the ante. I moved us to the table I'd reserved at the edge of the patio so we could have an unobstructed view. An Absolut on the rocks and her second drink followed soon behind.

"Thanks for coming," I said, after a casual toast.

"Months of nothing but around-the-clock shifts tending to stressed-out nurses as they look after sick, desperate people, and some private eye appears out of nowhere to ask me out to dinner at the most expensive place in a hundred miles. Hmm, tough decision."

My native social skills were one of my ex-wife's first crushing disappointments. As a young engineer they didn't matter that much. Abby was happy to carry the load at neighborhood functions since her taciturn husband hanging around the bar looking unapproachable carried no real penalty. But after I started the upward corporate trajectory and we got invited to business gatherings by guys with titles that made Abby almost lick her chops, it became an issue.

Having grown up blue collar, then schooled in technology, with some finishing touches courtesy of amateur and professional boxing, I'd never heard of small talk much less knew how to do it. Nor cared, not a whit.

"It's not that hard," Abby would tell me.

"For you. You actually think all that mindless blather is fun."

"You don't have to *say* to be in a *conversation*."

"What does that mean?"

"You just have to *ask*."

It turned out to be good advice. Whenever I was alarmed by the threat of social interaction, I'd just start to ask questions. In the process, I learned that people liked being interviewed, that nothing was more satisfying than talking about themselves.

"So what brought you down here?" I asked Charlotte.

"A divorce, what else?"

She'd married her husband while he was still in medical school in a moment of what she called temporary insanity. Even though her life as a nurse proved conclusively that most male doctors were assholes, she thought she was brilliant enough to see through her beloved's imperious exterior to the benevolent and sensitive soul within.

"You can guess how that turned out," she said.

To be fair to her husband, she told me, she had other reasons for feeling existential dread, a prevailing sense of worthlessness and lack of meaning in the world. The cure for that, she felt, was either to drown herself in substance abuse or retreat to a nunnery for a lifetime of penitence and prayer.

"So I split the difference and joined an overseas NGO where they let you drink. Cheers."

I asked her about the staff paying their own way, one of the claims made on the Loventeers' website. It made her laugh.

"I know, right? We pay for the privilege of putting ourselves through all this impossible bullshit. Stupid."

"Generous?"

"I told you my ex is a doctor. My price for letting him out of the marriage."

Not to give me a false impression, she said the work had been totally redemptive, with enough personal satisfaction and fulfillment to last a lifetime. Every day she saw men, women, and children who wouldn't have survived if it hadn't been for her and the crew she led. She'd committed to a total of five years, so with four under her belt, she'd soon be on to something else.

"Like what?" I asked.

"I don't know. Wall Street?"

I asked her what it was like to work for the Loventeers. She said it depended on which Loventeers I was talking about. There were the social workers and medical staff at the Caring Center, to whom she was devoted, and then the administrative people on top of the hill, and the twain had yet to meet.

"I have no idea what those people do. Every year, the practice supervisors submit a budget, they give us less than we need, and that's the last we hear from them till the next year."

"What about Daniel Osterman?" I asked.

"Who's he?"

"The executive director of the La Selva Bendita campus."

"No kidding. His predecessor killed herself. Must have been a tough recruiting process."

"Did you know her?" I asked.

She leaned into the table.

"I did actually. Had a big head of white hair, which I admired. A superficial thing to remember, I know. She was the only one of those hacienda people who ever came down to talk to us. Had a bit of spark. Spent a long time in the nursery with the orphan babies."

"How did she die?" I asked.

"Jumped off one of our lovely jungle cliffs. It was only a few months ago. We only knew because the Puerto Ricans working with us read it in the local paper."

"When she visited the Caring Center, was she on her own?"

"I didn't see anyone else from up on the hill. I honestly didn't think much about it. There's so much to keep track of every day it's all-consuming."

"How do people qualify to be cared for here? Do they turn up at your gate?"

"No, they have to go through an office in downtown La Selva Bendita. I meant that as a joke. Downtown is some beat-up-looking gas station, a rusted-out water tank, tumbled-down fritter joint, and the Loventeers' concrete box where people wait outside before going in one at a time to get qualified, which can take weeks. I've only been there once. Won't go back. Too depressing."

I tried to keep the questioning momentum going after that, but she got wise to me and turned the tables. I first told her I was also divorced but had a steady girlfriend who lived next door. Then I had to confess I was only a private investigator because my friend Jackie Swaitkowski made me get certified so the cops wouldn't bust us for obstructing justice. Then I talked about the charge against Burton Lewis for killing Elton Darby, the chief fund-raiser for Worldwide Loventeers, though no more than she could have read in the media through a simple Google search. I said a visit to one of their field operations was just a routine part of our work for Burton.

"As an undercover carpenter?" she asked.

"Stick with what you know."

"I have a feeling you've done other things."

"A little large-scale hydrocarbon processing for a global engineering firm, but you have to start out somewhere."

We were in the parking lot after dinner about to go our separate ways when I remembered to close our deal. I took the battery out of my pocket to show her.

"Where did you get it?" she asked.

I'd noticed a utility room the first time Ramon and I went through the back door to the hacienda. Assuming they used the same HVAC equipment as the Caring Center, there should have been a discrete cooling system for the air handlers that would have its own thermostatic control. After Ramon left for the day, I proved the theory.

"Won't that shut down their air conditioning?" she asked.

"More's the pity. I'll come down there tomorrow and stick it in. Should work for at least a year."

I got an enthusiastic kiss on the lips, which wasn't part of the deal, but every negotiation takes unexpected turns.

Chapter Eighteen

I waited a few days for the vodka to filter out of my system before breaking into the hacienda. I also used the time to locate all the security cameras, I hoped, and find lapses in coverage. I'd installed similar systems and knew the difficulty in keeping every square inch in view. But I was also handicapped by the need to look like a guy just ambling around on a cigarette break, so it took both nights and about a half pack of smokes to complete the assessment.

What any good security breach needs is a diversion. I found a promising candidate at the security hut guarding the front gate. The installers had run the coaxial cable from the conspicuously menacing camera on the upper corner of the gate through an eight-foot metal conduit. However, the distance from corner to ground was more like eight feet, two inches, leaving a small section of black cable fully exposed.

The rear of the hut was also conveniently located within a few feet of the natural foliage, thick, but easily passable. So, at about two A.M., I took a brief, deliberate, and I hoped silent, walk in the woods. My greatest ally in this was the incessant, chirpy racket from the coqui. I wore a jacket, baseball cap, and pack on my back, all black. I'd rubbed some dark topsoil on my face and hands, on which I also wore surgical gloves. When I reached the building, I crouched down and waited about ten minutes before crawling on my belly over to the exposed cable and snipping it with a pair of wire cutters.

Within seconds, I could hear the guard calling back to the monitoring room in the hacienda reporting the failure, something the guy in the room would know simultaneously as his own front-gate monitor winked to black. I did a fast crawl back into the underbrush where I lay still to see what would happen next.

Soon the front gate guard was outside looking up at the camera, making the natural assumption that some electronic trouble had caused the outage. A vehicle soon arrived bringing what I hoped was the guy from the hacienda so two of them could stare dumbly up at the camera, as if strength in numbers would fix the problem.

Moving as quickly and quietly as possible, I retraced my steps to the hacienda where I followed my planned route to the ground floor, which was utterly obscured by the landscaping, and I hoped overlooked by the security system.

Squatting down next to the building, I waited again for signs that I'd been spotted. Things like flashlight beams, yells, and waving sidearms. But all I heard were a billion coquis and whatever else was out there competing for love and sustenance.

I felt along the wall for the access door I'd scoped out in the daylight. It was a single-panel, metal-sheathed door with a common exterior lock, a brand I'd learned to pick during some long-ago act of juvenile delinquency. Since most breaking and entering involved just that, a lot of breaking of doors and dead bolts, there'd been few advancements in the design of the locks themselves. It wasn't my personal best for speed of entry, but it wasn't long before I felt the satisfying turn of the handle.

I'd seen no evidence of alarm sensors at individual windows and doors, probably considered an unneeded expense given the cameras and armed security detail. So far, I was

right. The door opened into a darkly lit hallway that led to
a stairwell up to the second floor where all the action was.

First I had to make an important stop. At the other end
of the hall was the utility room where I'd pilfered Charlotte's
new thermostat battery. In addition to the HVAC system,
there was other important equipment, such as the telecom-
munications hub, computer servers, and most important of
all, the electrical panel.

I unscrewed the big faceplate so I could get to all the
wiring. I followed the heavy gauge lines from the main
breakers to where they entered from the bottom of the panel.
Using a box cutter, I sliced the insulation around the bundle
and identified the principal ground wire. Then I reinstalled
the faceplate, and with wire snips in hand, prepared myself
for the impending total blackout.

The hallway was carpeted and I wore rubber-soled
boots, but my footfalls still sounded horribly loud, though
this was a time for speed over stealth. Using the back of my
hand against the wall to guide my progress, I trotted to the
stairwell and went up to the second-floor office area.

Now it had to be all by memory. I had a panicky moment
of disorientation until I found the big open room filled by
day with the young telemarketers. From there, I could feel
my way to the hall that led to the director's office, and adjacent, the office of Ruth Bellingham.

I 'd just shut the door to her office behind me when the
shouting started. It came from inside the building, but not
in close proximity. I set to fast work.

Using the flashlight in my smartphone, I looked for computer gear, but aside from an untethered power cord and
Ethernet cable, there was nothing. So I opened the only file
cabinet in the room. It was organized by date. I pulled out
the last five years, files about five inches thick, and stuffed
them in the backpack. I gathered up all the loose papers
on the desk, and checked the drawers, which were nearly

empty. I scanned around and saw nothing else of potential value.

The voice outside the door grew louder. A man on a walkie-talkie. The choices were to leave the office and try to evade notice, or just confront the guy, or go out the window, which opened easily enough, but it was too dark to see where I'd land after dropping at least a single story, enough to break a leg.

I chose option two. Waiting until he was past the office door, I stepped out behind him. I tapped him on the shoulder, which must have been alarming, though he had little time to fully grasp the moment, since I tried to channel Muhammad Ali's Liston-felling right jab, which apparently worked, since the guard went off his feet and hard into the carpet.

I picked up the radio and apologized for dropping it, responding to the other caller's urgent questions. When the caller said the Spanish equivalent of "Pay attention, dumbass," I put the radio on the floor and picked up the guard's flashlight, turning it off, but keeping it in hand, comforted by its heft.

The only back exit I was sure of went past the utility room. As predicted, men were in there with flashlights focused on the electrical panel, giving each other instructions, and still unaware that the cause of the problem was a single cut wire hidden behind a slender slit in the insulation.

I gently eased open the outside door and closed it silently behind me.

The Wrangler was where I'd left it, all my gear locked in the back and full of gas. I kept the headlights off until I reached the connecting drive down to the Caring Center, which I'd never be able to follow in the dark. I was happy to see the lights were still on as I broke through the forest and headed for the exit, the elation of imminent escape overturned by a pair of headlights darting in behind me just as I cleared the entranceway.

My pursuer knew the roads better than I did, but I think I made up for the advantage with heightened motivation. I forced myself to concentrate on the road ahead and ignore the glare of the high beams behind me as they closed in, then dropped back, depending on how each of us assessed the immediate risk of overturning or catching a wheel in the deep drainage ditches to either side of the road surface.

Slaloming down the steep mountain path, bouncing on the big tires, buffeted by potholes and crude asphalt patches, propelled by engines and gravity, it was a type of vehicular ballet. A dance contest where the only important variable wasn't grace or strength, or endurance, but nerve.

His gave out when we hit a T intersection. The smart choice would have been to hit the brakes, but instead, I downshifted and made a right turn under full power. After a weightless moment on two wheels, I dropped to the road surface and struggled to get the careening Jeep under control. A quick look in the rearview showed the other guy skidding across the intersection and disappearing into the forest.

I saw no point in letting up until I reached flatter terrain, and light traffic, into which I eased with both hands on the wheel and a dry mouth and runaway heart rate.

Which I slowly brought under control, breathing in through the nose and out from the mouth.

I drove to the hotel in Condado and persuaded Slope to give up my two-grand deposit on the spot, thanked him again, and caught a cab to the airport. I grabbed the first flight I could get to JFK, by way of a connection in Philadelphia, doing my best not to think about the time it would take for the cops to trace the Jeep's plates to Carlito, and from there to Slippery Slope, to the credit card I used at the hotel, to Jackie's law office, and finally to me.

CHAPTER NINETEEN

"Oh good, you're still with us," said Amanda, when I called her after leaving the parking lot at JFK.

"Glad you're not disappointed."

"Eddie might be. He's come to rely on my menu. I think it's the presentation."

It was early afternoon and I'd lost a night of sleep. My goal was to stay awake long enough to make it to the Adirondack chairs above the breakwater, reckoning I could say hello to Eddie, then doze for at least an hour before Amanda came home from work. As it transpired, she decided to leave me there comatose well into the evening, when she came by with some take-out from the Pequot, breaded shrimp and a basket of heart-seizing french fries covered in cheddar.

Foggy, but conscious, I ate under the light from the lanterns hung from the market umbrella. The air was as warm as Puerto Rico's, though many percentage points lower in humidity, and the trades had been replaced by our prevailing south southwesterly.

One of the most congenial aspects of our relationship was a mutual pleasure at evading pressing conversation, the type normal people relished, such as catching up on everything we'd been doing over the last week or so. Instead we had our own version of small talk, which could include the inconsequential as easily as the significant, as long as it didn't involve subjects that could wait for another time.

So she didn't tell me about progress on her latest rehab project, and I didn't discuss my time in Puerto Rico, and both were satisfied with leaving it at that.

No such dynamic was available with Jackie Swaitkowski.

"You did what?"

I met her at her office in Water Mill where I dumped the contents of my backpack out on the client coffee table. She was freshly risen from bed, her messy red hair in full chaos, wearing a men's Oxford cloth shirt, apparently Harry Goodlander's, given its immense size. The summer sun had turned her pale legs a pinkish tan, with freckled accents on thighs and knees.

"I have a theory," I said. "If it's correct, I doubt we'll be hearing from law enforcement. If not, you'll have another client whose prospects are worse than Burton's."

"Swell. What besides breaking and entering?"

"Carpentry and some minor electrical work."

"I think that's legal," she said.

"Mostly. And assault and battery. Not always my fault."

"That's a relief."

As I flipped through the paperwork, I told the story of renting Drunk Carlito's Wrangler and traveling up in the hills to the bed-and-breakfast in La Selva Bendita, the landlady's nephews' checkout approach, securing the building job under a false identity, and the satisfying work with the humble mason Ramon.

I described the office atmosphere in the hacienda, which appeared to be a circumscribed version of the phone-bank operation at the Loventeers' HQ in Manhattan, with palm trees and ceiling fans in lieu of floor-to-ceiling windows facing neighboring skyscrapers.

"I thought they were doing humanitarian work," said Jackie.

"That's a wholly separate operation. I didn't get a close look, but had a long talk with the nursing supervisor. It's what you'd expect, earnest care for the destitute and disadvantaged, though with little involvement from management on top of the hill."

"I don't get it."

I didn't either, though I had my theory, which I tried to explain.

"If you have a business, the money to run the operation comes from selling products or services. It's all a fully integrated enterprise, with direct cause and effect. You make stuff, you sell it, you make more stuff. If it stops selling, you're out of business. If you're a nonprofit, the money to provide free or cheap services has to come from donations. And there's no direct relationship between the money coming in and going out. You just have to convince people that your good works deserve financial support. Not an easy task, since no amount of money will ever be enough to satisfy the overwhelming need, so competition for funding is fierce. At the same time, accountability for ultimate outcomes is hard to track. Big-time donors—foundations and government agencies—have the wherewithal to make sure their philanthropic dollars are well spent, demanding audits and metrics, but individual givers just go on trust and the good feelings that come from writing that check at Christmas time, or when their tax accountants say they need to lower their gross income."

"So what about Worldwide Loventeers?"

"I want to believe that the majority of charitable organizations, NGOs, put the lion's share of donated funds into providing services. If that isn't true, I don't want to know about it. But if an NGO was so inclined, it might put most of their efforts into an effective fund-raising machine, focusing on individual donors, rich or otherwise, while maintaining just enough in the way of services to justify their existence."

"So you might have a lot of extra money sloshing around," she said.

"A cynic might say that would tempt the less than virtuous."

"So that's what they're all about?"

"Maybe, but I think it's worse than that," I said, putting my attention back on the stack of file folders in front of me. Jackie had to just sit there and watch me work, an impossible thing for her to do without constant fidgeting and making little snorting sounds of impatience. When she reached for one of the folders, as if her compulsive need to speed progress gave her special insight into the project, I swatted her hand, which shocked her, even though she'd done that kind of thing to me about a million times.

"Go do something," I said. "Take a shower or jog around the block."

"I'm trying to help."

"You have a kitchen in your apartment. I bet there's a way to make coffee. That would be a help."

She frowned at me and scratched an itch on her inner thigh, revealing a pair of plaid boxer shorts under the oversized shirt. In moments like that I often puzzled over our complete lack of erotic interest in each other, even though Jackie's presentation as all female was impossible to overlook.

Perhaps because the thought of Amanda, at any time, day or night, stirred my weary heart.

"I wish we hadn't given up smoking," she said, and I knew exactly what she meant.

Ten minutes later, we both had big mugs of coffee and I had a folder open on the table. It was a filled-out form with a head shot of a young Latina stapled to the upper left corner. Everything was in Spanish, which was okay for Jackie, who was barely fluent, but could get by enough to serve the bulk of her indigent clientele.

It looked a lot like an employment application, complete with vital statistics—age, birthplace, education level, immediate family members, personal interests and skills, extracurricular activities. There was also a comment box labeled "Interview," which was more telling.

"Pretty smile, nice figure if you like slim," said the handwritten notes. "Clear complexion, except for small scar on chin. Refused drink, but admitted to having some wine with friends. Nonsmoker. No drug use. Not a virgin. One boyfriend, former." Former was underlined twice. "Wants to model, maybe go into acting. No musical skills, though could sing a tune in key. Acceptable table etiquette. Minimum social media exposure, Puerto Rico only. Lives with mother. No father in the picture. One sister, no brothers. *Highly recommended.*"

Her birthdate put her age at sixteen. Jackie looked up at me over the file.

"Is this what I think it is?" she asked.

I described the little breakfast reception at the hacienda with a bunch of overfed middle-aged guys and nervous, but hopeful-looking Latinas dressed for the disco at nine A.M.

"What do you think?" I asked Jackie.

"A little too much love at the Loventeers."

"Of the wrong kind. I think you need to go through all this stuff and look for something dispositive. I'm heading back to New York."

"I'm fine with that, but how does this connect to Burton's case?"

"I don't know, but I think it does. And if not, it's an excellent way to shake the trees."

"Who're you planning to shake first?" she asked.

"You really want to know?"

She rolled up the sleeves of the giant shirt and did a better job with the buttons, as if just realizing the threat to her modesty, however poorly monitored.

"Not really," she said. "And you wouldn't tell me anyway."

I was driving my '67 Pontiac Grand Prix, having had my fill of Jeeps and needing to give it a little exercise. I'd discovered the old car in a shed at the back of the property when I took possession of the cottage after my mother checked out of the house and into a nursing home for the last few months of her life. My father was a mechanic by trade and had kept the car's internal organs in good repair, though the paint had worn down and he protected what was left with a layer of grey primer.

Sailing skill came in handy when piloting the colossal land yacht. I'd stiffened the suspension with upgraded shocks and other modifications, but it still had a pitch and yaw comparable to the *Carpe Mañana's* under moderate seas.

After its first restoration, I'd used it to obliterate a pair of murderous thugs, basically totaling the car. For no good reason, I rebuilt it all over again. I told the guys at the frame-straightening shop, "They don't make 'em like this anymore," and neither should they.

I first went to see Frank Entwhistle to double-check the timeline for the cabinets I was building for him. He asked if six weeks was okay, and I grudgingly agreed, knowing that three would be all I needed to complete the job. Frank was never a slim man, but it looked like he'd padded on another fifty pounds since the last time I saw him. I wondered if three weeks was soon enough to outrace cardiac arrest.

I had other chores to catch up on—buying materials, settling my bill at the building supply store, restocking Big Dog biscuits from the pet shop and vodka from the liquor store—the prime underpinnings of my day-to-day existence. I also stopped by Mad Martha's, a cave-like joint that had the best seafood in town, all locally caught, and a reputation for hostility toward anyone above a fifty K annual income. Undeserved, I felt, though I'd never tried to get a drink there with the arms of my sweater tied around my neck à la Art Reynolds.

So it was dark by the time I got to Burton Lewis's house to check on things. Joe Sullivan let me through the gate, having requisitioned Isabella's security camera, I'm sure not without keen resistance. Confirmed when Sullivan met me at the front door.

"She would have had me run a whole separate line for my camera array," he said. "I got Burton to make the call."

"Orwell said people never seize power with the intention of relinquishing it," I told him.

"And that was way back in, what, '84?"

He said that Burton was somewhere upstairs, but he'd be glad to see me. I asked if we could have a private chat first. We went out to one of the screened-in patios.

"How's it been going?" I asked.

"Media dogs keep sniffing around but seem to respond to gentle suggestions that they get the fuck out of here. Other than that, it's been quiet. I think Burton is pretty blue, but you can't blame him for that. He'll watch the ball game with me, but doesn't seem to care when the Yankees lose. Bad sign."

"Has Jackie been around?"

"Sure, but I don't know what they talk about. Not a lot of fun and laughs, that's for sure."

He cracked us a couple of beers and checked his tablet when we sat down.

"I have all the cameras controlled from this thing. The monitors rotate through about every ten minutes. Motion sensors kick off an alarm once in a while. Usually squirrels. Sometimes a rabbit or small herd of deer. I'll let you know if I see any lions, tigers, or bears."

I'd noticed the Colt 9 mm holstered on his belt. Past experience told me there was a smaller pistol in an ankle holster and other ordnance stashed around the house in strategic locations.

"Just don't shoot them," I said. "We're getting enough bad publicity."

"So how's the investigation?"

I said we should bring Burton into the conversation so I didn't have to repeat the story, and he used his smartphone to call upstairs. Minutes later Burton showed up wearing jeans and a sweatshirt, and a pair of cashmere slippers probably sourced by a family retainer sometime in the last century.

We'd finished our beers, so it was easy to comply with his demand that everyone have a single-malt scotch on the rocks in massive cocktail glasses. As Sullivan suggested, he didn't look too good, even more gaunt than usual, hair too long, eyes too dark, laugh lines seemingly erased. It pained me to see, reminding me of the many times I'd sought refuge from my own dreary obsessions in the company of his abiding *joie de vivre*, however burdened with the responsibilities and absurdities of vast, generational wealth.

"So where you been?" he asked me. "Jackie says Puerto Rico. Love that island, but what on earth for?"

They let me start the story from when the Reverend Jerry Swanson came out to my boat, back-filling his association with Milton Flowers, former executive director of Worldwide Loventeers.

Having already gone through the whole thing with Jackie, the narrative flowed along easily, with only a few questions from Joe Sullivan, such as, "Did you glove up before breaking into that office?" and "Do you know how bad you hurt the security guard you suckered in the hallway?" anticipating, I realized, future prosecution, looking for answers to questions he knew I'd be asked.

Throughout, Burton listened keenly without comment, his tired face settling deeper into grim discontent.

"So you think they're trafficking young women," he said.

"Not just young, underaged," I said. "Could be the old scam promising fame and fortune, then have them turning tricks before they know what hit them. Might just get brokered off to the old business guys, let the sugar daddies handle the final transactions, which would provide a layer of deniability. No way to know, though Jackie might figure it out from the files I boosted out of Ruth Bellingham's office."

"Oh, my Lord," said Burton, downing his second scotch.

"I know, Burt. There's no way you could have known."

"There isn't? Don't be so sure," he said, and then left us, striding back into the house, his fancy slippers slapping on the tile floor. Sullivan looked over at me.

"We got a problem here," he said, when Burton was out of earshot.

I really didn't want to know what it was, but I asked anyway.

"I like Burton, you know that," he said. "Winner of least offensive billionaire contest. But I've been a detective for a while now, and a beat cop longer than that, and I know like my mother's face when somebody's hiding something. Even hardened assholes who lie professionally usually give it up eventually. Honorable people like Lewis, with little prior experience, usually stick it up on a neon billboard. If I'm seeing it, you damn well know Ross and Mike Cermanski are seeing it, and they could give a rat's ass about Burton's history of decency and good works. To them, he's just another collar, another lamb to toss into the meat processing plant they call the criminal justice system."

"Your mother lied?"

"All the time."

One of the things I think Burton valued most about our friendship was my respect for his privacy, my total lack of interest in the titillation inspired by the very rich. So I knew him well, though only that part of him that engaged with me, a circumscribed pool of knowledge, full and deep though it may have been.

"Maybe he did it," said Sullivan.

"Maybe he didn't. Presumption of innocence doesn't mean we won't find out the truth in the end."

"That's the theory. Meanwhile, you better operate on the presumption that he's totally fucked, because from where I sit, that's the case."

"Understood."

CHAPTER TWENTY

$\mathbf{M}$y phone rang as I was climbing into the Grand Prix. It was Amanda.

"They're here," she said.

"Who's they?"

"Men with guns. They're walking around your cottage."

"Where are you?"

"In the house. I locked Eddie in the basement. He's barking."

I could hear him.

"Call 911," I said.

"Did that. I can see people coming this way. Shotgun or automatic?"

"Shotgun. Lock all the doors. Go to the second floor and take a position at the top of the stairs. Now."

I could hear shuffling sounds and heavy breathing as she ran around the house. It wasn't the first time we'd been invaded out on Oak Point, only I was there, not fifteen minutes away feeling desperate and powerless. I gunned the Grand Prix through a stop sign, hoping a cop would jump on my tail. The giant V8 responded with glee, shoving me back into the driver's seat. The road stayed clear as I hurtled through the tight neighborhoods north of Burton's estate, until I flew into the denser regions of Southampton Village. I slammed on the brakes, barely avoiding a rear-ender with an oblivious Prius.

"I'm here," said Amanda. "I've got the shotgun and a handful of shells. Do you remember how to get them in the gun?"

I talked her through the process, unnecessary it turned out, since she had it locked and loaded in a few seconds, working it out on her own.

"Where're the cops?" she asked, in a half whisper.

"Coming. Don't shoot anyone wearing a uniform."

"Easy for you to say."

"I'm trying," I said, running a few red lights, still free of cop pursuit.

"I need to call Danny Izard," I said to Amanda. "Can you hang tight for a minute?"

"Sure, boss. Tell him I said hi."

That I had our local North Sea beat cop on speed dial probably said something about what I'd done to disrupt the equanimity of life on Oak Point.

"I'm there in five minutes tops," Danny told me as soon as he answered the phone. "Backup's on the way. Any ideas?"

"A good guess. Go straight to Amanda's. And be careful."

"Always am."

"I mean it, Danny."

"Roger that."

I called back Amanda.

"How many?" I asked her.

"Two? Not sure. How's Danny?"

"On the way."

"I think I hear a siren," she said. "Should I go see?"

"No. Stay put."

I had the phone in my lap on speaker. I'd blasted through the big intersection with Route 27 and onto North Sea Road, violating a long list of traffic rules and assuring nightmares of demonic '67 Pontiacs filling the minds of the other drivers. Now it was just a matter of navigating the curvy two-lane road up to Oak Point, just a few minutes under warp drive. I passed a few trucks on the last decent straightaway and had a clear shot until hitting the tight curves, which were filled with responsible, speed-limit-compliant citizens. I tried tailgating and intimidation by flashing my high beams, but they held their ground. I cursed and pounded on the steering wheel.

"Somebody's shooting," said Amanda.

"I'll call you back."

I hung up on her and called Danny. No answer.

I called back Amanda.

"Somebody's knocking on the front door," she whispered.

"Could be Danny. Hold your fire."

I heard a ragged smashing sound and she screamed. I floored the Grand Prix and took the last corner into oncoming traffic, forcing a car onto the shoulder, though not far enough to avoid smacking his side panel. The Grand Prix barely quivered and stayed on the pavement as I turned on two wheels onto Oak Point.

I yelled to Amanda over the phone, but she didn't answer.

Danny's patrol car was in the driveway behind my cottage, lights flashing. The driver's-side door was open, and he was lying on the ground holding his side.

"Shot right through the door," he said through clenched teeth. "Some kind of high-powered shit."

Blood painted his shirt front and seeped through his fingers. I tore off my T-shirt and had him push it into the wound.

"Sorry, Sam," he said. "You tried to warn me."

"Have to check on Amanda. Stay awake. Backup will be here any minute."

"Take my gun. It's over there on the ground."

It was only a couple hundred feet to Amanda's house, but I jumped back in the Grand Prix and spun tires around Danny's patrol car. The house was blacked out from the inside, but the outside was now lit up by the Grand Prix's high beams. I was looking at the open front door when just inside my peripheral vision I saw a man step out from behind a tree and point an assault rifle at my car. The windshield blew up, spraying my face with glass. I slid down in the seat and aimed the car blindly at the tree. I hit it under accelerating power, but there's a lot of car in the front end of a '67 Grand Prix, and it soaked up the blow and kept me safely shoved down in the wheel wells.

I shouldered open the car door and the Grand Prix's headlights, still in full blaze, showed a man sitting on the ground a few feet away, his rifle nowhere in sight, but he was digging around in the pockets of his field jacket.

I shot him in the forehead with Danny's service automatic. He looked surprised.

I ran to Amanda's house as fast as possible with the gun raised in front of me. Another man was lying on his back on the stone landing at the front door. In the pale light of the night sky, his torso looked like a blackened, incoherent mass. A stubby rapid-fire rifle lay by his side. I stepped behind a column that supported the portico above the door and called to Amanda.

"Up here," she yelled. "I'm okay."

Sirens and strobing red and blue lights filled the air. Then yells and voices over the police radio, urgent but controlled. Eddie kept up his barking in the basement.

"Don't move," I called to Amanda. "I'll wait for them here."

I sat next to the dead guy on the landing and put Danny's gun behind me—within easy reach, but with luck out of sight of the jumpy cops with weapons drawn and a comrade on the ground.

I had my hands up when they came down the driveway, tossing around flashlight beams and harsh commands.

"It's me, Sam," I said. "Be careful. There might be another shooter."

They immediately turned their flashlights on the woods behind our houses and lawn leading out to the bay, making themselves excellent targets, though it wasn't the time to argue tactics.

While the cops were occupied, I went through the front door and asked Amanda to lower the shotgun.

"Not until I see the whites of your eyes, buddy," she called down from the top of the stairs.

I walked into the foyer and flicked on the light. Blood was everywhere.

I said, "*C'est moi, honnêtement.*" It's me, honestly, I hoped unmistakably.

She walked down the stairs, holding the shotgun with the stock tucked under her arm and her finger on the trigger. When she could get a good look at my face, she dropped the gun and fell forward, making me catch her.

I gripped her slender body and dug my face into the nape of her neck, her smell filling my brain with joy and recollection. Her tears flowed onto my shoulder.

"Oh God, oh God," she squeezed out between sobs.

I picked her up and carried her into the living room so I could lay her out on the big sofa. I brushed her hair off her forehead and said I was going to let Eddie out of the basement, his anxious and persistent barking enough to wake the dead, two of whom were in close proximity.

He banged up against my legs and stayed near when I went back to the living room, where he found Amanda helpless on the couch. He bounded up on her and licked her face.

"Steady as she goes, matey," said Amanda. "Everything's fine."

A cop called from outside and I said it was clear to come in. He turned on every light switch he could find and had

his gun leading the way. I asked him how Danny Izard was
doing.

"Awake and alert, on his way to the hospital. Is this your
residence, sir?"

I nodded at Amanda.

"It's hers. The shotgun is on the stairs. Self-defense."

"We'll let the DA decide that. Please stay in place."

He started to walk through the house flicking on more
lights and holding his sidearm as if evil perpetrators were
about to jump out from behind the furniture. I tried to
follow him, but Amanda clung to my arm.

"Don't go," she said. "I like you here."

I sat down on the edge of the sofa.

"He broke down the door and pointed his gun at me,"
she said. "That makes it justifiable, right?"

"Yes," I said, hoping I was right.

"Oh, good. I think I'd rather hate prison. Limited outfit
choices."

"You're a tough girl," I said, brushing back her hair,
even though it really didn't need to be brushed.

"I told him to drop the gun, and instead he pointed it
up at me," she repeated. "That shotgun has an awful recoil.
I'll be bruised for weeks. And why is your face all bloody
and what happened to your shirt? Don't get me wrong, I
like it. Manly."

I noted that the wet bar was just outside the french
doors leading to the patio. She thought it was a swell idea,
as did Eddie, who jumped up as soon as I moved toward
the door. I had Amanda hold on to his collar while I went
outside to provision.

I clinked her red wine with my glass of vodka on the
rocks, offering the same to the cop as he came back down
the stairs.

"You people are something else," he said.

And I had to agree.

Chapter Twenty-One

Ross Semple was in a reflective mood.

We were out on my sunporch after about two hours of reenacting the shootings and letting the CSIs take a lot of photos. Mike Cermanski had been there for all that, but Semple told him to go home, that he could handle it from there. Cermanski shrugged it off and left.

Jackie had arrived right before Semple, so I had a few moments to prep her, though not enough to stop her from watching my every word the way Eddie watched me eat steak.

"I've been at this for quite a while," said Semple, "and I can't decide if things in the world are getting better or worse. The data says much better, but it doesn't usually feel that way."

"All mayhem is local," I said.

His adjunct was there, so we had to tell our stories one more time so she could record them. Outside, the crime scene people were still busy doing all the arcane things they do. Eddie was dying to join the fun, but I had him tied up to the table I kept out on the porch to thwart his talent for wily escape.

I kept my eye on Amanda, who looked a little pale, but her voice was steady as she walked Semple through the chain of events. He made her repeat some of her words, but she didn't waver or backtrack. Or avert her eyes.

Jackie, who had a live-and-let-live relationship with Amanda, stayed close to her and almost seemed solicitous. I wondered if she'd ask Amanda to join her in the Women Who've Shot People Dead Club.

"It must have been terrifying," said Ross, "to have that man come through your door."

"Have you ever had a gun pointed at you with intent to kill?" she asked.

"Yes."

"How did it feel?"

"Terrifying."

One of his cops came to the door and he went to meet him. While we waited, Jackie asked Amanda how she was doing.

"I've been better. I think I might be vomiting at some point. Sam was right. I should have gone to Burton's." I tried to wave that off, but she wouldn't let me. "I put you in an impossible position. Though maybe we could stay clear of aggressive people with firearms. Just for a little bit."

"Okay."

When Ross came back, he told us the ID in the pocket of the guy I shot had him as a Polish national here on an over-stayed visa. Apparently, the other guy's wallet had been in the inside pocket of his jacket, and thus now a shredded, unreadable wad.

"It'll have to go to the lab to pull the information," said Ross. "Will take a while. Spark any ideas?"

"He'll be Polish," I said. "Look for a guy named Mikolaj Galecki. I think they were working for him, and he works as muscle for Art Reynolds, the president of the board of Worldwide Loventeers. I bet you can tie all of them together."

"Why would somebody running a charity need muscle?" asked Ross.

"There's a lot more to it than that. I think they're recruiting girls out of their operations around the world and sending them here, and maybe other cities. I'm guessing under false pretenses, but I don't know that directly. Young girls, underage."

Semple didn't react to that the way he should have. Jackie saw it, too, and was about to say something when I grabbed her shoulder.

"You should have told us," I said.

"You're aware that we have a federal government. They prize confidentiality."

"Goddamn it, Ross," said Jackie. "I'm aware of the two bodies lying out there. Could have been Sam and Amanda."

"Wasn't relevant to your case," he said.

"The fuck it isn't," said Jackie, "obviously."

Ross had been leaning against a window frame, since all the seating space was tied up. He pulled away from the wall and said, "Neither of you will be charged. I'll take care of it."

Jackie was hardly placated.

"No shit you will. Tell us what you know."

"I know one of my officers is in Southampton Hospital getting his guts sewn together, so spare me the outrage, counselor, and take what you can get."

He left the room and I followed him out.

"We should be cooperating," I said. "I've learned things."

"I know we should. But if the FBI comes barreling in here, I'll lose all control. Just give me some air and get that Irish hell cat on a tighter leash."

"Nobody leashes Jackie, and I wouldn't even if I could. I'm not used to seeing you sucking the FBI's tit. What's up?"

"Five years," he said.

"What does that mean?"

"If I make it that far, I get full retirement. Otherwise, 60 percent, at most. I've been notified that this thing is over my head, and to stay back. It may surprise you, but I have a family too. I think a lot of you, Sam, but not as much as my wife and kids. And their kids."

He kept walking all the way to his plain-wrapper car, stopping only to tell a CSI that he was leaving and to get him the preliminary report as soon as it was ready. I followed him and watched him drop into his car, so I was standing there when he rolled down the window.

"One thing I can tell you," he said.

"What?"

"I just decided. Things are getting worse."

Then he drove off.

ISABELLA WAS delighted to see Amanda and Eddie come through the door. I often felt she showered this attention on my girlfriend and dog as a way to emphasize how little I deserved. Burton seemed equally pleased when he and Joe Sullivan joined us on the enclosed patio.

Jackie had gone on home to her place in Water Mill where Harry was waiting for her. There wasn't much else she could do, and the jousting with Ross Semple had taken its toll.

Amanda and I weren't exactly tip-top ourselves after all that had happened, so I saw no point in going through everything with Burton and Sullivan. I asked if we could just relax and leave all that for another time, and they said sure. I wanted the world to be on hold for just a little bit of time. To be in suspended animation, secured from ugly questions and unsatisfying answers, and recollections of guns and blood and death.

I just wanted to drink in peace, with my dog at my feet and my favorite woman next to me with her hand on my arm, and that's what I did.

It wasn't that hard to find Art Reynolds's house. Jackie got the address in about two seconds off the Internet using her special investigative software that proved nothing in the world was safe from prying eyes.

He lived in Scarsdale, which wasn't a big surprise. Well back from the street, but still visible, an early twentieth-century Tudor. I didn't know if he was home, or his wife. His one kid, probably not, since Jackie told me his Facebook page said he was working with the indigent in Venezuela, a country that had a bumper crop of indigents to work with.

I'd watched dawn slowly light up the neighborhood. I was almost through the big thermos of coffee I'd brought with me, and it still wasn't enough. An edgy, bleary call for sleep clung to my mind. I wondered why it used to be so much easier to defy the norms of sleep and wakefulness. I looked at my weathered and trampled face in the rearview mirror and basically had my answer.

Time hadn't been on my side before and wasn't about to start now.

A woman in a Mazda sports car drove out the driveway. I got a good look at her, good enough to easily see she wasn't his wife, unless she'd turned her black hair blonde and shed about twenty years in age.

Reynolds came shortly after, driving one of the bigger models of Mercedes. It rolled down the driveway and turned toward the Scarsdale train station, as expected. I fell in behind, as planned.

I knew that effectively tailing someone—keeping them in sight without giving yourself away—was a hard-earned skill, but I'd scoped out the route from Reynolds's house to the station, and it was pretty straightforward, and unlikely to raise suspicion if he noticed an old Jeep was always in his rearview mirror.

Early as it was, there were only a few spaces left at the station. Masters of the Universe had to be committed early birds. Reynolds had a sticker on his windshield that authorized him to park there. I didn't, but I'd be gone before they noticed.

I heard the click of the Mercedes's door locks and had my little automatic stuffed into Reynolds's stomach as soon as he got out of the car. I had him give me the car keys.

"Let's get back inside," I said, unlocking the doors and walking around to the passenger side.

"You know you're going to jail for this," he said, as soon as we were in the leathery comfort of the Mercedes.

"Maybe. I might see you there, if what I think is true."

"I don't know what you think."

"I think there's no such thing as an easy job. I learned that from years of carpentry. Even the smallest task can go awry if you aren't careful with measurements and tools, manual or power. It takes a lot of concentration. I also think the worst thing that can happen to some people is big success. It gives them the idea they can do whatever they want and get away with it. Creates the illusion of invulnerability."

"You're sore about your girlfriend. Trust me, she's not that interesting."

"How do you know I won't shoot you in the belly?"

"You won't."

I didn't shoot him in the belly, but I did shoot the Mercedes's radio, which was pretty startling for Reynolds.

"Jesus Christ!" he yelled. "What the fuck!"

Then I shot the speedometer.

"Getting closer," I said.

"You're out of your mind," he said. "Please stop."

"You stop. Keep Galecki away from me and Amanda. Two of his guys went down last night and that'll keep happening until I reach you. Understand?"

He nodded without saying anything, which I knew meant nothing, but it felt good to see him do it. Part of me wanted to stick the gun to his temple and pull the trigger, but that was a road I wasn't prepared to travel, as much as I wanted to.

"I hate people like you, Reynolds," I said. "Always have. Maybe someday I'll get over it."

"Class warfare, Acquillo. You'll never win."

I had to give him credit for having the balls to say that when they were within range of my little gun. I got a grip on my rancor and got the hell out of there, unsatisfied, but still in possession of the scant remains of my own principles and self-respect.

Chapter Twenty-Two

The late executive director of the Puerto Rico campus of Worldwide Loventeers was named Carolyn Harris. She had a daughter, Eulah, who lived in the northwest corner of Connecticut, according to Jackie's research.

I was in my old Jeep and the Grand Prix was in the shop that had put it back together the last time I'd used it as a defensive weapon.

"At least it's the front this time," said the guy at the counter. "I think our work in the back is fully intact. Next time get T-boned and you'll end up with a whole new car."

I took the ferry out of Port Jefferson, which landed in Bridgeport, and then drove up Route 8 till it terminated in Winsted, and then a few miles more over wooded hills to the address Jackie had given me. It was a gravel driveway that took another five minutes to traverse until I reached a small Cape Cod house with a few horses hanging around a paddock outside a big red barn.

Imagining attack dogs and shotguns, I took my time getting out of the Jeep. After Puerto Rico, it was a pleasure to be surrounded by tall New England hardwoods and hemlock. Jackie had also given me a phone number, which I dialed on my smartphone.

A woman answered and said, "Is that you in the drive?"

"It is. I'm here to talk to you about your mother."

"She's dead."

"I know. It's what I want to talk about."

"I'm alone here," she said.

"I can meet you someplace nearby. Get a cup of coffee or something."

The line went quiet for a moment, but then she gave me the name of a coffee shop in town. She told me to go there and she'd follow in about fifteen minutes. I thanked her and hung up.

Nature hadn't been kind to Eulah Harris. Short and overweight, with hair so thin and wispy you could see her scalp. It made me think of what Charlotte said about Carolyn's proud mane of white hair. A woman who thought naming her female child Eulah was a good idea.

When she sat down, I slid her my private investigator's license. She studied it carefully and wrote down my name and license number in a little address book she took out of her purse.

"First off, I'm sorry about your loss," I said.

"Thanks, I guess. It was a few months ago. I'm over it, I think. What's your interest?"

"I'm looking into the Worldwide Loventeers."

I didn't want to say more than that, and luckily, she didn't ask.

"Her *pobrecitos.* The wretched refuse she looked after. She loved them."

"That's what she was like? Loving?"

Eulah shook her head in a way that was hard to read as a yes or a no. Turned out to be both.

"Everyone will tell you my mother was the kindest, gentlest, most generous, and gracious person you'd ever meet. I didn't like her very much."

A waitress stopped at the table and Eulah said all she wanted was a cinnamon bun and some water. I got coffee.

"You didn't like her?" I asked.

"She didn't like me. Or my younger brother. As soon as he was born, she left us with our father and went to Africa. And then lived in every other rat hole around the world. We saw her exactly twice. At my brother's wedding and our father's funeral. What mother does that?"

A lifetime of harm and grievance seeped out of her and flooded the table between us. I wondered if all that toxicity had found its way to her depleted scalp.

"I'm sorry," I said, which was all I could say.

"Everybody's sorry. I appreciate it, though, since otherwise, what would human beings be worth?"

Her gaze was focused somewhere in the middle of my shirt, as if looking up toward my face was too painful an effort. When her cinnamon bun arrived, she picked it up and ate it with two hands, like a raccoon. She spoke in an urgent monotone that didn't entirely line up with the content of her speech.

"Do you have any idea why your mother took her own life?" I asked, as gently as I knew how.

Eulah scoffed.

"Who believes that? Morons."

"So you don't think she killed herself."

"Carolyn? Why would she do that? Was anybody happier with life?"

I wasn't sure how to converse with a person who spoke in rhetorical questions, but I tried anyway.

"A person who was ill, maybe, or hiding a mental illness, a depression?"

"Laughable," said Eulah.

When she'd gnawed the cinnamon bun down to a half-dollar-sized lump, she looked at it appraisingly, then popped it in her mouth.

"Can I have another one of those?" she asked. "I assume you're paying."

"Have all you want. Bottomless buns here at the Winsted coffee shop."

"That's funny," she said, though amusement didn't show on her face. "My father left me and my brother more than five million dollars each. Carolyn should have stuck around for that."

"So your father was good to you."

"He was. Outsourced a lot to nannies and caregivers, and didn't know which end of a screwdriver would turn a screw, but he hugged us a lot, and could act silly, and that probably saved our lives. Are you Jewish? You've got the nose."

"My mother's father was a Jew," I said, "but I'm mostly French Catholic with a little Italian mixed in for extra flavor. And the nose was modified in the boxing ring."

"My father was Jewish, even though he had this WASPY name Harris. But he didn't practice. I think that's too bad. We might have liked it. Carolyn was a Swede. My brother got all the blond."

Her second cinnamon bun arrived and she went at it with the same feral vigor. I wondered if she'd dip it in a stream if any were nearby.

"So if you don't think your mother committed suicide, what happened?" I asked, trying to drag the conversation back to relevance.

She shrugged.

"Somebody threw her off that cliff. Might've had it coming, who knows. But she didn't kill herself. That's absurd."

A thought jumped at me.

"Why are you so sure about your mother's state of mind if you only saw her twice in your life?"

"I wrote her every day," she said, with the same inflection-free voice. "She wrote back about every two weeks. Twelve thousand, seven hundred and seventy-five letters versus eight hundred and fifty-six. But who's counting."

"Every day," I said.

"Every day. Still do. They all get returned, but I'm not sure how to stop."

"And you saw no sign of suicidal thoughts."

"If my mother killed herself, pigs can fly faster than a Boeing 777 and lesbian leprechauns run the Pentagon."

She offered me the symmetrically fashioned circular remains of her second cinnamon bun. I said only if she was thoroughly sated. She said she was, so I ate it.

"What do you think?" she asked.

"Tasty. But not the best I've had."

She slapped the table top.

"That's what I'm talking about. Honesty. Why can't the world have more of it?"

"Honestly don't know."

And this time she gave up a little surreptitious grin and almost brought her gaze even with my eyes. I appreciated the effort, paid the bill, and let her get back to whatever life she'd carved out for herself.

"We need serious hacker help here," I told Jackie over the phone as I headed back south to Southampton. "Randall Dodge-grade help."

"He's resigned from the trade," said Jackie. "He blames it on you, by the way."

"I kept him out of jail, the ingrate."

"Only because you almost put him there. I'm not here to play chicken and egg."

Randall was a Shinnecock Indian and master of the digital world who'd done a lot of favors for me after Jackie and I had done a lot of favors for him. I wasn't sure how the tally sheet stacked up, but I still felt it was leaning in my direction.

I hung up on Jackie and called him.

"As I've told Jackie, fuck no," he said, without a lot of hesitation when he heard it was me on the line.

"I love you, Randall," I said. "Not in the carnal sense, of course, but you're one of my favorite people."

Randall seemed a little touched by that.

"Well, thank you, Sam. I guess I love you too."

"So just do this for me. I'll protect you."

"As if," he said. Then paused, and said, "What is it?"

So I told him. Not that hard, I suggested, which he didn't buy.

"Not that hard if you don't have to do it," he said.

Then I told him why it was important. As a Native American by designation, with a lot of black and Latino stirred into the mix, social causes resonated.

"All right, what the fuck," he said. "If I get nailed, Jackie needs to defend me for free."

"Have you ever paid her?"

"I guess not."

"So, same deal."

I gave him all the information Jackie had acquired on Carolyn Harris, enough to get him on the scent.

"All I need is her e-mail," I said. "Say over the last year of her life. Busting into the Loventeers' server would be dandy, but I'm guessing the good stuff will be in her private communications."

"You wouldn't happen to have her computer, would you?"

"Nah, that'd be too easy. You prefer a challenge."

"You're welcome to go screw yourself, Sam. And I mean that in the most loving way."

I HAD another computer project on my list, but not requiring Randall's level of expertise. I called Jackie and told her she could do it just fine.

"I need to get Ruth Bellingham's permanent address," I said. "I'm assuming it's somewhere in or around New York, not Puerto Rico."

"Do you know how many hours of research that can take?"

"You know what? You digital geniuses are all a bunch of whiners."

"Only you can compliment and insult a person in a single sentence," she said.

"I think it's important that we haven't heard from her. She couldn't get back the stolen files through legal means, so she got New York to send in the hit team. I warned Art Reynolds to keep Galecki and his goons away from us, and we haven't heard from him either. Innocent people would be raising holy hell by now. I know where to find Reynolds, but Bellingham is closer to the action, and maybe a softer target."

I got off the phone with her in mid-complaint and concentrated on piloting the convoluted path to the ferry dock in Bridgeport, Connecticut. The trip across the sound almost felt like a vacation, the air all stirred up with summerly breezes and the setting sun turning the water a dark steel-blue, casting magic-hour light that improved the complexions of all the people sitting outside on top of the ship. A woman about my age with straight black hair and a Schnauzer that was catching every treat she tossed him, no matter how challenging, asked me if I liked dogs. I said, sure, I had one myself, a mutt and not as good an infielder, but possessing other qualities.

"Good chick magnet?" she asked.

"Already attracted one of those," I said. "She's been looking after the dog lately, so maybe we both caught her."

"I can't imagine life without some dopey, furry thing to sleep with every night. Though I guess you could have said that about my ex-husband."

She also said she couldn't be friends with anyone her dog didn't like. She'd never trust them, believing the Schnauzer was a flawless judge of character.

I asked her to give me one of his treats, which I lobbed to him, an easy catch.

"If he didn't like you, he wouldn't even do that," she said. "He'd just let it drop on the floor. It's uncanny."

"I know some people whose character could use a little judging. Maybe you should hire him out."

"Ha, ha. Maybe cover the cost of all these treats. What is your girlfriend feeding yours?"

I didn't have the heart to tell her Fromager d'Affinois, pâté campagna, and biscotti, so I just said I didn't know, but I was sure it was okay. She said her ex-husband used to get drunk and feed the Schnauzer beer.

"Did he like your husband?" I asked.

She pondered that.

"Come to think of it, he did. I guess he's not that perfect."

"Might've been the beer."

"Might've been."

"I've got good news, bad news, and worse news," said Randall, when I picked up his call.

I was in my shop at the drawing table, trying to muscle through some tricky calculations.

"Let's take it in order."

"Carolyn Harris's personal e-mail account is still open."

"That's great."

"But the provider is very serious about security. It's a freaking steel vault."

"What's the worst part?" I asked.

"Have to have the password. Normally, you could use brute force. It's an app that tries random shit, like millions of word and number combinations an hour, until something clicks. I happen to possess one of the best of those things, though I deny ever having used it."

"So?"

"The provider also noticed this is a way to break into their customers' mailboxes, so they detect brute force attempts in about ten seconds and lock up the account. Even I can't get around that. Not unless I have the computer itself. Then there are ways. Maybe."

I asked him to give me a second to think. As he was talking, something slipped into my mind, a thought or a memory, with no words attached. But I could feel it in there, fluttering around the region between the conscious and subconscious.

When it didn't come, I said I'd call him back.

"For sure. I'm just here doing honest work."

I knew that recall wasn't easily forced. In fact, whenever I struggled to capture a fleeting thought, it would always scamper away. It was better to invoke the powers of Zen, to relax the jaw, slow the breathing, and seek the soundless void.

I slid off the stool and lay down on the concrete floor, closing my eyes. I was always lousy at clearing my brain, a hectoring, chaotic generator of furious noise if there ever was one. But I could divert the cacophony to something else, to more soothing contemplation.

So I thought about sailing. About how I'd motor out into the Little Peconic, well past the shallower water, where I could raise the mainsail and unfurl the jib. I thought about how the breeze would fill the sails as I turned off the wind, and as the boat began to heel, kill the motor, introducing a near perfect silence into the world. I thought about checking the anemometer and setting the ideal bearing in relation to wind direction and velocity. Snapping on the auto helm and dropping back on the padded seat behind the helm, releasing control of the wheel and whatever tension had accumulated around my heart and soul.

Free from operating the boat, I could look around the Little Peconic, at the familiar coastlines and scattering of speed boats and sails. The sky and slate grey water, whose power lay latent and unconcerned by the affairs of those like me, moving over the surface in blissful denial of the true nature of things.

I switched to Spanish to scour that feeling from emotional memory. I realized it made me feel wealthy beyond words. *Rico*. And its opposite, *pobre*.

I called Randall and asked him to access Carolyn's e-mail account. When he got there, I said, "Try *pobrecitos*."

"Okay. Why the hell not."

After a few seconds he said, "I'm in. How did you do that?"

"Ask the Buddha."

"Righteous hacker, for sure."

"The most."

I asked him to download everything he could and e-mail it to me. I could hear him tapping away, fingers moving over the keyboard like Arthur Rubinstein on speed.

"You know, dude, this is barely illegal," said Randall. "Not on the same scale as some of the shit you've had me do."

"I said I'd protect you."

"I'll never argue with you again."

"Yes, you will," I said.

"Okay, but I'll be nicer when I do it."

"Fair enough."

Soon after, an e-mail showed up from an unknown address with an attachment titled "Carolyn's Last Words." As her personal e-mail, it was predictably domestic in nature, over half being responses to Eulah's handwritten letters. I deleted all of that without looking. I searched for any e-mails to names connected to the Loventeers, with no success, until a bunch popped up as correspondence with a person named Ruth.

These I read. Starting six months before her death, Carolyn was becoming increasingly apprehensive about how some adolescent girls and young boys were being directed away from the Caring Center into a program run out of the hacienda. Ruth's replies were conciliatory, promising to dig into the situation and report back anything she found that may be of concern. Carolyn grew steadily frustrated with these assurances, which seemed to yield few tangible results.

Like a Hitchcock movie rendered in digital language, one could see the ever more frantic Carolyn Harris heading for a collision with the dissembling and evasive Ruth Bellingham, until Carolyn's final e-mail, written the day before her death, carried the words, "I've run out of patience. I intend on reporting this entire state of affairs to federal and Puerto Rican authorities."

Film goes to black.

CHAPTER TWENTY-THREE

Jackie was happy to confirm to me that she was, in fact, a digital genius, proven by having tracked down Ruth Bellingham's address.

"I knew you could do it," I said.

"No mean feat, you should know."

"I'm sure," I said. "So where is she?"

"London."

"Get the hell out of here."

"Specifically a London neighborhood called Islington. She's the daughter of the founders of Worldwide Loventeers. Married a rich bloke named Pendleton Bellingham, if you can believe that. Do you think people called him Penny? Or Ha'penny, if he was a little on the small side? He dropped dead about twenty years ago, nicely timed with her parents' deaths. Ruth inherited the charity, the house in Islington, and other houses around the world, including Patagonia and the Seychelles."

"The Loventeers executive director in Puerto Rico said she wasn't the big boss," I said.

"He's been deceived. She's the biggest boss they have, since she owns the joint. One hundred percent."

"You can own a nonprofit?"

"Sure. Like your age, your tax ID is just a number."

"Does Burton's expense account cover a trip to London?" I asked.

"It would cover a trip to Proxima Centauri if it helped one of our cases. But how do we know she's there?"

"Just a hunch. If I'm wrong, I'll reimburse the firm."

"Piffle."

I once spent more than 50 percent of the year in parts of the world other than my home in Stamford, Connecticut. Every part of the world you could possibly imagine, wherever there was a handy source of crude oil and investment capital. At first, Abby found that a cause to gripe, but after a while, she almost seemed cheered by the prospect of my absence. It came to be that she had a completely separate life from me, enjoyed with one of our neighbors. They liked to spend time in a cozy ski lodge in Vermont. I destroyed it, right around the time I gutted our Stamford house that had passed into Abby's ownership after the divorce. This turned into a legal encumbrance, though it felt therapeutic at the time. I've built a lot of houses since then, and I think figuring out how to tear them down was good preparation. It's a lot harder than you might think.

International travel had changed since I'd done a lot of it, but the basics stayed the same. Drive to JFK, park in a long-term lot about one hundred miles away, ride a tram with nervous, unhappy people, get stripped nearly naked by the TSA, find a bar near your gate, drink too much, but still get on the flight with more nervous, unhappy people, endure efforts to encroach on your armrests (I gave no quarter), fail to sleep, continue to drink too much, read the illiterate thriller novel nearly losing your eyesight because of the small type and lousy paper, pee frequently and suffer the terrifying sound of the toilet flushing, try to assure the British flight attendants that you really weren't flirting, just trying to be friendly and pleasant, stagger through the Heathrow gauntlet, and tell the person at the hotel desk that your room must be ready because if you don't lie down for a moment your brain will bleed out through your eye sockets, creating an awful, shall we say bloody, mess.

All of that awaited me, but first I had to go back to Burton's and check in on Amanda and tell her what I was up to. I stopped at the cottage on the way and threw essentials in a suitcase, like my laptop and clever Internet connector. While I was so engaged, Jackie had booked my flight and a hotel in London close to Islington, but not too close. Experience told me to always keep your home base a little distant from your quarry.

That evening, I sat with Amanda, Jackie, Harry, Burton, Eddie, and Sullivan out on one of Burton's big sun porches, open on three sides with a giant paddle fan on the ceiling double teaming with the sea breeze. His house wasn't right on the ocean, but we were close enough to hear the surf, which sounded a little worked up over something.

No one was feeling particularly festive, the stress of recent events weighing heavily. Burton had a device he'd brought back from Australia that he used to fling a hard rubber ball out onto the lawn, so Eddie was gleefully occupied.

I asked Burton if he'd ever met Ruth Bellingham.

"No," he said. "I didn't even know she existed. Not sure if the Edelsteins do either, and I'm not about to call and ask. I'm afraid of what I might say."

"I'll do it," said Jackie. "Tomorrow. Would be good to know."

Burton thanked her but said it really wouldn't make much difference one way or the other.

"I appreciate everything you all are doing," he said, "but I don't see how it improves my prospects with the case. It's going to come down to my testimony against the surviving witnesses that evening, two of whom are of unimpeachable standing legally and socially. Thoroughly damning."

I wanted to tell him that for some reason all the things we were discovering about the Worldwide Loventeers had an important bearing on the events of that night, but I couldn't tell him why. That it was a conviction based on pure gut, which wouldn't have assuaged me if our situations had been reversed.

But then Jackie did it for me.

"I think we're making progress," she said to him. "It just doesn't look like it."

"Very well," said Burton.

My cell phone rang, which I think relieved everyone. I took the call out on the lawn.

"Sam, it's Bill Fenton." My buddy from the NYPD. "Sorry to call so late, but I just got some news from Interpol. Damn Europeans always forget they're in a different time zone."

"No problem here. What's up?"

"Your boy Mikolaj Galecki, aka, Zayna Dabrowski, Addey Mazur, Krzysztof Zalewski, take your pick, is major bad news. Picked a fight with a Polish Olympic heavyweight when he was only eighteen. Beat the shit out of him. From there had a career in hurting people for the Polish version of Cosa Nostra, then went international, moved into drugs, arms dealing, and human smuggling, currently most wanted for white slavery. Big business out of Eastern Europe. I guess easier to transport than Russian grenade launchers. And would you believe it, has an advanced degree from the University of London. Speaks like a dozen languages. If he's over here, and the smart money says he's lurking around Brooklyn, the FBI would very much like to show him a little hospitality."

I told him about the attack by a pair of Polish guys out on Oak Point. That they hadn't hesitated to shoot one of our cops.

"That's the way it is with these foreign nationals," said Fenton. "They get sent out on a job, they either get their man, or die trying, since failure is apparently not an option. Almost makes you nostalgic for the old gumbas."

I thanked him and said I'd definitely call it in if I caught wind of Galecki.

"Listen, Sam. I'm not trying to insult you, but he's out of your league. Even if you weren't on the wrong end of middle age, there's some evil shit out there that's bigger than anything you can imagine. Bigger money, bigger power, bigger motherfuckers. Nothing you can handle on your own. I'm just saying."

I said I heard him, but had one more question.

"What's Galecki's degree in?"

"Philosophy. Isn't that some shit?"

I FILLED everyone in on my call with Bill Fenton and asked Sullivan if he could pass along the information about Mikolaj Galecki to Ross Semple, and he said sure.

"I'll call Bill myself just to get all the details. I know the stuff Ross will want to hear."

"For what it's worth, London is full of Polish import-export people," said Harry, a guy in the import-export business. "It's the perfect hub for any EU citizen. Though I suppose Brexit will screw that up and they'll have to move somewhere else."

"So these Polish shippers and handlers, legal or illegal?" I asked.

"Both. Ever since the war, the Brits and Poles have been woven into the same illicit networks. Keeping the naughty goods flowing from East to West and back again. Dollars to dimes it's where Galecki hooked up with Bellingham, who hooked him into New York."

In no hurry to leave the soothing fellowship, however dimmed by current misfortune, I forced myself to get up and kiss Amanda farewell.

"I think you can forgo packing shorts and T-shirts for this trip," she said. "Though an umbrella might be in order."

Burton rose with me and asked if we could have a private word before I left. Only Jackie raised an eyebrow.

He brought me into a small library near the front door that I'd forgotten was there, shutting the door behind us.

"This is horrible, but I have to tell you something," he said. "I hope it can stay between us."

The only way to describe the expression on his face was agonized.

"Of course, Burt."

He forced it out, with great difficulty.

"Elton Darby was attempting to gain my financial support through a variety of incentives. Of relevance here was the prospect of certain liaisons, anonymous, discreet, in foreign locales. I'm a fool who should have shut these offers down immediately, but I was a little intrigued. It's hard for me, you must know. I'm not the flamboyant, public type. I know that's all passé, but I can't depart from habit. But I get lonely. That damned Darby really knew how to work on me."

"Listen, Burt, that's no big deal. Everybody deserves a little romance."

He closed his eyes and shook his head hard as if to cast away the horrid thing he was about to say.

"That night, at the Edelsteins, I was still resisting Darby's entreaties, so he must have been desperate enough to raise the stakes." He paused before saying, "He said I could have any age I wanted. Just order it up. I was horrified, and told him so. What kind of monster did he think I was? I told him I was going to report him to Loventeers management. That's when he grabbed my arm and pulled me in to say he'd claim it was me who asked for this. It would be my word against his. And the media would surely get his story first."

He gripped my arm, as if re-creating the moment, and shuddered.

"I ripped my arm away and he ended up with my watch," he said. "There were threatening words. Shouting. He said he was keeping the watch as a donation. He taunted me. I just walked away. Looked for Joshua and Rosie, but couldn't find them, so I left the house. And you know the rest. I trust you with this, Sam, but no one else. Jackie doesn't need to know. It doesn't change anything about the facts of the case."

I told him it connected a few dots for me, but I would keep his confidence.

"One thing in return," I said.

"What?"

"Stop being so hard on yourself. You're still the best person I know."

"Then you might question your other associations," he said, but smiled a tired smile, genuine for all of that.

JACKIE HAD me in business class, so I was comfortable, though wide awake for the whole flight. I brought along an architect's scale, mechanical pencil, and an eight-and-a-half-by-eleven pad of drawing paper that I used to design a giant built-in wall unit Frank had assigned to me. The very finest kind of project: big, open budget, and very long time frame. And no other designers involved to muddy the waters.

The English flight attendant asked me if I was an architect.

"Cabinetmaker," I said. "Architects take themselves too seriously. Though I like some of them. The good ones."

"That looks appallingly complicated," she said.

"It's only scale, proportion, symmetry, and common sense in three dimensions."

"Still sounds rather complicated."

"Do you know how to knit a sweater?" I asked.

"I do, actually."

"That's complicated. This is child's play. You just need to bring me another belt of vodka to help with my concentration."

"That I can accomplish right away. You'll have to wait a bit for the sweater."

I'd made the run to Heathrow a hundred times during my tenure with the company, since in those days London was the hub through which you had to pass to get almost anywhere. It had been a few years, but it was neither better nor worse to negotiate the massive infrastructure and find my way into the city.

The sun was bright and the sky blue on the ride in, which didn't seem natural or particularly fair, given the bleary, sand-filled condition of my eyes. The cabbie, a Hungarian who claimed to have lived in every country in Europe, and was planning his next move to Sri Lanka, said the traffic in London had achieved astonishing levels of congestion in the two years he'd been there, but driving people around was still his favorite occupation.

"I need to keep moving all the time. My girlfriend thinks it's a sickness, but she keeps moving with me, so how bad really?"

"I like sitting on my ass in one place," I said. "You should give it a try."

"Maybe in Sri Lanka."

Jackie had put me in a hotel on the South Bank with a nice view of the Thames and Saint Paul's Cathedral. I would have appreciated the scenery more if I hadn't passed out and slept all the way around to the next morning, with only a few interruptions to pee and watch Saint Paul's experience various phases—grey daylight, somber dusk, stellar artificial lights of night, rosy dawn. I was reminded of Monet's obsessive paintings of Notre Dame, every moment a new vision.

At breakfast in the hotel, everyone was from somewhere other than the UK, the servers and guests alike. Just like New York. I felt right at home.

I was on my second run to the buffet table, brimming with eggs, sausage, mushrooms, and bacon, when Jackie called me, even though it was only about three in the morning her time.

"I went through the Carolyn Harris e-mails you sent me. I see what you mean. Makes the threat, then the next day, she's dead. Coincidence?"

"Only if lesbian leprechauns are in charge of the Pentagon."

I caught a ride over to Islington, which took about an hour of circuitous travail through construction sites and frequent long waits at intersections. The driver was a skinny guy from Nepal who smelled of grilled cuisine, though the car was cleaned to standards I hadn't experienced outside Japan. He held up his smartphone, jacked into the car's stereo system, and asked my taste in music, suggesting punk rock. I went for late Ellington, a choice he found surprising, but as we listened, also inspired.

Islington was as I remembered, only with a lot more fresh paint and nicer cars. I walked past Bellingham's townhouse, and was disappointed to find no reasonable place to establish a stakeout. So I went down the block to a pub and hung out working on my built-ins over coffee until noon, when I had a Guinness and pondered next moves.

I called Jackie, waking her up, as usual.

"So Bellingham doesn't have a separate office. Does that mean she's usually there at her house?" I asked.

"I guess. She could be in some Loventeers' outpost for the next few months. No way to know."

"That'd be inconvenient."

"That's all I can tell you. This is your hunch, not mine."

I thanked her and got another Guinness. When the barmaid came back around, I asked if the pub delivered food in the neighborhood.

"Aye, for the discerning. Our shepherd's pie in particular. Where you from, if you don't mind me askin'?"

"Southampton, New York. It's on Long Island."

"Never been to New York. It's on my list. Have a cousin there who works in banking. My mum tells me you need a gun if you go out at night. I tell her, don't be ridiculous."

"Don't need a gun," I said, "but a credit card is essential. It's actually the weapon of choice."

"Can't be more expensive than this place. I don't know how people afford to live here, though I live here, so there it is. You want another Guinness?"

"I do," I said. "And the bill, and a takeaway of your famous shepherd's pie."

She brought it to me in a Styrofoam clamshell stuffed in a plastic bag. It smelled great and I was tempted to order another one on a plate, despite stuffing myself at the hotel's buffet.

"I have to graduate before thinkin' of international travel," she said, handing me the bag.

"What are you studying?"

"Psychiatric pharmacology," she said.

"There's a route to campus popularity."

"Never heard that one before. You Yanks certainly are the clever ones."

I walked the shepherd's pie over to Ruth's place, which was a brick Georgian row house behind a wall, also brick. The gate had a call box and a security cam. I pulled my

Oxford University baseball cap down over my face and pushed the button.

"Who the fuck," came out of the call box. A deep, grainy male voice.

"Shepherd's pie for the madam, sir," I said, trying to sound like an Australian mate I used to have at the company, a guy I liked imitating, usually at the end of a long night in an evil bar most would consider an ill-advised choice, especially when inebriated, which we certainly were.

After a few moments, he came back on.

"Nobody orderin' shepherd's pie here. You got the wrong house. So fuck off."

"So that's how it is," I said. "Maybe if you come out here and fuck me proper, you wanker."

The mechanics of the exchange weren't that easy, since we had to push a button to speak, then wait for the reply, and the fidelity wasn't first rate, but the essence of the content was communicated.

It's easy to see at this historical remove that Muhammad Ali was the greatest psychological fighter in history. The fine boxers who went up against him, people like George Foreman and Joe Frazier, his match physically, fell for it every time. What Ali understood intuitively is a scientific fact. That anger makes you stupid. It transfers mental function from your higher-level prefrontal cortex to the bottom of the brain, the amygdala, which only knows rage, fear, hunger, and the nice smell of the cute hominid sitting next to you.

The bloke on the intercom came out of the gate in the prehistoric way I expected—arms back, chest, head, and center of gravity thrust forward. All I had to do was grab him from the side by his shirtfront, stick out my foot, and propel his momentum into the street, where he landed face-first.

He was pretty big, so not that quick to get back on his feet, giving me plenty of time to kick him in the head, the kind of kick that would impress a striker for Manchester United.

I dragged his inert body up against the wall and went through the gate.

The front door was at the top of a steep flight of masonry stairs. The door was closed but unlocked. I went through.

"Trevor!" called out a female voice. I presumed Ruth's. "What on earth are you going on about?"

I followed the sound to a sitting room down the front hall. Ruth Bellingham was settled on a Victorian love seat wearing a silk robe, her feet up on a low stool, a digital tablet in her lap. I took off my Oxford University ball cap when she looked up at me, more confused than startled.

"Where is Trevor?" she asked, in a level voice.

"Taking a nap outside."

I took a few steps into the room and relieved her of the tablet and turned it off.

"You might think I don't remember you, but I do," she said.

"Good. Saves on introductions."

"I had my suspicions. That idiot Osterman."

"Not his fault. He was just trying to build an addition to the hacienda," I said.

"Then you can explain to me this horrid behavior," she said.

"More horrid than selling impoverished kids into sexual slavery?"

She settled her hands in her lap, composed, back straight. I wondered for the first time if she might have a little revolver in the pocket of that silk gown. I found the balls of my feet and got ready to jump, one way or the other.

"Well, that's preposterous," she said.

"You scumbags really focused on the Puerto Rico campus, especially after Maria, with all the upheaval and distressed families. Even better, the kids are US citizens and easy to bring to the mainland. Which also means there're no jurisidictional issues. And we have your files. It's all there. In your handwriting, your DNA all over it. A first-year federal prosecutor with an inferiority complex could nail the case with one hand tied behind her back."

She wasn't about to concede the point, though she didn't put up an argument.

"If you're so sure, why the inappropriate visit?"

"I want to know who in New York was involved. Art Reynolds, Milton Flowers, Elton Darby." I paused for a breath. "Burton Lewis."

I could see her weighing the implications, doing the math.

"I have no idea what you're talking about," she said. "And even if I did, why would I share any information with you?"

"The file is safe with me. For now."

She seemed to relax a bit.

"Ah. An exchange? Is that what it is?"

"Yeah," I said, in the way only a tired, shopworn Yank could say. "I don't care about you. I just want those bastards."

Her eyes drifted from my face to a corner of the room. I followed the gaze and saw a laptop sitting on an antique writing desk. She caught herself and flew her eyes back into mine, but it was too late. It was only a few steps for me over to the desk, where I snapped the laptop closed and stuck it under my arm with the tablet. Bellingham was on her feet, holding both fists in the air.

"Too late," I said. "Deal's off."

"Do not dare," she yelled.

I put my hand over her face, stuck my heel behind hers, and pushed hard enough to drop her back on her ass. She rolled over on her side and put her hands to her ears, as if willing the sound of her destruction from reaching her mind.

"You miserable spick," she said into the carpet.

"Miserable Canuck. Get your pejoratives straight."

Her whimpers were more in anger than pity. I wanted to kick her like I did her meatball bodyguard, but that would bring me too close to her level. Instead, I knelt down and said, softly, "I'm coming after you. I'm after those guys in the States as well, but you're the source of the evil. I don't know why you did it. I don't care. You hurt a lot of innocent people, but you also tried to hurt the people I love. Fear and anger make you stupid. Rage makes you crazy."

And then I stood up, shook out my shoulders, and walked out of there. Trevor was back on his feet, reeling a bit, and wobbled up to me on the path to the house. I had the devices under my left arm, so I had my right available to give him a parting shot to the face. He fell backward, eyes open, but blank to the world. It was more than I should have delivered, maybe less than he deserved, though I still felt a little bad when my head cleared.

But not all that bad.

Chapter Twenty-Four

When I got off the plane, I called Jackie and gave her a brief update on my fun in London. She told me to go straight from the airport to the Pequot, bringing everything with me. The journey was brief enough to avoid jet lag, but I was still jangled by the time differences, so I had to concentrate on driving. The sun was up, the day approaching midafternoon, the traffic in my favor.

My next call was to Amanda.

"How can I miss you if you keep coming home?" she asked.

"Sorry. Just couldn't take all that jolly British cheer."

I asked if she could meet me at the Pequot, where I'd likely arrive just after quitting time.

"Easily. They don't care if I show up covered in sawdust."

"Everything okay?"

"Joe Sullivan added a new member to my crew. First construction manager I've had with a pistol stuck in the back of his blue jeans. He never lets me out of his sight. Doesn't talk a lot, but is very polite. I thought you'd like to know that."

She thought right.

"Bring him along to the Pequot," I said.

"Unavoidable, I'm afraid. Door-to-door service."

"Call ahead and they'll have the catch-of-the-day waiting."

"With or without chips?"

I made one stop on the way to the East End—at a computer services company in Islip, where I invested an hour copying all the corrrespondence off Bellingham's hard drive. So I got to the Pequot a little later than planned, and Amanda's red pickup was already in the parking lot. Next to Jackie's Volvo station wagon. No apparent threats, though I still felt uneasy leaving the Jeep, wearing my backpack, and heading into the restaurant. I tried to calm my nerves, but all the travel and altercations were catching up to me.

They were at my regular booth, Jackie and Amanda and a sturdy young guy with short-cropped black hair and an aura of vigilance. I introduced myself.

"Joel MacGregor. Nice to meet you, sir," he said, standing and gripping my hand in a way that would allow him to toss me over his shoulder if he wanted to.

Amanda stood as well so she could give me an enthusiastic bear hug.

"Joel's ex-military," she said. "He calls me ma'am. I've grown accustomed."

He waited for us to sit before sitting down himself, his eyes scanning the Pequot's dusky interior.

"He calls me miss," said Jackie. MacGregor looked concerned. "Don't stop," she said to him, grabbing his meaty bicep with both hands. "I like it."

After going through all the ordering and delivery rituals, including a brief visit by Dorothy Hodges, Jackie got down to business.

"Where is it?" she asked.

"In my backpack," I said. "I got through customs free and clear, so I'm guessing she didn't report the theft."

"I have her files from La Selva in here," she said, holding up a tote bag. "I want to give everything to Hodges to hide somewhere. But you need to ask. He's your friend."

I said that wouldn't be a problem. But I asked her why.

"Things are getting a little too hairy, and I don't know enough to know if the sanctity of my office is sanctified enough to stop the FBI from paying a visit with a search warrant. We don't know enough, period. It's way too risky."

When Dorothy came back over, I asked if her father was around. She said he was in the kitchen bossing around the cooks, who were ignoring him, though it would be good to get him the hell out of there. We were happy to oblige.

He had his chef's apron on when he came over to the table. I asked him how things were cooking.

"Kids today think they were born knowing everything," he said.

"When did you learn?" I asked.

"When I was about five. Maybe four and a half."

We introduced him to MacGregor and listened to them describe their respective military units and experience in the field. Hodges made points by serving in a Swift Boat in Vietnam, though he wouldn't let MacGregor call his time in Kandahar Province any less worthy. The rest of us just sat there and honored the two of them with a series of toasts.

When they seemed spent of reminiscence, I brought up the business at hand.

"So, Paul, if we gave you some stuff to hide, do you think you could hide it where it would be completely safe and guaranteed retrievable?"

He thought about it.

"Safe from who?" he asked.

"Anyone. Including the FBI," said Jackie.

"Ah. That kind of safe."

He thought some more, then nodded.

"I could. Any chance I'd have to lie to the FBI?"

"Remote, but not zero," said Jackie.

He nodded again.

"Of course, they'd have to find me first. Not easy when a man is hunting up in New Hampshire, is what I'm thinking. Been planning to do that for a while."

"Dorothy is going to miss you terribly," said Amanda.

He grinned at that. "I can almost hear the cryin' and wailin'."

We were able to stuff Bellingham's laptop, her tablet, my own tablet, and the hard drive from my PC in my backpack and slide it over to him under the table.

He grunted when pulling the heavy bag into his lap.

"Must be weighty information," he said.

"The weightiest," said Jackie.

On the way out the door, I slipped Jackie the copy of Ruth Bellingham's correspondence that the computer people had stuck on a flash drive.

"Insurance policy," I said. "Plus you can give it a look over at your leisure."

"You think I'm leisuring?"

"I think it'll give us everything we need. Just keep it somewhere safe. Like your bra. Plenty of room in there."

She did just that when I handed her the hard drive. The significance not lost on either one of us.

"It's just till I get home," she said.

One of my least favorite things to see in my driveway is a big white van with US government license plates. There were two guys sitting in the front seat, who got out when I pulled the Jeep in behind.

About the same age and size as Joel MacGregor wearing nearly matching grey suits, just loose enough to conceal their weapons. I kept my own hands in clear view.

"Sam Acquillo?" one of them asked.

"That's me. What's up?"

"I'm Special Agent Carson, this is Special Agent Darrow. We're from the Federal Bureau of Investigation. We need to search your house."

I got up close enough to look at their IDs, as if I'd know if they were legit or not.

"Not without my lawyer," I said.

Carson held up a piece of paper.

"You can call her if you want, but we're searching your home."

"How do you know she's a she?"

"You can let us in, or we can use kinetic methods."

"And get those nice suits all sweaty?"

They looked inside the Jeep and saw my duffel bag, telling me I might as well bring it along since the warrant covered any of my vehicles. I did as asked and had them follow me to the cottage and through the side door. They snapped on surgical gloves.

"Want to tell me what you're looking for?" I asked, tossing the duffel on the kitchen table. "I might be able to just get it for you."

Darrow went right to my laptop, flipped it over, and used a tiny screwdriver to remove the cover from the hard drive.

"Want to tell me where it is?" he asked.

"Damn things keep disappearing on me," I said. "Put that cover back on, if you would. Easy to lose track of those little screws."

Carson went through all the duffel's contents and nooks and crannies, then took a photo of it with his smartphone. So I took photos of them with mine.

"Fair's fair," I said.

I called Jackie, who'd made a futile attempt to get to bed early, so I had the pleasure of waking her up again.

"Shit, shit," was about all she said before hanging up.

Before they got started, I told them about my registered automatic in a drawer next to my bed. I let them retrieve it, assuring them it was the only weapon in the house, unless they counted the three-quarter-sized Harmon Killebrew baseball bat I used to hit golf balls for my dog.

While I waited for Jackie, I sat on the screened-in porch and read some Spinoza, in case I had a chance to discuss the wily Sephardic philosopher with Mikolaj Galecki.

Carson and Darrow were only partway through the bedroom search when she showed up. They stood there while she studied their IDs and the search warrant, grilling them on probable cause and specified items they could seize, which included paper files and any computing devices, though not my phone.

"Don't let it disappear," said Carson. "We'll be back for that."

"You still haven't provided adequate probable cause," said Jackie. "Conspiracy to withhold evidence from a federal investigation? That's it?"

"Take it up with the judge," said Darrow.

She assured them she would, and before they had a chance to ask, told them I wouldn't say another word.

"Your choice. Won't make things any easier," said Carson.

"For you, maybe."

Jackie looked ready to watch them go through a long and tedious process, so I went back to Spinoza. She eventually relented, though only after they stipulated my design drawings were not files and to leave them the hell alone.

She sat on the daybed and said, "No talking."

I tossed her a copy of my favorite Immanuel Kant, but she opted to just sit and stew. It was after two in the morning when they finally wrapped up and Jackie had a chance to look over the haul, which mostly amounted to a pair of Bankers Boxes full of files I hadn't gotten around to tossing out, and my hard-drive-free laptop.

It wasn't until they left and we felt completely secure that I said, "Good call on stowing all that stuff with Hodges."

"They're only getting started. It's going to get nasty."

"What are we going to do?"

"Take a ride to New York. After we get some sleep and my brain has a chance to regain full function."

"What about mine?"

"That's up to you."

IT WASN'T the first time I'd paid a visit to the FBI's Manhattan field office, so Jackie drove and I navigated. On the way, Jackie and I went over what we knew, what we guessed, and where we didn't have a clue.

I asked her why we didn't just turn over all the stuff I'd swiped from Bellingham, along with my own computer and tablet. She said the first reason was it could land me in jail, though it would be a long and complicated prosecution, given the jurisdictional inconveniences of Puerto Rico and the United Kingdom. They might not think it was worth the effort, assuming Bellingham was the international criminal we thought she was. We were convinced we had the evidence to prove it, though it would be inadmissible in court, since boosting it after belting a few security people did not constitute a lawful search and seizure.

"Really? Pretty picky."

"However," said Jackie, "the FBI won't need it if they go looking themselves. They have ways. We just need to point them in the right direction. Which is the last reason we need to keep that information as long as possible."

"What's that?"

"Leverage."

JUDY PAOLINI's admin made it clear that Jackie should be very grateful to get on the assistant director's incredibly busy schedule on such short notice. Jackie told me she expressed her gratitude with an enthusiasm that bordered

on obsequiousness, which almost made her wretch up
breakfast. I asked if she really did want to speak with us,
and Jackie said absolutely.

"She really does have an incredibly busy schedule and
there are dozens of other agents in her office who would
normally handle this kind of thing. By the way, thanks for
being presentable, without me even having to tell you."

I was wearing my lightweight, grey dress pants and
blue blazer combination, with tie and light blue shirt, and
a pair of shoes that had been polished sometime within the
last decade. I said it made me look trustworthy.

"You look like a lawyer," she said. "Decide for yourself."

We timed the trip and our appointment to perfectly
coincide with the commuters trying to get into Manhattan from Long Island, so there was plenty of time to kick
around all these considerations, though we mostly sat there
and bitched about the traffic, since there wasn't much point
in speculating that much before hearing what Judy had to
say, something back at the company we used to call "pool-
ing our ignorance."

It took a while to get through security as the guards had
the experience of seeing just how much crap a woman can
cram into a bulging leather briefcase and giant handbag. I
had to hand over my Swiss Army Knife.

"Take care of that thing," I said. "It's been through a
lot."

He dropped it in a drawer nearly filled with knives just
like it.

Judy's admin had a low center of gravity and lousy eyesight. And little sense of humor, though I didn't give her
much of a chance. She brought us to the same conference
room I'd visited the last time, the only change being the portrait of the latest FBI director, who looked even more flinty
and determined than the last one.

She didn't offer coffee and I didn't ask.

Judy was a lot taller than her admin and eyeglass-free. Thin as a broom handle and even more sensibly dressed than me. She brought along a carbon copy of Carson and Darrow, likely from a cloning operation they had in the basement. He had a yellow legal pad and pen and she didn't introduce him.

Judy sat with her legs crossed and her hands folded in her lap.

"I don't have a lot of time," she said.

"Neither do we," said Jackie, a fiction I didn't correct. She put the search warrant on the table which only the clone looked at, carefully. "I allowed the search to go forward even though the probable cause noted in the warrant was egregiously insufficient. We're here to understand why and learn everything we can about this cited investigation."

"Which won't be very much," said Judy. I liked her voice. It was low and satiny, like a late-night DJ's. "The particulars are extremely sensitive and require the highest levels of confidentiality. All the files are sealed at the request of the US attorney and the grand jury is proceeding ex parte. Would you like me to explain further?"

Jackie barely blanched, but I'd known her long enough to see her mini blanches, and knew an insult when I heard one.

"I did catch that class in law school," she said. "Can we expect my client to be charged?"

"Mr. Acquillo?" she asked, as if I wasn't sitting there. "That's to be determined. Withholding evidence is a serious crime. As is lying to the FBI."

I tried to see what the clone was writing on his pad, but he caught me and moved it farther away.

"So there's nothing you can tell me," said Jackie.

"You requested the meeting," said Judy. "What do you have to tell me?"

"That we're out of here. You can go back to your more important work."

She stood up the way she does that seems to create a mighty updraft, dragging nearby objects and other meeting goers aloft in its wake. Judy held her seat.

"Please, counselor," she said. "Sit back down."

She did. I was still on my butt, so it was easy for me.

"You understand that federal investigations cannot succeed without the type of rigid rules of confidentiality we've put in place," said Judy. "The stakes are too high and the risks too great."

Jackie squeezed her eyes shut and I could almost hear the mustering of equipoise and self-control leaking out of her pores.

"Assistant Director Paolini," she said, "I perfectly understand the restrictions under which you have to operate. But I also understand that in many of these investigations, choices are made between preserving the reputations and welfare of individuals caught up in the proceedings, and success with the case overall. In more blunt terms, you pick who goes down, but also who gets screwed along the way. I am here to tell you, make sure you write this down," she added to the clone, "that I will not permit any of the people I represent, and who by the way, deeply admire, to be harmed by your disregard for fairness and common decency."

Judy gave up a tiny sigh. Of frustration or consonance, it was hard to tell.

"The information your client has in his possession . . ." she started to say.

"Allegedly," said Jackie.

"Allegedly, would be of value to our ongoing investigation. If he would relinquish it, that would be the end of the matter."

"Full immunity, in writing," said Jackie. "For both of us. And the deal doesn't include Sam's personal data. Not relevant to the case."

Judy made some semblance of a smile, though it wasn't one I'd seen that often outside pressure-cooker negotiations. Something between a grin and a snarl.

"Agreed," said Judy. "Write it up," she added to the clone, without looking at him. Then she looked at Jackie. "Contingent on us receiving the material in a very prompt fashion."

"One more thing," I said, causing Jackie to jerk in her chair. "Keep it quiet that you have the material. Don't tell anybody except people who absolutely have to know. No cops or field agents. Just give it a week."

"Care to tell me why?" asked Judy.

"You got your secrets, I've got mine," I said. "But I'm on your side. You won't be sorry."

She mulled it for a moment, then nodded.

"Very well," she said, "but only the immunity is specified in writing."

"Okay with me."

"We'll wait," said Jackie.

And wait we did, for about two hours, I think designed to amp up our already sky-high anxiety. At least for Jackie. I was fine looking out the window at the big buildings all around us, something I never tire of doing when trapped in a New York City office tower. Jackie had to tell me to stop humming an Ellington tune, something I also liked to do, though unconsciously.

The clone came in with two pieces of paper that Jackie read as if trying to see though the print to secret writing underneath. I waited for her to sign, then signed myself in the designated spot. The clone took the papers and pen he'd given us to use and left, saying the little admin troll would be by shortly to chase us out of the building.

Jackie stuffed our copy in her briefcase, put her finger up to her lips, and looked around the room before I had a chance to say anything. I nodded and made a little zipped lip gesture.

It wasn't until we got back in Jackie's Volvo that she let out a big gush of air.

"I don't want to go through that again anytime soon," she said.

"You did great. Right?"

"I did. And you gave me the rare gift of not fucking it up. Though I thought you were about to."

"My pleasure, I think."

"More importantly," she said. "How did they know you had that material? They didn't learn from Burton, or Sullivan, certainly not Hodges. Bellingham wouldn't call Scotland Yard and complain that a Yank just stole her computer full of incriminating evidence."

"Neither would any of Bellingham's buddies back in New York."

"No, they would just come straight for you," she said.

"Which they're going to do. That's why I bought the week."

"Making you bait," she said.

"I already am, but at least this way I've got some leverage. It worked with the FBI."

"Though we still don't know who killed Elton Darby. You might want to think about that now that you aren't under federal indictment."

"Sure. I wonder if Hodges has left for New Hampshire."

"Oh, Christ."

Chapter Twenty-Five

I had to drive all the way to Bellows Falls, Vermont, to pick up the backpack. Hodges claimed that was halfway to where he was hunting, and I didn't argue, since he was the one doing me the favor. It was a lot cooler up there than on Long Island, and the light richer, making all the greenery seem that much more green.

He was wearing his lightweight camouflage outfit and a bigger-than-usual froggy grin, proving the trip really was overdue and predictably salubrious.

"Shot anything yet?" I asked.

"No, but that's hardly the point. Just need to suck in all that moldering, insect-laden, New England mountain air. You should try it sometime."

"Insects give me welts."

"Women's skin lotion keeps 'em away," he said. "Not sure what to make of it."

"Just don't tell me how you know that."

When I got back to Southampton, I dropped off my tablet and hard drive at the cottage and took the backpack over to Jackie's office. She told me she'd be giving it to another attorney, who would give it to the FBI, for reasons she tried to explain, but it was all too arcane for me. I just asked her to put the stuff in a box and give me my backpack, since I'd had it for a while and didn't see the need to add it to the FBI storage room.

"Probably doesn't break the chain of custody," she said.

She'd wheeled in a giant whiteboard kept in her bedroom in the apartment next door. It was covered in diagrams and comments covering the night of Darby's death, delineating what we knew, and what we didn't, with names, times, and actions taken. We both took a long time staring at it.

I told her I used to do the same thing when trying to turn crude oil and natural gas into salable products. She asked me which was more difficult.

"This."

Having said that, I was delighted by her initiative. I loved nothing more than boxes and arrows, what-ifs and if-thens. It was even more my world than shop tools and architectural drawings, a world I'd spent decades navigating, conquering giant, pressurized steel vessels and convoluted piping filled with explosive admixtures that had to follow a perfectly circumscribed path, or result in exactly that. An explosion.

"We don't know enough," I said. "We never do."

"Back to basics, buddy," she said.

"You stay on Burton," I said. "I'll take the others. If you agree, boss."

"Oh, please."

I took a photo of her whiteboard and went back to Burton's, where all I did was slip into bed with Amanda and scrunch around Eddie's neck until we all fell asleep, content to let the next day sort itself out.

Not surprisingly, Mikolaj Galecki called me when I was about to eat breakfast with the gang at Burton's.

"You have some things that belong to people I work for," he said.

"I do. What of it?"

"I want them back."

"Really," I said. "Maybe I could do that. With provisos."

"I assumed."

"Stay away from my friends and family. If anything happens to anyone I know, or to me for that matter, the stuff will be in the hands of the FBI in a New York nanosecond."

"Then you'll go down with us," he said.

"I don't care. It'll be worth it."

"Not to you," he said. "You'll be dead before they get you in cuffs. Along with all your friends and family."

"This isn't that hard. We never meant to mess around with the Loventeers. We stumbled into all this trying to mount a defense for Burton Lewis. It isn't relevant to our case, and in fact, it's too much of a distraction. You'll get your stuff, we get free of you, and you'll be free of us. I'll tell you when and where to pick up the stuff."

"You're not telling me anything," he said. "This number disappears as soon as I hang up. I'm invisible."

"Don't count on it. And no more soldiers sent out to Oak Point."

"Those two boys were my cousins," he said. "Third cousins, but still family."

"I was just defending myself," I said.

"You and the woman. Brave girl. I will enjoy getting to know her better."

A pall settled over me like a wet quilt, unwelcomed, exhausting.

"We didn't start this fight," I said.

"I know. But it probably won't end so well for you."

"That's not true," I said. "*Sub specie aeternitatis.*"

"Spinoza. Not applicable here."

"Don't count on it. I'll take your Spinoza and raise you a pair of Kants."

"There's no free will," said Galecki. "It's all deterministic. All of us succumb to that reality eventually."

"How about this reality. Go fuck yourself."

It wasn't a very erudite thing to say, but it felt good to say it.

"I almost hope you don't deliver the goods, Acquillo. It'd be a real pleasure to break your neck."

"*Adversus solem ne loquitor*," I said, essentially I'm not arguing with any more of your bullshit, and hung up on him, realizing that rhetorical thugs were the same everywhere. Boringly rhetorical.

ONCE AGAIN I was packing my duffel bag, unhappily, given all the fun cabinet work, snuggling with Amanda, and goofing around with Eddie Van Halen I was leaving behind.

I told everyone I'd be gone for a few days, and only Amanda let me go without a lot of irritating questions. I asked her to stick close to Sullivan and MacGregor and try to keep that impulsivity under control.

"That might be too much to ask," she said. "I've been holding back an urge to chase rabbits in Malta."

"Go for it. I'll catch up with you."

In addition to a few changes of clothes, I stopped at the cottage to pick up my backpack filled with the laptop, tablet, and semiautomatic, and the Harmon Killebrew baseball bat, because, who knew. I threw it all in the old Jeep and headed for Brooklyn. On the way, I called Bill Fenton and asked him who was the borough's most notorious Polish criminal.

"That'd be Janko Kowalski, though I'm not sure I should be telling you that. What do you have in mind, if you don't mind me asking."

"Biting off the head of the snake."

"I'd advise against that."

"I know. Just stay tuned and let your brothers in Brooklyn know I'm on the side of the righteous," I said.

"You know they shoot first and check religious credentials afterward."

"I'll take my chances."

"You sure as shit are."

The upward mobility of Brooklyn had taken off like a rocket, and I didn't see any reason not to take advantage of that. I paused on a street corner and located a four-star hotel with a view of the East River and the Manhattan skyline. All they had available was a two-bedroom suite, which I took, assuming I wouldn't live long enough to pay off the credit card.

I self-parked the Jeep in the basement garage and hauled my stuff up to the room. Then I started making phone calls until I tracked down an old acquaintance I'd met around the same time as Bill Fenton, only this guy worked the other side of the legal divide. He had a successful excavation business with a sideline running one of New York's traditional mob families. We'd exchanged favors, so we were even, which is what you want with mob bosses.

"Sam Acquillo," he said on the phone. "So you haven't gotten yourself killed yet."

"Still a work in progress. How do you feel about the Polish mob?"

"I feel fine as long as they stay in Brooklyn and out of the Bronx."

I explained I was looking for one of them, an outsider from Europe, who I guessed would have to be in contact with the locals. As a courtesy if nothing else.

"That's likely," he said. "You'd have to clear things with Janko Kowalski. He's very particular about who plays around in his neighborhood."

"You know Janko?"

"I do, good enough to nod to and share an understanding. There're not people to mess around with, the Polish. They're smart and do a lot of subcontracting with the Russians, who have very exacting standards."

"Where would I find him?" I asked.

He gave me the address of a club in Greenpoint, at the north end of Brooklyn.

"You're not planning to do anything stupid over there, are you, Sam?"

"Not if it would offend you."

He chuckled.

"No sweat off my back," he said. "Like I said, long as it stays in Brooklyn."

I thanked him, but didn't say I owe you one, hoping it would stay off the ledger books.

It was getting dark and I wanted to make my first pass in the daylight, so I sat out on the balcony that overlooked the East River and gazed at the mighty wall of the Manhattan skyline, a star-filled galaxy of its own, exceeding defiance, the pulsing heart of the universe.

To me, always living close, but never within, it wasn't a city exactly, more a transcendent state of collective psychoses. A madness of anxiety and striving, a type of perilous mountain range of glass towers over thousands of compact, weathered joints that made you feel as embraced and secure as a fire-lit hearth.

It wasn't the Little Peconic Bay, but that night it served a similar role for me, gigantic and fearsome in lieu of serene, but a good way to settle the nerves before heading back into the breach.

My tablet GPS took me directly to The Krakus 24-Hour Bar & Grill, on the corner at the end of a row of stalwart brick buildings. It was far enough away from the river and deep enough in the old Polish neighborhood to have thus far avoided the tide of gentrification, and many of the other storefronts carried Polish names, with delis promising the best perogies and galumpkis in town.

I knew what a lot of that food tasted like, since my father would journey from the Bronx to stock up. Or send me on the bus with a big cloth bag to lug home, checking the receipt against the change to make sure I wasn't skimming the house. His father-in-law, my grandfather, was from Poland, and successfully inculcated the household in a lust for his native cuisine. I'd drifted away from the habit in adulthood, but just seeing the signs in the storefronts for kiszka and stuffed veal on sale ignited my taste buds and olfactory memories.

Though an unreconstructed Frenchman, despite his Italian name, my father wasn't much of a gourmand, though one could argue those deli meats would rival anything you might find at the Boucherie Moderne in Paris.

It was about eight in the morning, and true to its name, I saw a pair of men duck into The Krakus, the windows of which were opaque, reflecting back the passing cars and pedestrians. I found a place to park on the street and walked over there.

My Italian friend had called it a club, but there was no sign that someone off the street couldn't just walk in, so I did. The street exposure on the corner failed to signal the scale within. The bar ran about a mile down the right side of the room with a lot of standing room, though booths lined the other wall, interrupted by a staircase that led to a second story cantilevered over the main room, with windows covered in curtains. The ambience was also cavernous, and barely lit by isolated lanterns on the wall and feeble ceiling fixtures. There were a few wide-screen TVs showing a soccer game, with the sound blessedly turned down.

There were maybe a half-dozen people dispersed along the bar eating breakfast. When I sat down, a large woman in blue jeans shorts and T-shirt set a cup of coffee and glass of ice water in front of me. And a menu, that looked about an inch thick. If you favored cuisine of the home country, you were all set, but if not, you could be served any breakfast dish you could imagine. Or lunch, or dinner. Or between-meal snacks.

I ordered a breakfast plate with a side of house-made kielbasa and mustard.

"How do you keep track of all this food?" I asked the bartender.

"By doin' it a million years. We feed a lot of people with funny hours. I know bartenders that only catch a few hours of daylight. Them and the musicians. And the cleaning crews. Live like bats."

"Sleep upside down?"

She laughed.

"I like that. I'm gonna start calling those dudes vampires."

"Just don't tell them it was my joke."

Her T-shirt was apparently purchased at a showing of *The Best Little Whorehouse in Texas*. It was a big logo, but she had plenty of chest to handle the display.

The coffee, in a chunky ceramic mug, was delicious. I told her so.

"Them ten-ton percolators in the back have been cranking it out for forty years. Better be good by now."

She left for a bit, and when she came back I told her I'd heard the place was a club.

"That's upstairs. Invitation only. You thinkin' about joinin'?"

I made it clear that was not my intent.

"I'm from the Bronx," I said, truthfully enough. "We got plenty of clubs over there."

"Good, because that's a fucking exclusive club. Whole different clientele. Which is why I come on at four A.M. Want no part of the late-night festivities."

"Me neither," I said. "Too old for that shit."

"That's what I'm talkin' about. Bad enough with these knees."

She didn't look much past forty, but I commiserated anyway.

When the food came, she left me alone to wolf it down. Before I was done, she brought me an excellent coffee refill.

"I used to live in the Bronx," she said. "Just north of Broadway."

"What brought you over here?"

"Married a Polack, what else? You're not working here if you aren't at least married into the nationality. I'm actually Italian, in case you couldn't tell."

I couldn't, but said I could. I wondered if she came from people who hauled boulders for the stone masons.

"I know you're not around, but what time does the club start revving up?" I asked.

"Still interested in that? I'd say about eleven, maybe midnight. I know some of the girls who work straight through for the extra shift. Running on coke and nicotine. Skinny little things, mostly. Don't know how they do it. Youth, I guess."

"I feel sorry for kids like that. How young do you think?"

"Legal, but not by much," she said. "I hope. Most of them barely speak English. I don't know where they come from."

I shook my head in legitimate sympathy.

"We grew up in better times," I said.

"At least we thought so. You want more of that coffee? You drink a lot."

"Some have said."

I finished up there and left a big tip before going back outside to look around The Krakus exterior, working my way around to the back of the building to assess rear entry. There was a steel door on a loading dock and a dumpster. Standard stuff.

With not much else to do but drive around the neighborhood some more, I headed back to my fancy hotel, where

I surprised myself by lying down and taking a nap, something I rarely did. But I was glad for it, since I had an interesting night ahead of me.

IN CONTRAST to the sparsely attended breakfast hour, The
Krakus was now crammed to the rafters with revelers.
Mostly young mating-age people from the working class
and weather-beaten bar flies who'd contentedly dispensed
with meaningful work. The sound system was loud, but not
deafening, which I appreciated. It was standing room only,
including the audience around the pool table in the back.

The bartenders were a diverse mix of men and women,
all looking perfectly capable of handling bouncer duties. As
suggested by the woman at breakfast, the waitresses snak-
ing their way through the crowd with loaded trays were
young and exhausted-looking.

I found a place to lean against the wall and asked one
of them to bring me a beer. I had a good view of the staircase up to the door of the upstairs club, and saw a few men
make their way up there. They knocked, likely stated their
bona fides, and were let in by a bald man of impressive
stature.

I finished my beer and walked up the steps. I knocked
on the door, when the bald guy asked who I was, I said,
"I'm here to see Janko."

He opened the door and said, "You're joking, right?"

"Orfio Pagliero said I could find him here."

Which was technically true, though it had the feel of an
introduction.

"Wait here," he said, and shut the door.

A few minutes later he let me in.

"Keep your hands where I can see them," he said, before
patting me down.

The club had a lot nicer bar and loads of comfy furniture, well made, not unlike you'd find in a gentlemen's
club in the West End of London. I guessed about twenty
men and an equal number of women were scattered about,
though there was room for plenty more. A giant Polish coat
of arms, a white eagle on a field of red, was hung over the
bar. The decor followed that aesthetic, with maroon plush
felt, mahogany, and brass. The male bartender wore a black
suit, and his waitresses were in white shirts and black slacks.
The other women were plenty dolled up, paired off with the
men, and attentive.

They'd taken advantage of New York City's smoking
waiver for private clubs, and the air was thick with it, min-
gling in a familiar way with a hard liquor aroma.

Second only in size to the eagle was a portrait of Carl
Yastrzemski, a Southampton home town hero. Other Polish
heroes were also honored, including Zbigniew Brzezinski,
Tadeusz Kościuszko, and Jerzy Kosiński, though I doubted
anyone in the room had read *The Painted Bird*.

The doorman nodded at someone in the room, who
stood up and came over.

Janko carried a sizable portion of his weight below the
breastbone in a pot belly covered by a grey, long-sleeved
cashmere polo shirt, but was otherwise slim. Thin clumps
of dyed hair stuck out from his head and his face resembled
the color and consistency of wet cement. I guessed his age
around mid-seventies.

He kept his distance and didn't bother to shake hands.

"You got a name?"

"Sam Acquillo."

"You in Pagliero's crew?"

"No, but my father used to do some work for his father."

"What sort of work?"

"Wheelman. Andre Acquillo. Had a repair shop in the
Bronx."

"I heard of him," said Janko. "Good with fast engines."

"That's him."

"We don't need that kind of work around here."

"Not looking for it," I said. "I just want to arrange a meet with somebody you probably know."

"Who's that?"

"Mikolaj Galecki."

Janko moved his mouth around as if he'd just taken a bite of something. The doorman had been watching me, but at the sound of Galecki's name, flashed an uneasy look at his boss.

"He wouldn't be here, would he?" I asked, praying to every god ever conceived by man that he wasn't.

Janko shook his head, but still didn't react for a painfully long time before asking, "Why do you want to meet with him?"

"I don't. He wants to meet me. I took some stuff he's keenly interested in getting back. We need to set up a meet."

He considered that for another hunk of uncomfortable time. I tried to speed the process.

"Galecki would look well on anyone helping solve this problem he's got," I said. "If you know what he's about, you know what that means."

Self-interest works as well on Polish criminals as it does on every other mortal on the planet. I kept at it.

"What have you got to lose?" I asked. "Just pass along the request and if he doesn't want to do it, not your problem."

"Maybe we could stick you in the kitchen freezer and have him come over and get you," said the doorman, showing some spirited initiative.

"That would trigger something very bad for Galecki, and consequently, even worse for you," I said to Janko.

The doorman stood back and clasped his hands over his midriff, docilely returning to his lane. Janko didn't bother to look at him.

"Do you want a drink, or a girl or something?" Janko asked me, apparently making up his mind.

"No thanks. Just want to give you this," I said, handing him a folded piece of paper taken from my back pocket. "It's my instructions for the meet. Tell him no changes, just yes or no. He's got my number."

Janko slipped the note into his pants pocket.

"I met your father, you know," he said. "One fucking hard-headed son of a bitch. Always pissed off about something."

"That's about all you needed to know about him," I said, and turned to leave, after glancing at the doorman to make sure it was okay. He looked over at Janko, who nodded, and I walked down the stairs and into the boisterous and oblivious throng below.

Chapter Twenty-Six

I'd given myself twenty-four hours to settle my mind before meeting Galecki, and decided they were best spent in Brooklyn in the nice hotel overlooking the East River. My time at a similar spot in Puerto Rico had reinforced my appreciation for beds both soft and firm, daily replacement of shampoo and towels, and minibars bursting with top-label little bottles.

They had a world-class gym as well, but I never liked all those machines. I assumed a boxing ring with stinking locker rooms and angry ethnic malcontents wasn't within their demographic parameters. But I did take a dip in the pool, where I just sat in a swimsuit bought at the hotel store for more than I'd usually pay for a load of lumber and felt the perfectly heated water caress my stiff and contrary body.

While in the pool, I called my half-sister, Rozele Mikutavičienė, just to say hello, not telling her I was in Brooklyn, an easy trip to her apartment on the Upper West Side.

"Sam, you're a stitch," she said.

"What does that mean?"

"You never call, but send me funny things in the mail. And then you call."

"I like to be unpredictable."

"I think you're lazy, but it's okay. I know you're thinking of me."

"I am," I said. "How are things?"

"Things are fine. I'm doing well. I hear from your daughter all the time, who is not as lazy."

"She's in France, though you probably know that. She never writes to me, though what would I write back?" I said. "My life's too boring."

"Is everything okay?" she asked.

"Everything's fine. I'm just checking in."

"No, you're not. You know I know."

We talked for another hour about nothing important except that we wanted to talk about it, till I finally let her get back to her life.

"Call me when you really are fine, okay?" she said. "Don't make me worry."

I agreed and hung up with the sense that I'd underestimated my sister's intuitive powers. The urge to call others lingered, but I wondered who else might attach greater significance to the call than intended. I tried Joe Sullivan.

"Just checking in," I said, when he answered.

"We're good here."

"How's Danny Izard?"

"On the mend. Bullet seemed to make it through without taking out much of the kidney. Lucky."

"I know you're always on high alert, but the next day will be critical," I said. "You might bring somebody else in to cover you when you're sleeping."

"That bad."

"Just a little touchy."

"Where are you?"

"Sitting in a swimming pool," I said. "It's nice."

"Got a little drink with an umbrella?"

"This is Brooklyn. Drinks only come with a straw, if you're lucky."

"Just don't do anything stupid."

"Why do people keep telling me that?"

"Maybe there's a history there?"

I thanked him and hung up, convinced any more calls would be counter to my purposes. Whatever they were.

I GOT to the meeting place two hours early. There was no one there to tell me I couldn't walk the grounds of the Nassau County cemetery where the remains of Elton Darby were interred, so I did.

The gravestone-free cemetery looked as I 'd remembered, like the manicured landscape it was. The day helped things along, with clear skies and persistently low humidity, even this far up island. I went deep into the section called English Glade, which looked just like that. A few old oak trees, with boughs hugging the ground, cushioned by mounds of tall grass and little ponds set there to reflect the wildflowers circling the water.

I wore my backpack, T-shirt, and blue jeans, and running shoes on my feet. Even with the automatic slipped into my front pants pocket, I was comfortable as I walked around taking in the pastoral tranquility.

That day, using the verdant landscape as a repository for the dead didn't seem like such a bad idea. In marked contrast to the grandiose statues crammed into Westminster Abbey, a horde of forgotten Ozmandiases cluttering up a perfectly nice old building. I thought maybe I should ask Amanda if she really did pick out a pair of spots for us. I could use my vast carpentry earnings to put down a deposit.

I knew where my parents were, in the big cemetery in Southampton. Though not the exact location, since I hadn't been back since burying my mother. No animus toward visiting, I just didn't see the point. If I wanted to honor her memory, I just had to look out on the Little Peconic Bay, a body of water she'd spent most of her life gazing at, I hoped as a source of solace from her unfortunate marital circumstances.

I'd specified the cemetery as the meeting place, but not the exact coordinates. Even in the English Glade, I had good sight lines, assuring Galecki couldn't get to me without me knowing it. Or bring along reinforcements, contrary to the arrangement. I'd arrived two hours ahead of time assuming he'd be there early for the same purpose, and he didn't disappoint me.

He was standing on the edge of a more sparsely treed, viny area. Probably called Poison Ivy Pasture. Even at some distance, he projected mass, a well-proportioned man, just big all over. He had on a white dress shirt, untucked, and a pair of striped synthetic pants. Black leather shoes, I hoped with slippery leather soles.

I walked over and stopped about twenty feet away.

"You're an amusing little man," he said to me, not that insulting, since to him, we were all little. I pointed that out.

"I've got the files and hard drives in the backpack," I said. "I want to toss it to you and leave."

"How do I know it's everything you've stolen?"

"You won't until your bosses go through it. But why would I put us back at square one?"

"Because foolishness seems to be your specialty."

I moved closer, slipping off the backpack and holding it by the soft handle sewn into the top.

"Look, Galecki, you got what you wanted. Let's go back to our corners and declare a draw."

He gestured for me to come closer still, which I did, until I was nearly within his long reach.

"You'll give me the bag," he said. "And I will still take everything you have. Because that is what I do."

There wasn't time to discuss human nature, in any language, nor trade parables on the eternal contest between good and evil, so I just gave him the bag. Meaning I swung it into his face with all the velocity inherent in a stack of lead weights, which I'd brought along instead of the files and hard drives, which were safely in the hands of the FBI.

The blow stunned him as much as the surprise, though he stayed on his feet, raising his fists, yelling obscenities, I think in Polish, and telling me to stand and fight, but I had a better idea.

I turned and ran.

Sprinting was never my thing, but I was a good long-distance jogger and hoped I could get far enough ahead to pull out the automatic and get off a shot. Unfortunately, sprinting was one of his talents, and he caught me after less than a hundred-yard dash.

He pushed me between the shoulder blades and I went down hard on the ground, breaking the fall with my face and sliding to a stop against a rotting tree stump.

He had about six inches of height on me, which is a lot when you think about how that scales up to the rest of a human being. To prove the point, he grabbed me by the scruff of the neck and seat of the pants and tossed me into a clump of untamed forsythia. It was an easy landing. The hard part was getting clear of the thick cluster of stems and back on my feet.

I made it just in time to get a brawler's haymaker right to the face, which sent me another few feet away from the forsythia, but now unsure of which way the world was turning, where was up and where was down.

I'd been a professional boxer, and I knew what it was like to take a punch, I just never thought it would have the force of an industrial crushing machine. Though I was still able to find my feet, and dance backward, trying to focus on the plodding mass before me.

I ducked the next punch, and the one after that. This gave me hope that Galecki's fighting style was all brutality and no finesse, until he crouched into a perfectly proper fighter's posture and shot a right jab directly into my face.

I caught it pulling back, so it could have been worse. I danced quickly to his left, which surprised him, and he stumbled a bit trying to bring an awkward left fist into play. I blocked it and scored my first hit to his nose. It wasn't my best shot, but it clearly hurt enough to make him take a step back and bring his fists up to protect his face. So I planted one in his midriff, which was a lot worse for my hand than his stomach. He smiled at the attempt.

I was still afraid to pull out the gun, thinking it was too easy for him to grab it. Instead I searched around for a weapon, but the groundskeepers had done a nice job of keeping things tidy for their dead clientele. Galecki took advantage of that moment's distraction to throw another pile driver at my head, but I was quick enough to get out of the way, though he nicked the end of my nose, and I could feel the wind stirred up by his fist passing by.

This was the terrible disadvantage guys in my weight class always had against the big men. The only way to do any damage was to get inside their reach, but then it had to work, because otherwise you were locked in, and in a street fight, there were no refs to break up the clinch.

So I did what all smaller, quicker fighters do. I danced around and tried to find an opening. He just grinned at me, a sight made more horrifying by the giant red welt on the side of his face. We both knew where this was headed, and there was nothing I could do about it.

He stepped in and threw a hard right into my chest. I'd blocked it with my forearm, but it didn't seem to matter. The blow took me off my feet and I went sprawling into the tall grass. I thought for a moment that my heart had stopped, but it was just the raw pain of newly bruised sternum and ribs. I struggled to breathe, but got back up on my feet, knowing that it was keep moving or die.

With that in mind, I turned and started running again. When I heard him quickly catch up behind me, I stopped and took a pen out of my shirt pocket. I fingered off the cap, and when he grabbed my arm, I swiveled around and stabbed him in the cheek. He cursed and dropped back a step, dabbing at his face. This gave me a chance to throw a left-right combination at his nose, which was already bleeding from my first score.

He stopped smiling, and the next punch came out of nowhere, catching me in the rib cage, right above the kidney. The kind of punch that doesn't look like much to a boxing audience but can drop you to your knees. Which was what happened to me.

I hugged myself and tried to get my breathing under control, sitting back on my heels. He stood over me, I assumed picking the right spot to smash me into oblivion. I shook my head and he let me stagger up to my feet.

I put my hand over my heart and whispered a few words in French. He said he couldn't hear me. I said to come closer, which he did, lowering his fists.

"You think you've won, but just look up there," I said, pointing at the sky.

Sometimes the oldest tricks are the best. He looked and I slammed my right fist directly into his Adam's apple. A lot of complicated little webs of flesh and cartilage gave way. A startled rage lit up his face and both hands went to his throat. I kicked him in the balls, which didn't seem to have much effect, so I kicked him again. This time he backed away to gather himself.

Even if I was the doomed one, I took some satisfaction that he was the one with the bloody face. Though I hardly lingered over it, turning again and running hard to gather some distance.

I took a chance and looked over my shoulder, seeing him just a few long strides away from catching me. Still running, I dug out the automatic, spun around, and started firing while running backward. I got off the fourth shot as he barreled into me, already off balance, so I hit the ground under all the force of his weight.

Dead weight, it turned out.

I CALLED Judy Paolini and got her admin. I said I needed to talk to Judy immediately. The admin started to do her little bureaucratic dance, so I just yelled, "Put her on the fucking phone!"—an approach that worked, making me think I should have tried it before.

I told her the FBI could have Mikolaj Galecki, though not in the form they'd likely hoped for. I gave her a sketch of what happened and told her where Galecki and I would be waiting for the responding officers.

They got there pretty quickly, fortunately State Police, who knew how to secure the scene, keep the local cops away, and wait resolutely for the FBI to get there. I was almost honored to see Judy Paolini among the contingent, wearing a blue suit and a pair of aerobic workout shoes. Since I was lying on the ground at the time, I felt it only right to drag myself up to my feet.

"They said you refused medical treatment," she said.

"I'm wicked sore, but nothing's broken. I really just want to give my statement and get the hell out of here."

"You know our immunity agreement doesn't cover this."

I did, but she knew how we got there, and was willing to let me off on my own recognizance, at least for the time being. I told her Jackie knew nothing of this specific meet up with Galecki, and that I really shouldn't say a lot more before consulting with her.

"I'd suggest she assert self-defense and justifiable homicide," she said. "That's what it looks like to me."

"I'll pass that along."

ONCE I was on my way back to Southampton, pain in my side, chest, forearm, nose, and left cheek began to ramp up and would steal the show in a few hours.

I really didn't care, welcoming the pain like an old friend, appreciating that it was far better than being dead.

CHAPTER TWENTY-SEVEN

A week later, a *New York Times* headline announced the federal indictments of a half-dozen Worldwide Loventeers' executives and board members, prominently Ruth Bellingham and Arthur Reynolds, on charges including fraud, embezzlement, and misappropriation of the organization's funds, money laundering—and most shockingly—human trafficking.

Other indictments were expected to follow, though Rosie and Joshua Edelstein, and Milton Flowers, were not on the list, to my vast relief. Also unindicted, due to being dead, was Elton Darby, though he was cited as one of the principal players in the long-running illegal operation. An aside noted that billionaire Burton Lewis was awaiting trial for Darby's death, though there was no known link between that incident and the NGO scandal.

No mention of Mikolaj Galecki.

THE DA was generous in giving us as much time as we needed to prepare Burton's case. It didn't hurt that he and Burton had a long, if not particularly close, personal relationship. Jackie and I agreed we'd take all the rich, white privilege we could get if it helped save Burton.

The irony was we didn't really need all that time. The facts and testimonies had solidified, and nothing we'd uncovered promised to change that. Our only hope was that time would shake something loose that would open things up, but that became seemingly unlikely.

Eddie and Amanda eventually moved out of Burton's house, but Sullivan stayed on as security, and Burton admitted, good company. In this way summer capitulated to fall, and the case began to feel like a free-floating malaise versus full-blown fever. I was grateful for the slower tempo, needing those weeks to allow my bruised ribs to go from searing pain to nagging ache. Over that time, everything calmed down.

Jackie kept her big whiteboard at the ready, and whenever I was over there, I'd wheel it out and stare at it with a yellow legal pad in my lap, and the various statements given by the witnesses, looking for cracks in continuity and consistency.

At the sound of Darby crashing through the window, Joshua, Rosie, and Violeta were on the first floor, in different places, but within close enough proximity to call to each other when they heard the crash. In our scenario, Burton was on the front walk heading for his car.

Rosie sent Violeta outside. That's why Violeta got to Darby first, then Burton, then Rosie. Then Joshua.

Johnnie Mercado was heading their way when Rosie stopped him and pulled him back into the house, not wanting him to see Darby's body.

If Burton was the killer, did he have time to toss Darby out the window, then get down to the first floor and outside ahead of Rosie, though not Violeta? Had anyone seen Burton running down the stairs? No, something in Burt's favor, but the Edelsteins' house is big enough to have three separate staircases. One out of three chances they'd see each other.

I remembered many long hours in bland, industrial conference rooms with junior engineers anguishing over a seemingly insurmountable problem. The system wasn't working, even though all the component parts were operating according to spec. It made no sense, and engineers don't believe in black magic, so they were thrown into a type of existential cognitive dissonance.

I didn't believe in magic either, so I usually said to them, "Pick a spec and change it. See if that yields the results we're getting. If it doesn't, pick another one."

I also remember Ross Semple saying to me after initial interviews with the witnesses:

"They're all lying."

I knew Burton's lie, or at least evasion, so that left the rest of them.

When Jackie came into her office to attend to her work, I said this to her.

"Joshua, Rosie, and Violeta are lying."

"Why do you say that?"

"Because that's the only explanation. Mercado might have lied as well, but we can't know that. Though we do know Burton is telling the truth, so his version of events is what we base everything on, and question anything that contradicts it."

She put the stack of files she was holding down on her desk.

"You remember they changed their stories between Cermanski's first interview at the scene and when Joshua got hauled in for a grilling," she said. "It felt like their efforts to shield Burton had broken down once they fully realized the implications of lying, or even evading, the truth. The wages of perjury."

"Yeah, but what if they just needed time to get their stories straight. Coordinated, settled into a realistic narrative."

Jackie tapped out a rhythm on the desktop with her pen.

"But why?" she asked.

"Because they know who actually killed Elton Darby, and they're willing to let Burton Lewis go to jail to keep it hidden."

She changed up the pen tapping, moving into a three-four-time signature.

"We got distracted by the Loventeers," she said.

"We did. All that really matters is what happened that night. Why can be answered later."

"What do you think we should do?" she asked.

"Change the specs."

I KNEW a place that sold salvaged building materials, nice stuff, like moldings, architectural detail and windows and doors. It was in an area north of Bridgehampton in an old farmhouse whose fields had long ago been overrun by scrub pines and pin oaks.

It took some looking through dusty rows of windows leaning up against the wall of the barn to select the right size and configuration, as close as I could remember. I stuck them inside the Jeep and up on the roof and took them back to Oak Point.

When I got there, I built a two-by-four structure next to the shed at the back of the property that allowed me to set the windows into a freestanding, rigid frame. I put on my cold-weather jumpsuit, made of a heavy cotton and polyester weave, the type worn by year-round construction workers in Northern New England. Then called Amanda, who'd recently driven down our common driveway.

She showed up with a wine glass, Eddie following along.

"Okay," she said. "I'm curious."

"Here's what we're going to do. I'm going to stand here, and you're going to put everything you have into shoving me through that window."

"It's a six-over-six," she said. "Lots of wood frame."

"I know. But you really want to send me through it."

"I think I know where this is going."

"Just put down the wine glass."

I stood there and watched her prepare herself.

"Not sure I can give it my all," she said. "What's my motivation?"

"I'm a fucking slimy piece of shit who has done you terrible harm. And I made you drink that white wine with boeuf bourguignon."

She let out a banshee scream and charged into me. We both went through the window, which I hadn't anticipated, but it somewhat proved the point. We got cut up a little bit, but no arteries were slashed in the process.

As we lay there amid the splintered wood and glass shards, assessing our wounds, I asked if she thought she was stronger than Rosie Edelstein.

"I am, though she has at least twenty pounds on me. When you're shoving someone through a window, a little heft will make up the difference."

"So she could have done the deed."

"In my nonexistent forensics experience, yes. Especially if she was sufficiently pissed, which imparts herculean strength."

"Thanks."

"Anytime, Sam. It was kinda fun."

"You seemed pretty enthusiastic."

"I have my own motivations."

PEOPLE WHO visit Southampton and gobble up all the glossy magazines littering the sidewalk might think fund-raisers are the only thing we do. That's far from true, though certain wealthy people do a lot of them, and they're well promoted in digital and traditional media.

People like me would rather be found dead than at one of those fund-raisers, though we have our own version for sick kids of construction workers, or Latino day laborers with burned-down houses, so I never paid much attention to the breathy commentary. But luck made me look at the local paper one morning, and I saw that Rosie Edelstein was co-chair of an event benefitting a historical house in the village, with hopes of sustaining it into the future. Most of the local builders would be hoping they'd get the job of doing the actual preserving and sustaining, so there was a chance I'd see some of my friends there lapping up cocktails and finger food.

The cost of entry was a modest two hundred bucks, which I went online and paid, getting tickets for both me and Amanda. I told her she had to dress up, but also that I was stalking Rosie, so to dress appropriately.

"Then I'm thinking that claw-proof Kevlar number," she said.

"Perfect."

She actually wore something I wanted to immediately take off, but that happened all the time, so I kept my deviant thoughts to myself.

The event was in the estate section directly south of the Village center. We drove Amanda's Audi to blend into the crowd of cars overtaxing the valets. I took another approach, parking on the street a few blocks south so we could control how we got out of there, even if it meant a short sprint toward the ocean.

It was a strange experience to hand over legitimate tickets, having mostly crashed these absurd events over the years. I noted that to Amanda and she said it made her proud.

"Movin' up in the world, Acquillo."

Walking into the crowd with Amanda's light touch on my arm caused a little burst of euphoria. While everyone around me was trying to advance their social station, I just luxuriated in the feel of her moving next to me and delighted in looking at her and making stupid faces, getting a subtle smile as reward.

"So what's your plan, Sam?" Amanda asked.

"Whenever Dashiell Hammett's Continental Op wanted to break up an investigative deadlock, he'd do some random thing that would set new patterns in motion. Shake the can."

The backyard of the historic house was a relatively small space for so many people, so it was a challenge to locate and take advantage of the bar. Amanda was good in these situations, having the skill to advance our position with minimal cause for offense along the way.

It was an open bar, with top-shelf liquor, so I thought maybe I'd be able to make up the ticket investment with a little enterprise. I started off with a double and the best label I could identify for Amanda.

An undernourished woman behind me in a plunge-neck dress that mostly revealed a bony sternum, felt compelled to comment on how well the historical society had maintained the grounds. I agreed, even though I didn't have much of an opinion.

"I hear the problem is the interior," she said. "Not good."

"They didn't have much in the way of decorators back in the seventeenth century," I said.

She looked unsure.

"That's not really what I meant."

"I've been in there," I said. "Not a right angle in the place."

"Oh," she said, hopefully, "so it's really just a fixer-upper."

"You must be in real estate."

She finally felt on firmer ground.

"I am," she said with a thousand-watt smile that seemed to come out of nowhere. "Are you looking to sell or buy?"

"Neither. I just want to rot in place."

"I'm sure we can help you with that."

Amanda, who'd heard most of this, gripped my arm and pulled me into the crowd.

"Come on, Tiger. You've already got a real estate lady."

Fortified, we moved deep into the swell, trying to search out Rosie Edelstein. I did run into some builders I knew, including Frank Entwhistle, and his wife, who was about a tenth his size. A cheerful woman with a compulsive laugh, she was a good audience, since she thought everything anybody said was funny. It actually made me pull back on the wisecracks. Afraid too much humor might cause her internal injury. Frank asked me about his job, and I said it was on schedule. He said he never had any doubt, and he shouldn't have, since I hadn't missed a deadline yet.

One of the servers came by with a tray full of crisp pastry things stuffed with crab. I offered her fifty bucks for the whole tray, and she almost took me up on it before Amanda stepped in and quashed the deal.

"Killjoy."

"You need room for the veggie spring rolls."

We made two more trips to the bar before finally spotting Rosie Edelstein, standing inside a crowd of young people displaying their characteristic vanity, confidence, and insecurity. I moved in and yelled in her ear, "I know you did it."

She jerked her head back and stared at me. The light was too dim to show the blood seeping away from her face, but I knew it did.

"What the hell are you talking about?" she said, her voice barely cresting over the din.

"You killed Darby. I can prove it," I yelled into her right ear. "Unless you know something I don't know. If so, you better tell me now. Otherwise I'm on my way to the DA."

She arched her head back, like a predatory bird about to strike.

"You will never," she said. "Never."

"Watch me," I said, then moved away, though before I did, Amanda said, "Watch him."

I hoped we'd bump up against her again, but when I looked around later, she was nowhere to be found. I never saw Joshua, so he must not have been there. That didn't matter.

The can had been shaken, if not stirred.

CHAPTER TWENTY-EIGHT

I called Jackie the next day and asked if she'd held on to Violeta's cell phone number.

"I did."

"Call her and see if she'll take five hundred bucks to tell us when the Edelsteins are away from the house and let me go in and poke around."

"I'll try. She's pretty skittish. Justifiably."

"Let me know."

I spent the rest of the day finishing the giant wall unit for Frank Entwhistle. I was eager to get it done, since it had filled up most of the available space in the shop. I called Frank and asked to have his guys come over and haul it out of there. As always, he was appreciative and gracious.

"They'll bring another set of drawings," he said. "Call me after you give a look."

"Another accommodating client?"

"No, this guy's sort of a shit. I'll deal with him."

"Thanks for that. I've had my share of shits in my other line of work."

The sun had started its shift into the hard light along the horizon, but the temperatures had stayed warm, so the oaks around the house were still mostly green. Amanda and I had taken advantage of the extended season by spending evenings out on the Adirondacks, bringing along blankets if needed, to catch the sunset and ease into the night.

I'd been notified by the body shop that the Grand Prix was nearly rehabilitated. The claims adjuster took it as a total, but seemed a little disgruntled about another outlay for a car he felt overdue for retirement. It was hard to argue, but I was all paid up on the premiums and not ready to let it go.

The other big wound from that night was Amanda's disposition, less easily remedied. Steadfast woman that she was, killing another person, however warranted, leaves something behind. An ugly tragedy had cost her a young daughter, the greatest trauma of her life, which ironically provided some perspective. Not one to relish talking through abiding emotional pain, she did mention that surviving that gave her an advantage, an established path toward reconciling acceptance with the intolerable.

Maybe I should have been more affected by my own lethal deeds. It made me wonder a little about the health of my conscience. But I'd known those men who died would never rest until we were both killed, along with who knows what other cherished beings, which made me feel far more relieved than penitent.

Danny Izard made a full recovery, faster than anyone expected, though I'd known him since he was a kid chasing after my daughter, Allison, not knowing that she'd secretly hoped to be caught. For no good reason, I believed he possessed preternatural defenses against calamity, as if his kind nature and unburdened optimism were talismans. I knew from knowledge and experience that people like Danny often attracted malignant forces, but I liked my own conclusion better.

I called off the security people I'd obtained for Allison and her boyfriend, Nathan, after calling to let them know. If I could do it, I'd have them under twenty-four-hour watch for all eternity, but I knew that was neither sane nor possible.

There was only one sufferer in my immediate circle who'd yet to have relief.

Burton Lewis.

JACKIE CUT the deal with Violeta, and it only took a few days for her to call and say the coast was clear. I drove over to Burton's, where I left the Jeep, and walked the rest of the way to the Edelsteins'.

When I used the intercom to ask her to open the gate, I checked the supporting column, pleased to feel it still had a satisfying wobble. Violeta met me at the front door.

"The señor and señora are both in the city for two days, so the timing is good," she said.

"Hang with me, if you would," I said, leading her to the base of the main stairwell.

I asked where she was when she heard Burton and Elton shouting at each other upstairs.

"I was here," she said, which had been her testimony.

"And the Edelsteins?"

"The señor was in the kitchen and the señora still in the living room talking to Johnnie Mercado."

"Burton says he came down these stairs and was out the door when he heard the crash. So you didn't see him?"

She shook her head.

"I went to find the señor. I didn't know what else to do."

"So Burton could have come down and left and you wouldn't have seen him."

"It's possible."

"So you went to get Joshua. Where was he?"

"I told you. In the kitchen."

"What did he do?"

"He looked annoyed and said he'd talk to Rosie. I don't think he was very happy that his guests were arguing."

"Embarrassed?" I asked.

"Yes. It was a very awkward night."

"What happened then?"

"I went to the pantry where I have a stool. I didn't want to be near all the frightening things going on. I could hear the señor and señora talking and moving around the house, but I don't know what they were saying. I was upset."

"Understandable. So you don't know who else could have gone upstairs."

"No, but the señor and señora told the policeman that they went back to the living room. When I heard the crash, I was really scared. I wanted to run to my room, but the señora ran into the pantry and told me to go outside to see what had happened. I didn't want to, but I had no choice."

"How much time went by between the crash and when she asked you to look?"

She had to think about this one.

"I don't know. A few minutes?"

"Long enough to get here from the upstairs? There's a separate stairway that lands just outside the pantry door."

She nodded as she thought about it.

"Yes. She came that way. But she could have also been in the living room."

"Okay."

We moved away from the main stairway and went to the kitchen, then into the pantry, which had another door to the dining area, with access to the separate set of stairs. She followed me up to the hall that served bedrooms and baths on either side, the closest of which was the room from where Darby took the deep dive.

It was a small room, but the window in question was directly across from the door and clear of furniture. Plenty of room to gather some momentum. I stood at the window, a tall six-over-six, with muntins of a lighter gauge than the one Amanda pushed me through. Below was bare earth, the bush, collateral damage, still unrestored.

The whole scene had been gone over countless times, and nothing in Violeta's recollection would change the prosecutor's determination. She hadn't seen and heard everything, but neither had the other witnesses, so there was nothing contradictory. Within a reasonable doubt.

I felt my smartphone vibrate in my pocket. It was Jackie.

"Are you alone?" she asked.

"I'm here with Violeta."

Jackie whispered for me to ditch her, so I told Violeta it was a private call, and to meet me back downstairs. She eagerly left the room.

"Okay," I told Jackie.

"You know I have a dedicated laptop where I keep Ruth Bellingham's hard drive."

"I do."

"Every once in a while, I pull it out and browse. The FBI doesn't need me to do a parallel investigation, so I just do a little hunting and pecking. Since you were over there with Violeta, it gave me a thought, so for the hell of it I searched for her name."

"Really."

"Those handwritten résumés of the girls you grabbed had all been scanned into searchable pdfs. This one's dated four years ago. Violeta Zaragoza. Age seventeen. Speaks decent English. Only child. Mother works on a plantation. House with no running water. Pump in the front, outhouse in the back. Very pretty. That's underlined," she added. "Wants to come to the States to go to college. Four-star candidate. The stars are little drawings."

"Same Violeta?"

"There's a photo. She's wearing makeup."

"Holy Christ."

"That's not the worst of it," said Jackie, her low voice filled with something odd.

"What?"

"At the bottom of the page is a name. Joshua Edelstein. It's circled."

"That chart you have on the big whiteboard," I said. "Some of the boxes get new arrows."

I told her my plan, then hung up and went downstairs, where Violeta was waiting on her pantry stool.

"That was Jackie Swaitkowski," I told her. "She really wants to speak with you, but she can't make it over here. It would be so incredibly helpful if you could come now while we know the señor and señora aren't around."

She didn't seem all that keen, so I suggested there'd be some more money in it for her. That did the trick. I was nervous on the walk back to Burton's to retrieve the Jeep that she'd have second thoughts and fly the coop, but she was waiting at the end of the drive when I got there. She'd changed into civilian clothes, though not all ritzed-out like last time.

On the quick drive to Jackie's office in Water Mill I practiced my small-talk skills by asking her about the day-to-day experiences as a full-time housekeeper. It was an easy subject, and she had no trouble expounding on what sounded cruelly mundane, though for her was just another day on the job.

Jackie had her chipper client attitude on as she made Violeta comfortable and poured her coffee. She told me the Japanese restaurant on the first floor was open for lunch, and maybe I should go down and have some. She said when she was ready, she'd call me and put in their order to go.

So I got to sit at the sushi bar and work my way through a series of small plates while I waited for the call. It didn't come for almost two hours, when my smartphone was almost out of battery power from watching the Yankees, a habit of mine.

"We're ready," she said. "And don't bother with lunch. Nobody up here is hungry."

Violeta was lying on the client couch with her legs pulled up. Her face was red and the coffee table scattered with used tissues. She held one up to her face and didn't look at me. Jackie took me out in the hall.

"Bellingham told all the girls before they shipped out that they had to do everything their sponsors told them to do, or harm might come to their families. The poor girl has lived in mortal fear every day that one slipup could cost her mother's life."

"Did Joshua?" I left the question hanging.

"She claims not. She said Rosie was the one who wanted to keep her around, though she had no idea Violeta had been imported from the Loventeers. She actually thought a nonexistent sister had given her the tip on the job. She said the Edelsteins argued over it, with Joshua wanting to let her get on with her life, eager to get her out of the house. Rosie seemed about to give in when all this happened."

"Has she changed her story?"

Jackie nodded yes.

"When Burton and Darby were yelling at each other, Joshua and Rosie didn't stay downstairs. They both went up the stairway off the pantry, first Joshua, then Rosie. She still doesn't know what happened after that, but they had her tell the cops they never left the first floor. She said she's been telling the lie for so long, she almost doesn't believe the truth."

"Most believable type of lie."

"She can't go back to that house," said Jackie. "I can keep her here for now."

"She'll do that?"

"I told her I'm armed and dangerous. And will send even more dangerous *compadres* to her mother's for protection. That assured her."

"And so it should."

ON THE way to the city, I stopped by the cottage to get a few things and tell Amanda what was up. I said this trip wasn't one for her to worry about.

"You wouldn't tell me if it was," she said.

"I might hint."

"Call me on your way back and tell me the world isn't as horrifying as it feels."

"Okay."

There might have been a ton of traffic on the way in, but I wouldn't remember, since my head was so full of erupting narratives I barely noticed getting there. The best moments as a professional troubleshooter were when one particular problem revealed itself, the solution for which had a cascading effect on the surrounding dysfunction. The flood of understanding would sometimes be enough to make me nauseous.

It should have been more of a pleasure, a triumph, but I think the human mind hates giving up paradigms, even when they hide what's real. The loss of false belief becomes a kind of tragic death.

Joshua Edelstein's office was downtown within a few blocks of One World Trade Center. In a pretty big building in its own right, Joshua's investment firm had a full floor near the top. I'd been there before when we were building his house, so I knew where I was going. As usual, coming unannounced, I ran the risk that he'd left for the day, but I got lucky. The security desk let me talk to him on the house phone.

"Honestly, Sam, I'm pretty busy up here."

"Need to see you, Joshua. Can't wait."

"Give me twenty minutes."

"No. Has to be now. Let me up and meet me in reception."

I handed the phone back to security, who had me sign the book and gave me a little paper badge to stick on my shirt. As requested, Joshua was waiting. He looked tired and thinner than usual, his yellow polo shirt having an easier time containing his gut.

"My office?" he asked.

"Wherever you want."

Joshua's office was a big box, but made for work, with lines of shelves filled with books and binders, and a work-station with three separate monitors. He directed me to a small circular table.

"So what's going on, Sam," he said as we sat down. "Rosie said you were yelling some crazy stuff at the fund-raiser. She won't say what. Is everything okay?"

"It's definitely not okay. I know what really happened that night at your house, and I know why."

He frowned and gave his head a little shake, as if he hadn't heard me.

"What are you talking about?"

"What did they trap you with, the Loventeers' operation or something else?"

He threw up his hands, exasperated.

"I really don't know what the hell you're talking about. You're not making any sense."

"The FBI flipped you. They were gunning for World-wide Loventeers and needed someone close to the action on the inside. You were perfect. In the know, but just outside enough to avoid suspicion. You've been feeding them intelligence all along. Including telling them someone had stolen Bellingham's files, and it was probably me."

Concern started to overtake the frustration on his face. He squinted at me.

"That's a very strange story. I had nothing to do with that atrocity."

Joe Sullivan had once told me the best way to work an interrogation was to achieve empathy, have the suspect feel you're on his side and understand his problems. The second best was to scare the shit out of him. I chose the second route.

"Yeah you did. How much did you pay for Violeta?"

He took a moment to answer.

"I never touched that woman."

"You think Rosie will believe that?"

"You bastard," he said.

"Might be, but you know what they say about glass houses."

He rose like a shot out of his seat, paced a few steps away, then came back and sat down.

"What's your game here, Acquillo?"

"Saving my friend Burton Lewis from you. You went upstairs when Darby and he were arguing, but when you got there, Burton had left. Darby was all in a lather, still hopped up after the altercation. He starting taking it out on you, throwing around threats and accusations, revealing your secrets, that just like Darby, you'd bought and paid for a companion, only to chicken out on consummating the relationship. That you were neck deep in the whole squalid operation. Rosie was coming up behind you. You were afraid she'd hear what he was saying. You got pissed, and frightened, and you panicked. You pulled him into the bedroom, hoping she wouldn't hear, but he kept at it. You shoved him to make him stop, a bit too hard. He stumbled backward and went through the window. Rosie either saw you do it, or came in the room right after. It was Rosie's idea to pin it on Burton, an act decided when she said in front of Violetta, 'Burton, what have you done?'"

Joshua started to shiver, as if the temperature in the room had suddenly dropped to zero.

"You can't prove any of this," he said.

"Jackie Swaitkowski has Violeta squirreled away, waiting for me to call her so she can go over to the Village police HQ to give her statement. She'll tell them that you brought her to the States under false pretenses, that you held her virtually captive for four years by threatening the life of her mother. This will be highly credible, given that the feds have a few hundred other young women testifying to the same thing. She'll also say that you told her to lie about that night, that you went upstairs before the crash, intimidating her in the same way that kept her a prisoner in that house."

A remarkable change came over Joshua Edelstein. His body sagged as if someone had pulled a plug and let out all the air. He hung his head, and like the blues song goes, began to cry.

"I'm a good person," he said. "I wanted Violeta to have a nice life, but Rosie wouldn't let me. She said I had to keep her there. Rosie didn't know how that would expose me to all sorts of horrible trouble, but I couldn't do anything about it."

He took in a deep sobbing breath, and like my involuntary surge of confession to Charlotte Ensler back in La Selva Bendita, it all came gushing out.

"I wanted to help all those poor people. Loventeers does wonderful work, I don't care what you say. It was those bastards Reynolds and Darby, those sick fucking perverted bastards, who just saw it as a way to get rich and have an endless supply of kids to exploit, and wound, and traumatize, and," he searched for other verbs, but only came up with, "destroy."

"So it was easy for you when the FBI approached you with some, say, persuasive encouragement."

He recovered enough to say, "Just a little tax thing. Okay, a pretty big tax thing. It would wreck the firm. Rosie's precious fortune could go up in smoke."

"She didn't know anything about the Loventeers' side projects, or any of this other stuff," I said, as kindly as I could manage.

He wobbled his head.

"She doesn't know shit, but thinks she knows everything. I was never as good as her father, who left us an inheritance from this piss-ass shopping center in Upstate New York and I turned it into a global empire. And she still treats me like I'm some schmuck from the Lower East Side. She's from, where, the *Upper* East Side? La-de-fuckin'-da. She blamed me for never having kids. I got tested, buddy, and you know what? Lots of great little swimmers."

"Did she see you push Darby out the window?"

He shook his head, his face hung so low it nearly rested on his chest.

"Just after. You know what she said? 'Don't say anything.' The man was dead, her own personal fuck toy, and all she could think about was keeping our hands clean. Protecting our so-called reputation. No matter that it would destroy another man's life in the process."

He picked up his head and said through his tears, "The woman has no shame. No heart. And I let her get away with it because I have no courage. I'm a coward, Sam. I always have been."

"So it's time to grow some balls. In exchange for cooperation, the FBI can let you off the hook for the Loventeers. But not this. Not when Burton's standing there falsely accused."

He put his face in his hands but gave a little nod.

"I know. It's over," he said. "I can't live with the guilt anymore anyway. I've been thinking of swallowing a gun."

I believed him.

"I'm going to have to call the police to come get you," I said.

He looked even more horrified.

"Oh, please, Sam, no. Not here."

"Then we take a trip over to the FBI field office. It's a short cab ride. Take your pick."

He was breathing heavily, his mind a stew of anger, fear, and remorse. And panic.

"I don't have to tell them anything," he said. "I'll have a lawyer."

"That's true," I said. "But they'll also have this."

I took a small digital recorder out of my pocket.

"It's still running, so think about what you're going to say."

He looked over at his big office window.

"Don't try it," I said. "That's tempered glass, not like the stuff at your house. You'll just bounce off. And then I'll knock you out and carry you down the elevator. Don't think I'm not in the mood to do that."

He wept a little more, which I guess was cathartic. I waited him out, then stood up and told him it was time to go. He looked up at me.

"Of all the people who worked on the house, I always liked you best, Sam," he said. "Even more than Frank. That offended Rosie. She said you were trash. That should have told me something."

I helped him up to his feet. I knew what it should have told him, but she'd already ruined his life, so I didn't see the point in telling him what it was.

Chapter Twenty-Nine

It took me a little while to figure out how to throw rubber balls with that Australian thing of Burton's, but I finally got the hang of it, winging the thing across Burton's backyard, about the length of a football field.

The spectacular distance only seemed to incite Eddie to greater heights of glory.

It had grown cold enough to force Burton to install the winter windows on the big patio and bring out a pair of tall, chrome-plated space heaters. It was a Sunday afternoon and none of the others felt the need to do more than sprawl on the cushioned, wrought-iron furniture and eat to excess.

Amanda and I were drinking a zesty mixture of seltzer and cranberry juice, since she'd pointed out that we were both boozing way too much, and that any future fun depended on avoiding cirrhosis of the liver. I admitted that the tense times had been taking their toll, so went along, and almost felt better as a consequence.

Burton and Joe Sullivan had abandoned the football game when it became apparent that the Giants were going down in ignominy. Harry Goodlander, a devoted supporter of the Eagles, found the situation satisfactory.

"Where are the Eagles from again?" asked Jackie.

"Philadelphia, darling," said Harry. "You need to improve your sports literacy."

"Maybe I could get a book."

The week before, we'd received word from the Suffolk County DA that Joshua and Rosie Edelstein were close to plea agreements on the Darby killing, and cover-up, and Joshua had been neatly folded into the ongoing federal prosecution of the Worldwide Loventeers, now outed as their star witness. The organization itself had been consigned to the stewardship of dignitaries from New York and the UK, led by a former MP whose wealth and dedication to philanthropy promised to preserve their legitimate good works, despite all the scandals, for the foreseeable future.

Milton Flowers, absolved of any knowledge of, or responsibility for, the slave trade, had been wooed out of retirement to serve as executive director. In recognition, I sent him a bottle of sacramental wine.

They changed Carolyn Harris's cause of death from suicide to homicide and left the case open, though no one thought it would be resolved any time soon. Eulah thanked me when I told her over the phone, saying, "I'll write her with the news."

Jackie's semi-obsessive study of Bellingham's files had unearthed Johnnie Mercado's history, ten years at a Loventeers' campus in Uruguay, sponsored as a refugee when he was eighteen, by Elton Darby.

Violeta Zaragoza joined a cleaning crew in town, earning enough money to bring her mother up from Puerto Rico. I knew that because the service cleaned Burton's house, giving him the opportunity to assure her beyond all doubt that he would have behaved the same as she if their situations had been reversed. That she, like him, was the victim, not the perpetrator.

His general manner mostly returned to its prior state, though he said he took a lesson away from the whole episode.

"In a way, I'm partially to blame," he said.

I tried to protest, but he interrupted me.

"I set myself up for happenstance to inflict the harm. I'd isolated myself, always fearful that getting close to someone would eventually bring me sorrow. Instead of warding off evil, I actually attracted it."

"You gotta find somebody to love."

"A thing devoutly to be wished."

Acknowledgments

Very indebted to Sonia Ortega, who helped with my Spanish, and put me in touch with her family in Puerto Rico—Edith and Junior Velilla, and Alicia Nieves, who provided invaluable guidance and information. Other folks in Puerto Rico who shared their time and experiences include Nahiomy Rodrigues, Scarlett Alguera, and Aida Bauza. They lived through it all. *Gracias a todos ustedes.*

Al Hershner gave me the rundown on buying a car in Puerto Rico, and rode me around in his white Wrangler on Vieques. As a bonus, his wife, Paige Goettle, checked out my French.

Jim Walter helped me with Jewish social dynamics and insults, a fine art. The Right Reverend Jep Striet, retired, helped with the Episcopalian priest, whom he apparently resembles, though that must have been a coincidence.

Birmingham lad Andrew Wood told me how a football player would kick a person's head if it was a soccer ball.

Jill Varick Fletcher, with roots in New Britain, CT, provided the Polish cuisine, and as with my other sixteen books, did the first edit. Barbara Anderson also pitched in on initial editing, and copy editing, as part of the gallant Permanent Press crew of Susan Ahlquist, Lon Kirschner, and Nick Collins. Final edit by Judy Shepard, who with co-publisher Marty Shepard, continues to stand by me.

My wife, Mary Farrell, also continues to endure all this, a kindness undermined by our dogs, Jack and Charlie, who'd much prefer I just toss the ball.